LAST NIGHT AT THE BLUE ANGEL

Last Night at the Blue Angel

REBECCA ROTERT

WILLIAM MORROW
An Imprint of HarperCollins*Publishers*

LAST NIGHT AT THE BLUE ANGEL. Copyright © 2014 by Rebecca Shaw. All rights reserved. Printed in the United States of America. No part of this book may be used or reproduced in any manner whatsoever without written permission except in the case of brief quotations embodied in critical articles and reviews. For information address HarperCollins Publishers, 195 Broadway, New York, NY 10007.

HarperCollins books may be purchased for educational, business, or sales promotional use. For information please e-mail the Specials Markets Department at SPsales@harpercollins.com.

FIRST EDITION

Designed by Jamie Lynn Kerner

Library of Congress Cataloging-in-Publication Data has been applied for.

ISBN 978-0-06-231528-1

14 15 16 17 18   OV/RRD   10 9 8 7 6 5 4 3 2 1

For Alice Mae and (late) Wild Bill

LAST NIGHT AT THE BLUE ANGEL

PROLOGUE

NAOMI HILL STANDS center stage in a pool of light. Silver sequins teeter on the surface of the pale dress, her white arms rise like ribbons, palms facing the crowd as though to say, *I can hold you all, I will.* A note comes out of her—fills the room, clean, unwavering, unending—until a little vibrato appears near the end like a shiver, much the way David shivered over her in another life. Tonight is her last show at the Blue Angel and you cannot tell by looking at her just how much has gone wrong. That our life, as it was, is over. Her face says, *I know exactly what I am and what I'm good at. It's this right here, right now. My voice. And your eyes on me. There is nothing else. Not anymore.*

The table lanterns are turned low, all the better to hide the club's decline—matchbooks shoved under table legs to stop the wobbling, the rotting floorboards, the dripping plumbing. It is a full house tonight.

The fullest it's ever been. Smoke hangs above the crowd like a big, wide ghost. It is a room full of people. It is a room full of ghosts.

A record-company guy sits in the front. He's come to watch the redhead he saw on the cover of *Look* magazine, and as he looks at her, he thinks she's lovelier in person, and as he listens to her, the black and gray hairs on his arms stand up. His evening had begun so disastrously with a pretty but dim blind date and now, only hours later, his luck has turned. He has found the woman who will put him—put the Canary label altogether—on the map. Of this he is certain. The hairs on his arms are never wrong.

In a table to the side sits David, who believes he still has a shot, because no matter what happens, he always believes he has a shot. He turns a cuff link, thinks the dress makes her body look like it's been dipped in diamonds. Laura sits beside him. She is smiling because when she sees Naomi onstage, she can see all the Naomis there ever were.

The LaFontaines, their friends, and my Elizabeth take up three tables near the stage. They have never been here before, never been allowed in, and they study the old place while the rest of the crowd studies them. Rita and Sister Eye say hello to them before curtain, welcome them like friends, and sit down near the back.

All of these people are here tonight—the friends, the family, the strangers, the lovers—because of Jim's pictures. Because just last week, Chicago woke up to find Mother on the cover of *Look* magazine and the whole city fell in love with her face and her struggle, which Jim has been recording, shot by shot, my whole life.

And if you look carefully, you can see the top of a girl's head peeking out from behind a curtain, red curls and a green eye, studying Naomi and studying the crowd.

That was me. It was the summer of 1965 and this was the night my mother became famous.

PART ONE

I Concentrate on You

Sophia

CHAPTER 1

MOTHER IS A singer. I live in her dark margin.

For the first ten years of my life, I watch her from the wings.

She just started working here a few months back. A club called the Blue Angel. She says it was a very important joint once upon a time. There she is taking a deep breath, arching her back, wiggling her jaw, shaking out her hands. Steve the stage manager stands at his station in front of the control board and all the backstage eyes are on him. He raises his arm, counts from five to one, and swings the air in front of him like he's whacking a fly. The guy on the pulley pulls with all his might so the tired old curtains open as smooth and slow as sheets of oil.

Jim turns the crank on his twin-lens reflex. He gives me the *behave* look—bushy eyebrows raised—and I'm not even doing anything. Taking pictures is somehow Jim's job. He photographs two things as far as I can tell: one, buildings that are mostly falling down (he says that soon there won't be a single beautiful building left). And two, Mother (all he has to say about this is that he can't help it).

Mother looks at Bennett, the piano player, who closes his eyes and nods like he's saying, *Okay, you can have the candy.* She steps up to the mike. I can see the audience if I lean forward a little, but only a little. Steve made an *X* out of yellow tape and this is where I sit. If I want to stay here, says Steve, says Jim, says Saul, *Stay on your* X.

When she appears onstage all the chatter and glass clanking gives over to applause. A little whistle here and there. I clap, too, because I want her to know I'm her biggest fan. Even though I know her better than anybody else.

Tonight I clap so hard I think she'll look over at me and pull me out of the wing into the spotlight and introduce me as her daughter, *whom I love more than anything,* she'll say. But she doesn't.

The lights get cranked up a little, shine off her white skin and dark red, shiny hair. She glows beneath the spotlight.

Jim opens the body of his camera and fixes a roll of film to its spool.

Mother smiles. *Hello,* she says to the crowd, as if to a neighbor dropped by for coffee. More applause. Some folks saying hello themselves. When she raises her arm, everybody settles down and waits. She breathes in, her belly against the bones of the dress, and lets out a single, clean note that says, *Let go. I've got you.*

She moves into the first song slowly, like she knows she might be too much for you. She lets you take your time getting used to her—the sounds she makes, the way she moves—and she won't proceed with all she's got until she's sure you can take it.

I pull my knees up, wrap my plaid uniform skirt around my legs, and set my chin on my knees. *You don't know her,* I think. *Only I know her.*

Jim takes one shot after another. He smiles while he does it, like they're talking to each other, like it's just the two of them. They go way back, he says. But when I ask how they met, he just says, *It's a long story, kid.*

Under her gown, Mother is standing with her legs apart like the sailor boy on the Cracker Jack box. All the dresses she chooses have to allow this position no matter how much Hilda nags. *You can wear nice-fitting gown like movie star,* Hilda always says. And every time Mother goes, *Hmm, we'll have to think about that, won't we?* But that's just her pretending to consider something you've said. It's one of her famous tricks.

She goes on and on, singing us through all our feelings, even old Steve with his headset half on. And though we do this several nights a week, when she rushes off the stage before the encore and waves me over with her *Hurry! Hurry!* gesture, I feel like I've been chosen before everyone else in the club—and maybe in the world. I run to her, hug her, my face pressed into tulle and sequins, steam coming off her like a racehorse, and she says, *Homestretch, kitten!*

She waits a second before returning to the stage, holding my hand in the wing, and says, *It just doesn't matter how small a crowd is, so long as they adore you.*

All night I wait for these tiny moments that are just between us.

She runs back out into the hot lights, revived enough, by me I think, for one last song.

When it's all over, Mother takes my hand and we walk to her dressing room. *How was I,* she says, *was I okay?*

It was great.

Oh, good. Good, kitten.

But you messed up the verses on "Stairway to Paradise," I tell her.

What?

You flip-flopped the third verse and the second.

Hunh, says Mother. *Think anyone noticed?*

I did. I'm sure Bennett did.

Think I'll get fired?

Probably.

And then we'll become hoboes?

Yes.

Eat beans out of a can?

I like canned beans.

We open the door to her dressing room. Her street clothes are laid out over the chaise.

When have you had canned beans?

With Jim, I tell her.

Help me. She turns her back to me.

I kneel on a stool, unfasten the hook and eye at the top of the zipper, and then pull the stiff zipper down. Heat escapes. Mother takes a deep breath. The bodice's boning leaves vertical marks on her skin that angle toward her waist. She steps out of the dress and hands it to me. Then she sits down on the end of the chaise, unhooks her stockings, and rolls them down. Hilda wants her to wear panty hose but Mother says, *Stop trying to modernize me.*

I hang up the dress with the others. Up close, you can see how beat-up they are—small rips in the tulle, sequins dangling from loose threads, pale gold half-moons at the armpits. The linings look like flour sacks—rough, stained. I wonder if their job is to protect Mother from the gowns or the gowns from Mother.

A knock on the door.

She stands, naked except for her tap pants, rolled-down stockings, and shoes. *Yes,* she says, lifting her turquoise robe from a hook.

Miss Hill, I have something for you.

She throws the robe around her and opens the door. Steve hands her a note. She carries it back to her station, whipping her robe out of the way so she can sit. She opens it and reads. *Jesus Christ,* she whispers as she leans back against the chair and looks at herself in the mirror, stares like she's looking for something she lost, then sits up straight. *Jesus Christ,* she says again, winded.

Language, I say.

She leans over her makeup station, scratches something on a piece of paper, and folds it in half. *Be right back,* she says as she leaves.

I wait for a second before reading the note left on the counter. *Flying through and saw your photo on a window. Imagine my surprise. I was just going to watch you and leave but I would like to see you. I understand if you don't want to see me. Always, L.*

When Mother comes back she is moving slowly again. She takes off her makeup, pulls the hairpins out of her hair.

Are you going out tonight? I ask.

No, kitten. I'm coming home with you, she says this like it's what she always does.

What did you write on that piece of paper?

She rubs Pond's on her cheeks.

What's that, sweetie? Her lips stretch around her teeth.

The note.

She yanks a tissue out of its box and wipes her skin until it's pink and shiny. Then she begins to pull off her eyelashes very slowly. I take my Big Chief writing tablet out of my bag and write: *Eyelashes.*

An old friend is coming by this evening. She sticks the eyelashes to their tray and tugs at the leftover strands of glue on her eyelids.

When I turned ten, Mother stopped lying to me. I'd say that neither of us is used to it yet.

I tell myself, Do not fall asleep tonight no matter what.

Jim knocks on the door. Always the same. A little dance-step knock—one, two, one-two-three.

I'll meet you two out front, says Mother, so I grab my book bag and leave with Jim.

We open the door to the sparkling night, the wind boxing a sheet of newspaper all the way up to the sky, the El whining up the block, its girders the black legs of giants. I kick at the base of a light pole.

Hey, says Jim. *What'd that pole ever do to you?*

Jim's camera hangs from his neck still. He fishes for his pack of cigarettes. His shirt is denim with pearl buttons and a long collar. There's a rectangular square of wear in the pocket where he keeps his pack. That's how much he wears this shirt.

You okay, kid? he asks.

I don't answer. He studies me over the top of his horn-rimmed glasses. His black hair always looks like he just cut it himself.

I love you. You know that.

I know, I say.

And your ma. I love her, too, he says.

Doesn't everybody? I say.

But one day she's going to love me back.

There's a way adults smile at you when you want something you're never going to get. That's how I smile at Jim.

You can call me if you ever need— he says, but I already know this and I interrupt him.

I know.

Okay. He tucks his cigarette between his lips. *Gotta be sure.*

I'm trying to count how many seconds the red light is red but Jim keeps interrupting me.

I'm walking you both home, right? he asks, looking down the alley. *Not just you?*

She's coming, I say. I look up at the lights and the power lines. Up in the air. A couple years ago somebody hung speakers all over the Loop and a man's voice came out of all the speakers telling us the president had been shot. Jim was walking me home from school and all the people froze in the streets and looked up. Some of them fell on their knees or yelled or leaned on the person next to them. Downtown just stopped, the bad news falling down on all of us from the sky. Now everybody's driving as fast as they can. In a hurry. All the bad things forgotten. I get out my notebook and write: *Lights. Streetlamps. Car lights. Stoplights. All different kinds.*

Mother rushes out of the club like she's making an entrance onto the street. She's in her wool trousers, satin blouse, wool fedora, the stole with the fox's head that I cannot stand to look at.

What took you so long? says Jim.

Bennett was giving me some notes, says Mother. *He says I'm straining in my midrange, where I should be moving into my head voice. Do you think I'm straining?*

I think you sound great, he says.

We walk by Paolo's with the check curtains and Jim stops. *What do you say we get a bite?*

Yes, let's! I say.

No, darling. We need to get you home and to bed. I'll fix a little something while I run your bath, okay? she says to me. The rush in her voice. The disguise. *And besides, I'm done in. Just done.*

A young couple pops out the front door of Paolo's with a paper place mat. Mother turns her back to us when they call to her. They ask her to sign it and one of them says, *In case you make it big someday.*

Someone's coming over, I tell Jim while Mother's back is turned.

Who?

I shrug.

Who told you? he says.

She did.

He looks at me and stands up straight. Then he does that thing with his eyeballs where they go up and to the left, like he maybe saw a bat but is afraid to look. He starts walking and I follow. He goes slowly so Mother can catch up when she's done.

You don't have to walk us, I tell him.

Yes, I do, he says.

Mother joins us. Sighs. She likes to pretend she's tired of all the attention.

Jim jogs ahead and turns around to take a picture of us walking.

Honestly, darling, why all the photographs? says Mother.

Well, if you DO make it big someday, I'm gonna be flush.

You should be off photographing people who can pay you. That would be the wise thing, Jimmy.

I'm shooting a Bar Mitzvah next week.

Are they paying you?

No, I'm doing it for fun.

She smiles and pushes him. You can see him fill with warmth. It's all he wants—this smile, this little push. It's how we're exactly alike, Jim and me. We love the crumbs we get.

I take a bath with lots of Mr. Bubbles when we get home. Mother makes me fried eggs and toast and smiles at me across the table with a drink in her hand. I get up before I'm done and run to my room.

Hey, where you going? she shouts.

I write *Toaster* in my tablet and run back to the kitchen to finish my dinner.

Do you think I keep you up too late?

I shrug.

Later than normal? she adds.

What time are kids supposed to go to bed? I ask, food in my mouth.

Earlier, I think. She looks at the clock and takes a deep breath.

How do clocks work?

Mother looks at the clock again. *There's a little engine in there.*

I pick it up and look at the back. I start to unscrew it.

Don't do that. I need to be able to tell the time.

But I need to see the engine.

You can take it apart tomorrow. Really, kitten. Why are you so nervous all the time?

You don't understand.

C'mon, let's be done. She stands and stretches.

Mother hums while she walks me to my room, tucks me in, and strokes my damp hair. I am determined not to fall asleep. After she leaves, I lie awake wondering how the little red wires inside the toaster are made when I hear someone knock at the door. It seems to take Mother a long time to open it. I get out of bed and press my ear to the door. It's another woman. I open my tablet to the list. There was one named Margaret a while back. I saw her sneaking out in the morning, and when I told Jim about it he said maybe it was Mother's fairy godmother.

I press my ear back to the door. Mother and the other woman are talking about how long it's been. The other woman says, *I'm surprised you agreed to see me,* and she sounds very serious. I don't think this is Margaret.

Do you come to Chicago often? says Mother, loud and cheerful.

The woman says, *When I can. Davie comes all the time. We like to meet here. He's good for an expensive dinner.*

It's suddenly silent out there.

And why does he come here? says Mother.

Poker, says the woman. *You haven't seen him?*

No.

How about that, says the woman.

Would you mind lowering your voice? I have a child. Asleep.

You what?

I don't hear the rest.

CHAPTER 2

IT'S ALMOST LIGHT when I wake up, curled on the floor by my door, and I kick myself. I slip down the long hallway to her room, avoiding the spots where the floor creaks. The door is open and I stand there looking at them, Mother sort of facedown, her arm hanging over the side of the bed and the other woman on her back, one arm resting on her stomach.

She has dark hair, shorter than Mother's, her skin is darker, too. The room smells like some entirely different season. A few bottles here and there, clothes thrown around like they were looking for something, the ashtray full.

I start picking up. The woman opens her eyes and squints at me.

Excuse me, I say, reaching over her to collect a champagne flute from the bed. She puts her hand on Mother's butt and wiggles her.

Naomi, she says.

Mother rolls over. *Kitten, what are you doing?*

I shrug. *Picking up.*

Later, says Mother.

When I get to the kitchen, I let the bottles fall into the trash can with a loud crash. I fill the percolator and put it on the stove. The woman stops for a moment in the kitchen doorway and stares at me. She's wearing a yellow jacket with black trim and a dark tight skirt, and has large brown eyes with long dark eyelashes. I stare back.

Coffee? I say.

No thanks, she says, but it seems like she hasn't heard me. She's staring still, her mouth open a little.

I turn my back to her and study the top of the percolator. The little see-through knob. I wait for something to happen.

You must be Sophia.

I turn around. *Who are you?*

The woman steps forward and tries to smile. *I'm sorry. I'm Laura. How old are you?*

Almost eleven. How old are you? I ask.

Almost thirty.

Pretty old.

It sure is. Do you mind? she asks, pointing at a chair.

She doesn't wait for me to answer before she sits, slips off her black shoes so she can adjust the Band-Aids on the back of each foot, and then puts them back on.

Do you have any kids? I ask.

No, she says.

Are you a singer, too?

Not at all. She takes a small black hat out of her purse and attaches it to her head, opening hairpins with her teeth.

What are you, then?

I'm a stewardess. You ever been on an airplane?

I shake my head. *Is it fun?*

Not particularly, she says. *But I get to go all kinds of places.*

Aren't you afraid of crashing into another plane?

She frowns. *Not particularly.* She stares at me. Forever.

It's not polite to stare.

I'm sorry.

She opens her purse again, takes out a small round box, and hands it to me. *Open it.*

The wood is very thin. I shimmy the lid off and inside there are five little dolls made of brightly colored threads with little scraps of fabric for clothes. Some of them wear hats made of ribbon or yarn.

Where'd you get these?

They're called trouble dolls. A woman in Guatemala gave them to me. That's in South America.

I know, I say, though I don't. *How do you know my mother?*

She leans forward like she has a secret. *I've known her since she was smaller than you.*

I try to imagine Mother as a child but all I can see is her in her green gown and heels, but shorter. *What was she like?*

Naughty, she says. *Don't tell her I said that.*

Did she worry a lot?

Let me think. Yes, I suppose she did, actually.

Just then Mother comes down the hallway, barefoot, robe open, the tiny key she wears around her neck on a ratty bit of silk hanging between her bare breasts.

Laura stands and walks toward her. I think she's going to hug her or something but Mother looks my way and Laura stops.

Sophia and I were just getting to know each other, Laura tells her.

That's nice. Is the coffee done?

I pour her a cup and leave it on the table. She's looking at Laura.

I suppose I should be going, says Laura. Mother nods, lights a cigarette, then tosses the lighter on the table. Laura doesn't leave. She seems to be waiting for something.

She clears her throat. *Could I have a word?*

They step into the hallway.

I'd hoped for this for a long time, I hear Laura say. *I'm glad . . . I'm just so happy we could make everything right again.*

Who says we made everything right? says Mother. *We had a good time is all.*

Laura doesn't say anything. I hear her moving toward the door. I run after her with the tiny box.

Your dolls! I say.

Keep them. And don't forget to tell them your troubles.

She looks back toward the kitchen but Mother is already gone.

I run to my bedroom and take out my notebook and flip to the list again. I write the name *Laura* under *Margaret, Paul, Elsa, Guy with ring on pinkie,* and *Jonathan.* I write the date and then I write: *from the airplanes/curly hair/gave me her dolls.* I hold them in my hands for a minute. Maybe the dolls could help me with the other list. I go back to the kitchen.

When I come out, Mother is looking for her slippers—little marabou heels. One in the hall. She puts it on and walks around, one foot in slipper, the other on tippy-toe. She gets a cigarette from the living room, collects the round glass lighter while she's there, and carries them around, one in each hand, searching; she is a human puzzle that's about to come together.

I don't tell her that the other slipper is under the kitchen table. I pull a loaf of bread out of the bread box.

Maybe she has it, I say instead.

Has what? says Mother, barely listening.

The slipper.

Darling, what are you talking about?

Your fairy godmother. Maybe she needs to fix it or something.

She leans on the doorjamb and lights her cigarette, holding up the bare foot now like it's hurt. *Where are you getting these fairy tales?* she says, blowing smoke my way. *I know for a fact there are no fairy tales in this house.*

I don't answer, wanting her to think there are many things she doesn't know about me.

She hobbles over and puts her arms around me for some reason.

I wriggle out. The toast is going to burn.

Oh, for God's sake, she says, discovering the slipper, smiling, like, aren't we crazy girls? No, I think. No, we are not.

How do you know her? I ask, pretending to look for creamed honey in the Frigidaire.

Mother glances at my mouth. When she gets like this she'll look anyplace but your eyes. She wanders into the living room. *Ka-tee, Ka-ta* go the heels on the dull wood floor.

Another windy day, she says, looking across the living room toward the windows, across the turquoise walls and low, white furniture, the black-and-white photographs of her framed and hung like rows of square portholes, past the ferns and paperweights, out the window, into the wind. She has this way of looking out, looking past. She does it on-stage, too. When you're in the audience it's like you're caught between her and a lover in the back of the house.

I left Kansas to get away from that wind and here we are! she says. *Can you believe it?*

Kansas talk makes me nervous. I better start being good.

Come eat some toast, I say, hoping to distract her. *Honey and butter.*

My favorite, she says.

She takes two bites and looks past me. *All you could see was just wheat and wheat and sky and sky and wind. Oh, kitten, the wind never, never stopped.*

I need to come up with a way to keep her thoughts from going to Kansas.

It was just—nothingness. It filled us with nothingness. It made you feel so . . . trapped. Isn't that funny? With so much space around you? Trapped? Can you explain that?

Didn't you have a family?

Of course, darling, she says. *Most people do.*

18

The sadness comes over her. It's like when the clouds move in and everything in the apartment goes dull.

How come you never see them?

My heart pounds. I know I'm pushing. Jim is always saying, *Don't push, Sophia.*

Just because you love someone, doesn't mean they'll love you back, she says, poking the toast and studying the honey on her finger. *You may as well know that now.*

You shouldn't play with your food, I say, but she doesn't hear me.

Mother has many kinds of smiles. This one is the *I'm sad and all alone but I don't want you to worry* smile.

She opens her cigarette case and looks around the table for matches. The blue Diamond matchbox on the stove surprises her, like it's not been sitting there as long as I can remember. The paper crackles as she lights her cigarette, then she stares at the wall with the dead match in her hand. *It just came crashing down,* she says. *Sometimes in life it just all comes crashing down.*

Hey, I know! Let's go to Riverview Park today! I say.

But she's gone. All bad days start with Kansas.

I go to my bedroom and write in my tablet: *Matches.*

The door opens suddenly. *Call Jim. See if he'll take you,* she says, and I want her to come into my room, to help me with my list, to read with me or something, but she's back in her room before I can even ask.

Jim and I go to Riverview without her.

What'd he look like? he asks the second we get in the elevator.

I shrug. *Can we go to Aladdin's Castle first?*

Jim scowls. *Well, was he big, small, old, young?*

Last time you said you'd go on rides with me next time, I tell him. *Do you remember saying that?*

Sure, says Jim, *we'll see.*

I don't believe him.

Was it a fella you've seen before?

It wasn't a fella.

A gal?

Yup.

Well, what'd SHE *look like?*

What are you, Perry Mason now? I ask him.

He points his finger in the air. *Was she real skinny?*

No. She had very long eyelashes.

Anything else?

Nope. She was just regular.

He opens the car door for me. *Regular with lashes. That narrows it down.*

Can I get cotton candy?

We climb into his car and he pulls into traffic, yelling at a taxi as he does.

I open the ashtray in my armrest and let it click shut. Open. *Click.* Open. *Click.* Open. *Click.*

Sophia, says Jim. I stop.

He looks at me during a red light. *Does it bother you?*

What?

I don't know. The men, the women. All the coming and going.

I shrug. *I don't know.*

He continues to stare at me.

The light's green.

Riverview is crowded today. Lots of families. If a bomb got dropped here, so many people would die at the exact same time. I'm not paying attention and run into some guy.

Hey, watch where you're going, says Jim. So I try to watch and look around at the same time.

You looking for somebody?

If the bomb siren went off right now, where would you hide?

He stops walking and frowns at me, takes a deep breath, and studies the buildings closest to us. He's a buildings expert. *Tunnel of Love? That'd be a good place.*

He points at the Tunnel of Love and I memorize where it is—across from the Chutes, next to the Comet—and I feel better.

I ride all the roller coasters—the Bobs twice, the Jetstream, the Silver Flash—and the Carousel. The Carousel is not one of my favorites but it's the only ride Jim will go on with me. *I have enough excitement,* is his reason. I beg him to take me on the Tilt-a-Whirl.

We have to get going, he says.

But I didn't get to ride it! I say. *Not even once!* My hands are in the air. They are covered in a cotton-candy-saliva crust.

Next time, he says, and we are walking toward the parking lot.

We scope out buildings on the way home and park the car on the street in front of the Chicago Stock Exchange.

Jim says, *They'll take down every beautiful building in all of downtown if they have their way.*

I don't know who "they" is.

Welcome to progress. Jim says this a lot.

I look at the arch above the entrance, try to count the floors.

Why do you love buildings?

He combs his mustache with his fingers while he thinks. *This town . . . it's all hustlers and thieves from top to bottom. It always has been. But this . . .* He points to the building. *I don't know, kid. Sometimes we do something right. Make something worth taking care of.*

Can we go inside?

We'll come shoot her soon. You'll love it. Very ornate. I been in there so many times but there's always something new, something you missed before. A very small detail. You'll see. He leans back and looks at me. *That's how you know real beauty. Real beauty never changes. But it's always new to you. See what I mean? I should write that down.*

I nod.

Do you have homework? he says.

I shrug. *I hate Sundays.*

They're not so bad, says Jim.

Jim spends the afternoon with us. He and Mother smoke and laugh in the kitchen and now and then he takes a picture of one of us. They play gin rummy. Mother gets up to go to the bathroom. Jim looks at my tablet.

Homework? he says.

I shake my head.

What is it?

I'm making a list of all the rides I rode at Riverview and then I circle that list and write *very difficult* next to them. I also write *cotton candy*. I think about it. It can't be that hard, the way it disappears just by touching you—your tongue, your hands.

How hard would it be to make cotton candy? I ask.

Not hard. If you have that machine.

How hard would it be to make that machine?

Can't be that complicated, he says. *Why?*

I put a question mark next to *cotton candy*.

It's hard to explain.

Try, he says.

It's a list of things I might have to reinvent someday, I tell him.

Jim taps the ash of his cigarette into the ashtray and squints at me. *Why would you have to do that?*

I don't answer.

Do you think something bad is going to happen?

I add *machine* to *cotton candy* and put a little star next to it.

So . . . what sort of things would you have to reinvent?

Well, not easy things like . . . I look around. *Chair. The harder stuff. The stuff where I don't know how they work.*

Jim looks at me. *Let me see that list.*

I hand him my notebook. He studies it.

This is a long list, he says. *When did you start it?*

After they shot the president. When we came home that day and Mother was crying in front of the television.

I know, I know, says Jim. *Who do you think "they" is?*

The people who have guns. And bombs, I tell him. *She never cries.*

She probably does.

I would know if she did.

He hands the notebook back.

You forgot camera, he says.

I write down *camera*. I study the word and feel the fear swell inside me. *I have no idea how a camera works.*

It's okay, says Jim. *I do.*

Mother comes back. *What did I miss?*

Jim says, *I need to go to the darkroom. Want to come?*

The darkroom smells funny, I say. *You should stay here.*

He's looking at me like he feels sorry for me.

Can you spend the night? I ask.

Jim laughs. *No.*

It would be fun! says Mother. *We could watch* Ed Sullivan *and eat popcorn.*

He says, *Well, all right*, because no matter what Jim thinks, Mother can change his mind. We cook hamburgers and watch TV and make a bed for him on the couch, and while Mother tries to sing me to sleep in my bed, Jim leans in the door and listens.

I tiptoe into the living room in the middle of the night. He is snoring on the couch with all his clothes on, even his shoes. I cover him up with a blanket and pretend he's my dad. He stops snoring and opens one of his eyes.

You the tooth fairy? he says.

Yes.

He sits up slowly. *I'm fresh out of teeth. Will you take a cigarette?* He tugs one out of his shirt pocket.

No way.

He lights his cigarette and leans back. *Sit down, you dumb fairy.*

I sit next to him and we stare at the dark, still room.

How come you sleep on the couch when you spend the night? The others sleep in Mother's room.

He sucks on his cigarette; the end goes bright for a moment. *Because we're friends, your ma and me.*

You're my friend, too?

Of course, he says. *When you were a little baby, I said to you, "Kid, I'm gonna look after you whether you like it or not." Know what you said?*

What?

You said, "Gla, gla, gla." He rolls his eyes around and waves his arms in front of him like a baby.

He puts out his cigarette. *May I please go back to sleep now?*

CHAPTER 3

WHY ISN'T YOUR *homework done?* asks Sister Eye while the other kids are out on the playground.

I don't know.

Is Mama okay? she asks.

I nod.

Is there something you're not understanding?

I shrug.

Sister Eye sighs. She puts her hand on my head.

We had sleepovers all weekend, I say, trying to come up with something.

Who?

Jim last night. Some lady Saturday night.

I see, says Sister.

Don't be mad.

I'm not, peanut. She looks at the clock. *Let's work on your math for just a few minutes and then you can go outside for the rest of recess.*

I want to stay with you.

You spend an awful lot of time with adults, she says, erasing the board.

Did you give me my name? I love this story. I could hear it a hundred times.

Yes, she says. *Your mother wanted to call you Pearl.* She picks up bits of paper along the aisles. *"Let's call her Sophia," I said. And Jim was there. He said, "Much better," and Rita said, "I'll say."*

We always laugh at that part.

Why did you want to call me that? I ask.

Sophia was the name of my friend. She was smart and strong and a leader. She always knew exactly who she was.

She sits in front of me and folds her hands on my desk. I've known Sister Eye my whole life. And Rita. We all used to live together when we were poor. They're my best friends.

After all the kids are settled back in after recess, we bow our heads and say the Acts of Faith, Hope, and Love. When we're done, Sister says, *Please take out a clean sheet of paper.* But just then the civil defense drill siren sounds and we all get into balls under our desks. I cross my fingers and hope it's just practice. There are so many things not on my list. I just know it.

Sister Eye and Jim talk when we get out. It was Sister's idea for Jim to start picking me up from school. *Because Mama can be forgetful,* was what she told me. And Jim is always on time. He says punctuality is one of the few things a man can control.

He takes me all the way up to the apartment. He says it's so he can be sure I'm safe.

Oh, good, you're home! Mother says when we walk in. She's wearing a white dress with yellow and red flowers on it and a red apron. *The Good Mom Costume,* she calls it.

She talks while she walks to the coffee table in the main room. *The funniest thing happened today. I was just minding my own business and the postman shows up with a delivery. Look.* She lifts a blue dress from a giant box on the floor. The dress is the color of sky with navy beading and silver sequins. *Isn't it the most delicious thing you've ever seen?*

I step toward it. I want to touch it but I don't want to get it dirty.

Jim shrugs. *Nice dress.*

Well, the peculiar thing is this, she says, handing Jim a small, square card.

"Wear it tonight," Jim reads. He turns the card over to see if anything's written on the back.

Who on earth could it be? she asks.

Jim's eye twitches. *Well, anyone actually.*

Mother glances at him like he just tried to steal her cookie. She grabs the dress, holding it to her like they're going to dance. Then she floats down the hallway to her room, saying, *We'll have to see if it fits.*

Jim takes me into the kitchen and sits me down at the table. *I want you to get to work on your homework right away. I'll make you a snack.*

I don't want to do my homework.

Well, I know that. But it's what's going to happen.

I'm not a child.

Oh, yeah, he says. *You're Lady Bird Johnson. I forgot.*

I open my math book and try to look serious. *Don't be mean. It's unbeakening.*

It's what? says Jim.

Unbeakening, I say with some uncertainty.

What's the definition of that again?

Well, if you're mean, and you're a bird, your beak would fall off. For punishment.

Jim's eyebrows lift.

Mom said it.

The word is unbecoming, he says.

That doesn't make any sense.

Miss Rita shows up calling *Yoo-hoo! Yoo-hoo!* down the hallway. I run to hug her.

She takes my chin in her gloved hand and tilts my face up so she can study it. *Good,* she says.

Good what? I say. It's our little game.

You're still you. She bends over me. I study her face—the heavy pancake makeup, the line she draws just around the outside of her lips. Her eyelashes like little black fans. Her big twist of hair that she calls *platinum* instead of *blond.*

You're still Miss Rita, I tell her.

Well, now that that's settled, where's your mother?

Mother appears then in the dress. She is one curvy line after another, hugged in sparkly blue, hugged in the sky.

What on earth? says Miss Rita, circling Mother like she's the maypole.

It was a gift, says Mother.

I hate to think what ghastly favor inspired this, says Rita.

Mother waves her hand at Rita and glances at me. *For heaven's sake.*

Was I crude? Rita asks Jim.

But Jim isn't listening. He's just looking at the dress, trying not to look, looking some more.

I have new music for you, says Rita. They sit. *I know you love the old songs and God knows I do, too, but, darling, your audiences get older every night. We're going to have to start pouring Geritol at intermission. Do you listen to the radio? "Chapel of Love"? "My Guy"?*

Mother shudders. *Horrible, vulgar little songs. No talent whatsoever.*

Jim takes a picture of all of us at the kitchen table.

All I'm suggesting is that we perk up the act a bit. Rita stands and brushes her skirt. *I would say take your time but we're not getting any younger, darling, are we?*

Rita hugs me and says, *Show business is a barbaric life. Promise Miss Rita you'll be a . . . nurse. Or a teacher like Sister!*

I promise, I say.

She hugs me again. Usually four times. Enough that I smell like her perfume for the rest of the day. *Who's my favorite little bastard child?*

I am, I say.

Yes you are, yes you are, she sings.

Mother tosses the music on the table and goes back to admiring the new dress. She poses in the doorway of the kitchen. Dazzling us. *Like a glove*, she says, half turn to the left, half turn to the right.

Jim lifts his camera from around his neck and shoots another picture.

Oh, stop, she says, posing anyway just in case he shoots again. Which he does.

How did he know my size?

How do we know it's a he? says Jim, and then laughs.

Mother's jaw clenches. She doesn't laugh. She walks away.

What'd I do? asks Jim.

CHAPTER 4

Big doug says the Blue Angel was once the most important jazz club downtown. *All of the big shots came through this place.* People with names like Billy Strayhorn and Bix Beiderbecke and Dizzy Gillespie. Everyone around here shakes their heads when they tell stories about the good old days. I don't believe the good old days are happening anymore.

Big Doug runs the place and says his Blue Angel was every bit as good as New York's, maybe better. He tells Mother he's doing his best but *downtown's going to hell. What's a fella to do?* The club is a long dark room with lots of silver chrome and tubes of blue neon along the ceiling that fizzle and blink before they go out for good. Little tables with tablecloths and tiny blue lanterns fill the room and the dark blue curtains along the walls are all pulled to the side to hide the places where they're moth-eaten and threadbare. Behind the bar is an angel etched in glass with silver wings. She's looking down. I guess she doesn't want to see what's going on. *She's listening*, says Mother. *You should try it.*

The stage is raised and Bennett's big black piano takes up half of it. Behind the stage is a hallway with a few dressing rooms and a green-room.

During the show, I sit on my *X* and try to be still. Jim is studying the audience as they file in, rubbing his mustache. I watch, too.

Jim shakes his head and goes back to his stool. He fishes through his gear bag and becomes very focused on his camera.

Mother takes the stage and the blue dress is amazing under the lights. Jim moves in to photograph her but instead he just stares. Then, like he remembers why he's there, he takes a shot.

I lean forward and look at the first row. That's when I see the man at table A-5 for the first time. He's tall. Dark suit. Light blue tie. Cuff links. I try to figure out what's different about him. I look at the other men and women. It's how he looks at her that's different. It reminds me of the boys at recess burning ants with a magnifying glass.

Jim hooks a finger into the waistband of my pants and drags me by my butt back onto the *X*.

We have an agreement, he says.

I know.

He puts his hands on his thighs. *You don't want the audience to see you. It will distract them. They came to see your ma, not you. Not me neither.*

Sorry.

What's out there that you have to see so bad, huh?

That man there, I say.

Where?

The man at A-5.

Jim squints.

Mother feels pretty in the new blue dress. She's using her arms a lot, turning her upper body this way and that, winking, finger shaking, hand on hip, and so on. At one point she closes her eyes and lets a note fill the house, then become soft. It's like she trusts you enough to close her eyes. Like she knows you're not going to hurt her. Or leave her.

When she lets go of the last note, pulling her arms slowly into her sides, she notices the man at A-5, and for a moment, her stage-face goes away. She rushes into the wings.

Bennett watches her leave, smiles at the crowd, and begins a little tune on the piano.

Miss Hill, we've got four more songs before intermission, says Steve.

Intermission is now. She runs to her dressing room.

The crowd claps and starts up its conversations again, its clanking of glasses and shuffling of chairs. Except for A-5, alone at his table, who sits there in his own silence and waits.

Mother returns several minutes later. *We'll start here*, she says to Steve, pointing to his list of cues.

Yes, ma'am, he says.

The show is back on but Mother cannot seem to find her footing. She's either rushing ahead of the accompaniment or lagging behind it.

Take it easy, kid, Bennett says, just loud enough for her to hear.

She forgets the words a few times, inverts verses, and then gets lost. When the show is done, the crowd claps happily. But no encore.

Think they liked it! I tell Mother.

They're being polite, she says, flying past me and heading straight for her room before I can catch her.

I look in the audience for A-5 but he's gone. Just a few dollar bills on his table.

Jim takes me by the hand. *Come to the greenroom with us. Big Doug bought us sandwiches.*

I have to ask Mother.

Already did. She said it's fine. Take this will you? He hands me his tripod.

I sling it over my shoulder and carry it to the greenroom. It's one of his tricks, sticking me with his gear.

We get our sandwiches and sit in the greenroom. Somebody plugs in the old Zenith and we pull our chairs around to watch Johnny Carson. He stands in the center aisle in the audience reading questions from little white cards in his hands. His microphone cord trails behind him on the carpeted stairs like a pet snake. I laugh when the guys laugh. Johnny Carson acts like he doesn't know what's so funny. Neither does Jim, who looks at the television but doesn't seem to be watching it. Usually he has a good time with the crew. *They're good people*, he always says.

I finish my grilled cheese, drop my paper plate with its slippery yellow stain into the trash, and start to make my way through the maze of the lower level toward Mother's dressing room, but Jim scrambles after me.

Hey, he says, *Where you going?*

Mom's room.

But Carson's going to have those monkeys on.

I don't care about monkeys. I want to be with Mother.

Come on, kid. Come back with us for just a little while longer.

I wave at him and run to her room.

The door is locked. I put my ear to it and don't hear anything. I walk to the end of the hallway. The walls are concrete painted pink and the floor is concrete as well but smooth, the color of a blackboard. Nothing could get you back here, not even the bomb. I'm pretty sure.

I try another door. It's open. I turn on the lights. It's like Mother's dressing room but smaller.

Before the bulbs get hot, I unscrew all but every third one. This is how Mother does it; it cuts down on the heat and, as she says, keeps her face from melting.

There's an abandoned smock draped over a metal chair. Pepto-Bismol pink with snaps along the shoulder, worn to protect costumes from hairspray and pancake foundation. A sign posted by the door reads: WHEN YOU ARE IN COSTUME DO NOT: SMOKE, EAT, ROUGHHOUSE, GO OUT OF DOORS, RUN, SIT ON THE FLOOR. ALSO DO NOT: FORCE ZIPPERS, LACING, HOOK-AND-EYES, OR SNAPS. PLEASE REPORT ANY DAMAGE TO COSTUME SHOP IMMEDIATELY SO THAT SITUATION IS NOT MAKE WORSE. This has to be Hilda's sign. Her English gets bad when she's worried.

I sit at the vanity and look in the mirror. I don't usually look at myself because I'm busy looking at Mother all the time, her beauty crashing over me. It makes you not want to look at your ordinary self. Your red haywire hair. Your round moon face. Your four million freckles and your buckteeth. Eyelashes and eyebrows so pale you can't see them. I lean in close. Turns out I even have freckles on my lips.

You're the type a girl turns pretty overnight, Jim said once, after hearing Paul call me Howdy Doody after school.

I get up and lay the smock on the floor. The globe lights warm the small room and I fall asleep curled up on the smock.

When I wake up, it takes awhile to figure out where I am. Steve is shouting, *Sophia!* And I can hear Jim and Mother fighting.

Sophia, Steve calls. From a distance I hear Jim. He's saying, *It IS your life. YOUR life. And SO am I and so is EVERYONE here. We are ALL YOUR LIFE.*

I'm facing the door when Steve opens it. He drops down to his haunches so he can hug me face-to-face. *I was worried. We couldn't find you.*

I was in here, I say.

I see that.

We stand there a minute before turning out the lights and leaving the small, warm room.

Mother runs down the hallway, allowing her robe to fly open, showing her peach-colored bra and garter belt. The elastic of her garters is shot and knocks against her bare legs as she rushes toward me looking like a giant butterfly. Almost sliding into me, she squats and grabs me by the arms, shaking me. Her hair is down and there's mascara under her eyes.

God damn it, she shouts. *God damn it, Sophia. What were you thinking? God damn it.*

Enough now, says Steve.

This is not your affair, she says, standing up and facing him, trying to make herself tall.

I get away from her and run. I'm wearing my tennis shoes. She's wearing little heels and can't catch me, but Jim does.

Let's all just slow down, he says as we walk back to Mother's dressing room.

Damn it, she shouts from behind us. *A moment alone! One moment!* She storms into the bathroom. *I need to collect myself.* The doors swing shut behind her.

I think of my Tugboat Annie puzzle. All the parts it takes to make Tugboat Annie Tugboat Annie. Mother in the bathroom, collecting all her parts.

I open the door to Mother's dressing room and A-5 is sitting on the chaise. He gets up. He has tan skin and dark whiskers, and when he stands, he's tall as a tree.

And who are you? asks Jim.

A friend, he says. He tugs at his pants just above his knees and lowers his body down to squat in front of me.

Hello, doll, he says.

I look at him. I don't let go of Jim.

Quite a head of hair you got there, he says, touching my head. I step out of his reach.

He studies me, turning a cigarette in his long fingers.

You locked me out, I tell him.

I realize that now. I'm awful sorry.

You should probably be going, says Jim.

A-5 doesn't look at him.

Can you forgive me? he asks.

I don't even know you.

The girls are tired, says Jim.

A-5 stands, nods. *You look out for them?*

Jim glares at him over the top of his glasses.

A-5 puts on his coat and lifts his hat from Mother's vanity. He places it carefully on his head and stares at me. Then he smiles.

What are you looking at? I ask.

Sophia, says Jim.

It's all right. I'm just glad to meet you is all, says A-5.

I nod. I don't look at him until he's left and then I scramble into the hallway to watch him leave. He walks like there's all the time in the world.

I stand in the hallway a long time after he's left. Finally I turn into the dressing room and put my books in my bag. I wrap my scarf around my neck; the neck must always be covered, Mother says.

Jim looks at the room through the top of the camera and takes two pictures. I try to see what he sees but all I see is Mother's usual mess.

Jim gathers a few of her items from the counter—her hairbrush, her song folder, her watch—and places them in her big leather duffel. He lifts her gray trousers off the floor, shakes them, and drapes them over the back of her chaise. He turns her sweater right side out and sets it on the trousers, finds her socks, unrolls them, and places them on her shoes. There's something small on the floor, which he picks up, crumples, and throws in the wastepaper basket. His slowness makes me sleepy.

Behind me stands Mother, leaning in the doorframe. She smiles. *A little detective work? For old time's sake?*

She cocks her head at him. He steps in front of her and she stands up straighter. I sometimes think they're just going to start punching each other.

Someone needs to know what you're doing, he whispers. *I mean, you don't.*

Mother takes a quick breath like she's going to say something terrible but then she looks over at me.

CHAPTER 5

Jim KISSES MY head and tells me good-bye at the club and Mother is quiet on the walk home. I think she's still angry with me, though her feelings tend to spill out past the little boundary of us. Mother's feelings are the curb I walk, trying to keep my balance, and I get tired of it, being careful, and mad at her at the same time. But then she takes my hand and smiles at me.

You're my favorite, she says. And suddenly I'm on solid footing again, struck smooth, the moment perfect, our life perfect, and me, perfectly loved.

We live in an old hotel not too far from the club. Mother says it used to be a very fancy place. She says it's ideal for us because it's so close to work.

There is a seat built into our living room window. I perch there on top of a folded blanket, and if I sit just right, I can see a sliver of lake between two buildings, and if I sit long enough, I might see a fishing boat pass by the sliver, its lantern swinging. There is a whole world out there that has nothing to do with us. I write *fishing boats* in the front of my Big Chief tablet.

Let's tuck you in, kitten, says Mother.

She puts me in my nightgown and into bed.

Jim was mad, I say.

She touches my hair and looks at my face. *It's okay.*

Is he going to come back?

Of course, darling. He never stays sore for long.

He said he'd help me with my list. I need help with my list.

Shhh, shhh, she says. *Enough with the talking now.*

She gets up to leave.

Sing to me, I ask.

I've been singing all night.

But just to me.

She sings. *"The water is wide. I cannot get over. And neither have I wings to fly. Give me a boat that can carry two and both shall row, my love and I."*

When she notices me, all the times she doesn't notice me get erased. Like I imagined them.

I can hear the tired in her voice. I pretend to be asleep so she can leave.

She's very quiet as she gets ready for him but her trying to be quiet is so loud. It's like sitting on the floor of the orchestra pit, her quiet. I fall asleep in all her noise, thinking about her and me alone in a boat.

The next morning I go quietly into Mother's room, certain A-5 is there, but she is alone, asleep on top of the covers in her peach satin gown.

She wakes. *Come here*, she says, waving me onto the bed.

I lie down in front of her and she holds me from behind.

I memorize this feeling, her smell—hairspray and worn-out perfume. Nothing else in the world but us. She breathes slowly like she's still asleep but I can hear her thoughts whirring around.

You'll come to Hilda's with me today?

Yes, I say.

She pulls off her clip earrings and tosses them on the nightstand.

Did you think that man was going to come over last night? This comes out of my mouth before I really think about it.

Yes. I thought he'd come.

What's his name?

She's quiet for a long time. *David.*

We take a taxi to Hilda's. The El rattles overhead and I stare at Mother's face. When she thinks no one is looking at her, her mouth moves a little, like she's talking to someone she's mad at.

Stop staring. You're worse than Jim, she says, like she's just very tired of everyone looking at her all the time.

Hilda is dressed in her church clothes when we arrive at her shop.

Come in, come in. She flips on the lights, bends over the radiator, and turns it on. It hisses and moans.

She pulls her pincushion strap over her wrist and waves Mother forward. Mother removes her coat and trousers and blouse like she's alone in her room.

I sit down on a little bench and write *sewing machine* in my notebook.

Hilda pulls the beginnings of a dress over Mother's head and turns her this way and that by the hips. *You're distracted*, she says.

Mother ignores her.

A new lover? says Hilda. She pins several darts around Mother's waist and Mother has her arms up in the air like she's surrendering. *I know there is someone. Hilda knows. You're not talking?* She's the only person I know who is allowed to scold Mother, handle her, and I like to watch.

Hilda sighs. *It's nice to sing. You are young still. But soon you must settle down. For her*, she says.

I have plans for myself, Hilda. Big plans. Why should I settle down?

Not just you. You have the child. You forget you have the child, I think.

I most certainly do not, says Mother. *And besides, she's perfectly happy. She's fine.*

Hilda bends over and pins the hem, mumbling something in Polish.

I sit down at a sewing machine and turn the bobbin and pump it with my foot. The thread is trapped between the spool and the needle. I can tell that today Mother feels stuck with me, like I'm a chore she's trying to get out of. Sometimes it stays like this for weeks. I hook the thread with my finger and pull it a little; I pull too hard. It snaps and I take a deep breath.

What are you doing? says Hilda, rushing toward me. She speaks angrily in Polish and shakes her head.

I'm sorry.

She bends over me and pets my head. *The child needs attention.*

Hilda, says Mother, *come back. Come make me beautiful.* Mother's voice is hot coffee. Hilda is cream in it, dissolving. Like all of us.

After all the pinning and turning, Mother changes back into her regular clothes and we start home, her quiet.

I wish I had a brother or a sister, I say.

Why's that?

To play with. You had brothers and sisters.

And do you see me playing with them?

What were they like? I ask.

You know I'm not going to discuss this with you.

Why?

Someday, she says.

No, you're not. You never tell me anything, I say to her, louder than I'd meant to.

Where is this coming from, this outburst?

I imagine this big family someplace far away and Mother walking away from them because they're not good enough for her or beautiful enough and if she left them behind she'll leave me behind. I start to tell her all this but stop right away because I don't want to give her any ideas.

Well? says Mother, waiting. *I'm going home. You can stand there with your mouth open all day if you like.*

She walks quickly then. I catch up to her, but by the time I do, she has gone someplace else in her mind. Someplace that doesn't involve me one iota.

Wait for me, I say, but Mother is walking ahead and doesn't hear me or maybe she doesn't want to.

Naomi

CHAPTER 6

KANSAS, 1951

I WAS TEN WHEN Papa came home from Germany with a bullet in his shoulder and a shock of gray hair, and I was eleven when Mama had those twins. All I can tell you about them was that one was big and fat and the other was a runt with teeny raccoon fingers who lasted only a week. I didn't want Mama to have more babies and I thought the little one died because of me. We buried him behind the orchard, the wind trying to shred our ugly dresses while Daddy said a prayer, and then told us not to breathe a word. After that happened, Mama's mouth was set. I tried to make her laugh with my little made-up songs but she didn't.

There were seven of us. Thomas, the oldest, and then girls, girls, girls. We always had something to eat, we had shoes most of the time, we got baths on Saturday, girls first. By the time it was Thomas's turn, he just stared at that bathwater like it was slop. I heard Papa say to him once, *That water so filthy you be cleaner by staying out of it*, and they laughed with their heads touching because Papa loved Thomas more than anything.

People who live in Kansas will tell you how beautiful it is but all I can say is that in Kansas, the wind blows everything down or away, and if it can't do one of those two things, it just beats the shit out of it.

When I walked the long dirt road to school, I felt like a very small thing pushing my way along the edge of the world. The others walked in a huddle, hand in hand, but I stayed up ahead, not wanting to walk with them, not wanting to belong to them. I sometimes hoped the wind would carry them away. I walked as fast as I could. It's not that I was a cruel girl, I swear. I just had this feeling that our time together would be short.

By the time we reached the schoolhouse, we were stiff and quiet and warming up hurt worse than getting cold. I stood facing the stove, and when Sister Therese told me to sit down, I pretended not to hear her. So she grabbed my ears and bent down so our noses were almost touching. *Your sisters are good*, she said. *And Thomas is an angel. What's the matter with you? Answer me!*

David Miller stood nearby with firewood in his arms. He interrupted her. *I'm going to put this in the stove.*

Sister let go of me and said, *Well, you're not going to stand there holding it all day.*

Don't pay her any mind, he said as he passed me. He was the oldest boy in school and tall as two of me. Dark-haired and dark-eyed. Already shaving.

I looked at my sisters as I walked back to my seat and they looked at their books.

David's sister, Laura, was wearing another dress I hadn't seen before and her long black ringlets were so soft her ribbon slid right out of her hair. I dropped my pencil, and when I bent to fetch it, I took the ribbon and kept it. The girl sitting next to me saw me and raised her eyebrows, so I showed her my fist.

Laura absentmindedly touched her hair, and when she noticed

the ribbon was gone, looked for it on the bench and the floor. Then she looked back at me. She had large brown eyes that looked sad even though she had nothing to be sad about. We stared at each other for a minute, and then she turned back around.

Every day like clockwork Sister Therese ran around the schoolhouse opening all the windows even though it was getting cold. She stood in front of one for several minutes, fanning herself with her lesson book. When she turned back to us, her face was flushed and damp. Once I heard her whispering to herself, *It will pass, it will pass.*

When Father Eugene appeared in the doorway we stood quickly and greeted him in unison. He smiled and stomped his boots, speaking with Sister Therese quietly, their backs to us, glancing a few times at Thomas.

On the way home it was Thomas walking far ahead. I caught up to him and could tell he'd been crying.

Go on, he said, and started making longer strides.

Tell me what they said, I yelled.

They're taking me away. To become a priest.

I laughed at him. He wiped his face.

What the devil are you talking about? You're fifteen years old!

Well, that's when they take you, barked Thomas. I realized he was telling the truth and was scared to death.

I wish they'd take me, I said.

Easy for you to say.

The whole family was happy and proud about Thomas. *Father Thomas*, Murielle whispered to me in bed that night. *Won't that be something?*

It's horrible.

I don't think so, she said. *Special people can come from nowhere. Why, General Eisenhower was from right over in Abilene.*

A week later, Thomas was taken away empty-handed. He kissed me with his doll face.

You don't have to, I whispered to him. *We can run away.*

But all he did was blink.

After Thomas left, Papa took the older girls out of school to work on the farm. But not me. Mama told him I was too mean and lazy to be of any use there. *Let the nuns deal with her*, she had said.

My sisters became strong and lean, darker than me, and it was not hard to imagine them stuck in that filthy, tired life until they were like old swaybacked mares.

CHAPTER 7

WHILE SISTER THERESE was having one of her fever moments at an open window, I stole an arrowhead from the Land of Kansas diorama. She turned around just in time to catch me and put me in the corner for a week. The Monday my punishment was to end I went to school early with the head of an old hammer and a fistful of nails in my skirt pocket, and I angled the nails into every last window. Laura and David, because they were always the first ones to school, saw me doing this and smiled at each other. I raised the hammer up in the air, shook it like Sister did with her ruler, and they laughed again. Standing in front of them like that, their eyes on me, made me feel like I belonged to them, like I was one of them, like I was worth something—and I loved it so. I had stumbled upon the key to my happiness.

That afternoon when Sister Therese went hot and ran for the window, she couldn't get it open. So she tried the next one and then the next one until she finally said, *I am fed up with this!* and ran out of the schoolhouse.

Laura turned around to look at me with those big eyes and I said, *Yes?*

She continued to stare at me for the longest time, barely smiling. *You are terrible*, she whispered.

I wished I had something clever to say but I went blank, her face so close to mine. I learned two things that day: one, you ought not let yourself love a person until they've seen just how bad you are, and two, I loved Laura Miller.

Sister Therese's replacement was a novice all the way from Atchison.

Hello, children, she said, standing in front of the class. She had a large mouth and puffy green eyes, like she'd been crying or was just very tired.

Where's Sister Therese? asked Laura.

God needs her for other things right now, said the new nun.

I made a noise. Not a laugh exactly.

What does God want from you? said the new nun, looking right at me. *That will be our question*, she said, turning to the rest of the class.

She flipped through Sister Therese's lesson books and asked us where we were. We looked at one another. The older kids had a lot to say about what the younger ones were learning and then they argued about what they were studying. Laura and I didn't say anything because everyone was already talking at once. The conversation made the new nun rub her fingers under her coif where it seemed to be squeezing her forehead.

Maybe we should draw, she said as she pulled out a roll of brown paper and colored chalks. We covered our long tables with the paper and began to draw.

Laura was working very hard on a small drawing of a house when I reached forward and slid my finger into one of her long curls. It felt so soft as I dipped it very gently into my inkwell. The ink dripped on my hands and my desk and then onto her dress.

When she noticed she spun around and looked at me, hurt. The girl sitting next to us told on me and the new nun approached, looking down at us with her arms crossed.

You must be Naomi, she said. I looked down at my drawing, which was every color combined to make brown, and waited for her to strike me or send me to the corner.

She reached her hand toward me; I braced myself.

I'm Idalia. Sister Idalia, she said, and waited for me to shake her hand.

I slowly lifted my hand toward hers. She shook it gently. Her hand was rough and cold. I tried to pull my hand away but she pulled it toward her and then bent over it. She turned my fingers this way and that. They were stained black.

She moved my hand so that it was in front of my face.

You're not very good at this, you know, she said.

The whole class was turned and staring.

So, I said.

SO you might not have much of an aptitude for naughtiness. That's all I'm saying.

Then she looked at Laura and smiled, taking her by the hand. I looked at their hands holding and felt my bones clamp down on themselves, tightening like a spring.

Let's get you cleaned up, she said to Laura as they walked away. I feared I'd lost Laura for good.

The next day we spent practicing music for Mass. Sister separated us into several parts and began to teach us about harmony. Then she put her hands together in front of her chest and closed her eyes. *Lord Jesus, please bring us a piano. Surely someone has one they're not using.* Then she clapped her hands and said, *Let's go back to Attende Domine.*

We sang: *"O Attende Domine, et miserere, quia peccavimus tibi,"* which meant "Have mercy on us, oh God, for we have sinned against You," or something like that.

When we were done one of the boys asked, *What are we saying?*

Sister Idalia thought about this. She smiled and said, *It's Latin for "I am a child of God. I am loved. I am perfect just as I am,"* and then she kept on smiling like she was proud of something. It was a giant smile and she had a gap between her front teeth. I liked her so much already and I liked singing, and I loved Laura. All of these things in combination made me feel untethered, unable to protect myself, or worried that I'd forgotten how.

I leaned in behind Laura. *How come your brother hasn't been in school?* I asked.

He's working with my father at the bank, she said.

I tried to imagine David with his hair combed, counting dollars.

He is really good at numbers, I said.

He loves arithmetic more than anything, she said.

I was close enough to smell her breath. It smelled like hard candy.

I hate arithmetic, I said.

Laura giggled. *I noticed.*

The fire went low, so one of the boys got up to fetch some wood. He was small and wiry. I stuck my foot out and tripped him. He scrambled back up and looked at me but he was little and too afraid to say anything.

Are you all right, Clyde? said Sister Idalia. He nodded and ran off.

Naomi, she said, *come sit by me.*

I stared at her and walked slowly to her desk, keeping my arms folded across my chest as I often did because I had breasts and the other girls my age didn't have them yet. I wanted to explain myself to Sister. All of the feelings were right there under my skin but I didn't have the words for them. I sat down next to her on her little bench. *There we go,* she said.

We sang some more. Not just chants. Other songs, too. When I was singing I didn't want to hurt anyone. Singing made me warm from the inside out, like a lightbulb.

CHAPTER 8

THE NEXT DAY, as we were gathering our books to leave, Sister said, *Can you stay after?*

I looked around me. She smiled. *You're not in trouble. I want to share something with you.* She took my hand and we walked into the little room built onto the side of the schoolhouse. There was a bedroll, a crate of canned food, a small plug-in burner, a box of books, and a little stove. It was hardly big enough for the two of us to stand in and of course it was freezing.

You live here? I asked.

Mm-hmm, she said, smiling, like it was good news.

I can't wait for you to hear this, she said. She cleared a plate and a cup and a book off the top of a tall narrow cabinet and pulled a key on a string from her tunic. Bending over, she stuck the key into a tiny lock on the lid and opened it. There was a record player inside. She tucked the key on the string back in her tunic.

Do you have a record player at home?

We have a radio, I said. *I like* The Shadow.

She lifted a record out of its sleeve and placed it on the black disc. The sleeve said "The Boswell Sisters" across the top and there were three women dressed as sailors sitting in a boat. SHOUT, SISTER, SHOUT! was written on the boat. Crackling sounds filled the small room, then this beautiful burst of several voices sounding like one. It made me want to cry and dance all at once. My ears had never heard anything like it. I actually touched my ears, the sound was that strange and that beautiful.

She took my hands and we did a little dance as she sang all the words. When the song got slow, we stopped dancing and Sister Idalia put her hand to her heart, singing along: *"If that old devil should grab your hand, here's one thing that he can't stand. Shout, sister, shout!"* Then the music picked up again and we danced and danced until we were breathless. *Isn't it fun?* she said.

Why are you being nice to me? I asked, laughing.

Oh! This one! She pulled out another album.

Where'd you get all these?

My brother, she said. *You won't tell, will you? Father Eugene would have my hide.*

No.

I want you to hear everything.

Why? I asked.

She looked at me like it was obvious. *Because I think you've got a great voice. A big voice. But you don't know where to put it yet.*

Where would I put it?

It's hard to explain. For starters, you need to get as much music in your head as you can.

I just sat there and watched her talk to me. It all felt like an odd mistake. Nobody had ever really paid attention to me before. I'd gotten in plenty of trouble and heard a thousand orders, but this? I didn't know what to make of it. I felt it indirectly, like I was watching her be nice to someone else. To Laura, maybe. To someone good.

She put on another album. A woman with scared eyes on the sleeve named Dinah Washington. She was beautiful. Even her name made a little song. I said her name over and over in my mouth. Her voice was like cool water. Sister Idalia sang along. *"Love brings such misery and pain. I guess I'll never be the same."* This song made her eyes well up. I decided I wanted to sing. Not just stupid Latin church stuff but this, the kind of songs that made women cry.

We played it over and over until I knew the words and we could all sing together—me, Sister Idalia, and Dinah Washington.

She had other records, too. Sister kept saying, *Just one more.*

Then she looked at her watch on the chain she had attached to her belt. *Oh, dear, we have to get you home.* She straightened her coif and waved at me to follow her out of the room. I ran behind her down toward the well, where a rusty green pickup truck was parked. We jumped in and bounced up to the main road.

I didn't know nuns had trucks, I said.

My superior is a good egg, she said. *She let me come here on the condition that I have means of transportation, or, as she put it to me, "some way to get the hell out if you have to."*

I told her which direction to go. I was thinking two things on that ride. One, I am going to be whipped when I get home and two, Sister Idalia is not going to think I'm so special once she sees where I come from.

Dad and the girls were already in the yard when we pulled up.

You better let me do the talking, Sister Idalia said, setting the brake.

We walked up to my father, Sister with her back very straight, jaw stiff.

Mr. Hutnik, I presume? she said.

Yes, Sister, said my father.

I am Sister Idalia. The new teacher at Naomi's school.

Father looked down at the ground and shook his head. *What's she done now?* he asked.

I thought, This is going to be the end of school for me.

She's not in any trouble, but we do have a serious matter.

Father smoothed down his hair.

She's having some trouble with her multiplication tables, Mr. Hutnik. And this is affecting her grasp of mathematics as a whole.

Father frowned. I stared. My mouth hanging open.

If Naomi is ever to take a respectable job at, say, the bank or the grocery, or if she is ever to run a proper household, she will need at least a reasonable grasp of numbers. Now, there isn't need for alarm. I believe she has the necessary potential.

Father's brow was buckled and my sisters sneered at me. *What's to be done?* asked Father.

Sister Idalia sighed. *Well, I kept her late today but we are going to have to be vigilant. Do I have your permission to correct this . . .* she glanced down at me, searching for a word . . . *this troublesome issue?*

Father winced at that word but nodded anyway.

Sister Idalia shook father's hand. *Then I promise to do my best by Naomi. God bless you,* she said, turning on her heels.

I ran up beside her and walked her to her truck, giggling.

Quit it, she hissed.

You just told a huge lie to my father, I said.

She shot a look at me and hoisted herself into the truck. *In service of a greater cause,* she said as she fetched up her habit and shoved it under her thigh.

What cause? I asked.

The cause of you, Miss Hutnik. Then she leaned down and whispered, *Music might be the only thing could save you.*

She slammed the door.

I walked back toward the house and Murielle sidled up to me. *You're going to end up with us,* she said.

I looked at her.

If you don't do better at school, she said, smug.

Maybe so, I said to her with a sad little look on my face. A little kick of the dirt.

She's pretty in a way, Murielle said as we lay wide-awake that night. I looked at her face as she stared at the ceiling, absolutely certain I shouldn't open my mouth. *I wonder what her hair looks like.*

The moon had lit up the room with a strange, dark light.

Have you seen it? she asked.

What?

Her hair?

No, I said, turning away from her.

Seems like you know your tables. You been teaching them to us. Maybe you're teaching us wrong? she said. *One of your tricks.*

I'm not teaching you anything wrong, I said. *Go to sleep already.*

I lay there in the moonlight breathing deep until I was sure she was asleep. Then I just let my head run back to the music, to little phrases I'd committed to memory. I felt my throat move a little as I imagined singing. And I understood that this must be love, to visit a place in your mind where music is playing, to have such a place at all.

PART TWO

When I Fall in Love

Sophia

CHAPTER 9

CHICAGO, 1965

I HAVE TO START going to school early every single day, the Sisters say. Because I don't know my times tables yet. Jim says he's going to get me there on time, and if we get a move on, he'll let us stop for Danishes.

As we walk it's so windy that I hold Jim's arm and turn my face into his sleeve.

How come I have to?

Because every kid has to learn them. Your friends have to.

I don't have friends, I say, but I don't think he hears because of the wind and because he's working on his *math is important* speech.

I want you to do well in school, Jim kind of shouts. *I want you to have options.*

I don't know what that means.

A girl has to have options. You gotta trust me on this. I mean, what do you want to be when you grow up?

It depends, I say.

On what?

On bomb or no bomb.

He stops and looks down at me. *There's not going to be any bomb.*

You don't know.

You still have to learn math. Then he stops to pull his camera out from under his coat and photograph a door that is hanging by one hinge, its glass shattered into the shape of a star.

Can we stop at the bakery? I ask.

We don't have time.

You said!

He gets us Danishes but we have to eat them fast because the bakery is right by the school.

One of the nuns, Sister Marie, is sweeping the steps and the sidewalk when we walk up. She does this every morning, that or shoveling. As we get closer, she stops sweeping and smiles.

You could let the wind do that, Sister, says Jim.

She laughs. I think she seems a lot happier out here, sweeping, with no children around.

I say good-bye to Jim and run up the stairs to Sister Eye's room. She's looking out the window with her hands on her hips. She smiles big whenever she sees me, showing the big gap between her two front teeth.

There's my girl, she says, and hugs me hard. She smells like cigarettes and baby powder. *How are you today?*

Fine.

How's Mama?

Good. She told me to tell you to stop by after school and have coffee with her.

I will, then.

And Rita. Rita's coming, too, I tell her.

Oh, good.

Rita thinks I'm going to be pretty someday.

Sister puts her hands on my cheeks and puts her face right in front of mine. *You are the most beautiful creature*, she says. *Right now. You are perfectly you.*

Just then Sister Marie pokes her head in the door. *Hold on a minute, will you? You might have one more joining you.*

Of course, says Sister Eye.

I had thought it was just going to be us two and I don't want to share Sister with another kid.

Sister is wearing brown pants and a brown sweater today. She looks like a skinny bear. *Why don't you wear a habit like the other sisters?* I ask her.

Well, I'm not officially a sister any longer, she says. *But I've kept my vows.*

What are vows? I ask.

I think you already know this.

I forgot.

Promises to God, she says. *About the sort of person I hope to be.*

Then Sister Marie comes into the classroom holding hands with a girl my age but she is Negro, taller, and prettier. Bennett, Mother's piano player, is Negro, too. All of his kids go to their own school on the South Side. There's never been a Negro child here.

I would like you both to meet Elizabeth. She has just transferred from her school in Bronzeville to our school. Have a look around, Elizabeth, Sister Marie says. Elizabeth walks slowly over to the window and peers into the salamander cage.

Sister Marie tells Sister Eye, *Her father teaches at the school of sociology and is among the group fighting the board of education. He was instrumental in all of the school boycotts. But Elizabeth's school remains overburdened. She has attended only half days all year and her mother is at her wit's end.*

The girl and I look at each other. Her hair is gathered into two little poufs on the top of her head and tied with red ribbons. She is wearing red socks. They are cute but they are out of uniform. *You can sit here*, I tell her. *This desk is empty.*

She sits.

How come you're not at your own school? I ask.

She considers my face. *My mama thinks it's not good enough.*

Oh. This school's pretty good. I've been here since first. I lean in so I can whisper to her. *We have drills. For if a bomb gets dropped on us.*

Civil defense drills, says Elizabeth. *Every school does those.*

She doesn't seem to care about this.

Sister Marie is still talking to Sister Eye. *She might have some catching up to do.*

Elizabeth looks around the room, studies all the stuff on the walls.

Her mother assures me she's been supplementing at home but I thought it best she come early. To start to adjust, says Sister Marie.

It's going to be fine, says Sister Eye.

Elizabeth sits very straight.

Sister Eye hands us both a multiplication quiz. A row of numbers in no particular order runs down the left-hand side of the page and another row of numbers runs across the top. We are to fill in the grid that takes up the rest of the sheet.

I have filled in four squares and am counting on my fingers when Elizabeth puts down her pencil. She looks at me and at my page. When I look back at her she quickly turns her head.

After a few minutes, Sister approaches our desks. *How are we doing?* She turns Elizabeth's page so it's facing her and runs her finger over the grid.

Well, you've got your numbers down, don't you, dear? she says to Elizabeth.

Ma'am? says Elizabeth.

Yes, dear.

How come you let Negro children come here?

Sister takes a deep breath. *Well, Elizabeth, we haven't always.*

When did it change?

Sister looks at Elizabeth very seriously. *Today.*

Sister bends over me and my paper. *Take your time.*

I start putting numbers in the squares because I don't know the answers, and don't care what they are. Elizabeth turns in her seat to face me. *Hey, don't do that. It won't help. You just don't know them yet.*

Sister looks at her, smiling. *Elizabeth is very wise. Like you. I think you are going to be friends.*

Some of the pain the numbers cause goes away when Sister calls me wise, even more so when Elizabeth grins at the prospect of us being friends.

I just don't know them yet, I tell Elizabeth.

The other kids start filing in. Everyone stares at Elizabeth and whispers. Paul sits down behind me. He leans forward. *Who's your friend?*

Shut up, I say.

Does Howdy Doody have a friend?

They call me Howdy Doody because of my hair and freckles—and my teeth. *Cut it out.*

Your mama make a wrong turn this morning? Girl? says the boy behind Elizabeth.

She sits with her hands folded on her desk, her back straight.

I lean across the aisle. *Don't listen to them,* I whisper.

As she opens a book on her desk she says, *You're the one listening to them, not me.*

The whole room seems to be looking at us while Sister Marie and Sister Eye talk privately in the front of the room. Sister Eye waves at us both as she leaves.

Hey, Sophia, says Paul. *Is your dad coming to parent–teacher conferences? Oh, wait. I forgot you don't have a dad.*

Elizabeth glances at me and then back at her book.

Opening my Big Chief tablet to a blank page, I bend over it so no one can see and write: *Would you like to be my friend? I would like to be your friend.* Then I write down my phone number, tear out the page, and fold it into a very small triangle. The boys will see if I hand it to her, so I tuck it in the sleeve of my sweater.

Sister Marie raps her desk with a ruler in order to get our attention. She smiles as she introduces Elizabeth. *I am certain that in welcoming her you will be as kind and courteous as always.* Elizabeth glances up at Sister with one eyebrow raised. I can't conceal my laughter and it comes out in a quiet snort.

Ladies, says Sister.

Mother is waiting when Elizabeth and I walk out of the school. She is dressed up with hat and gloves and the fox stole. Mother is like the center of the world when she is anyplace. Everyone sort of turns to face her, watch her, even the mean boys.

There's my kitten, she says, waving. I'm anxious to introduce Elizabeth. I hope that Mother will make me seem more interesting.

Where's Jim? I ask.

She puts her hand on her hip like an actress. *Can't I pick up my own daughter?*

Mother, this is Elizabeth. She's new here, I say.

Mother bends over and offers her hand. *Well, hello, Miss Elizabeth*, she says.

Elizabeth slowly reaches out her hand. She stares at Mother like she's trying to figure something out. *Wait a minute. Is your name Naomi Hill?*

Well, now how on earth would you know my name? says Mother, touching her chest.

My dad has your record.

Well, he might be the only one.

He listens to it all the time. He sings along, too. It's horrible.

Mother laughs. A woman approaches us. *Mom*, says Elizabeth, *come here! Naomi Hill!*

Elizabeth's mother is tall and slim and wears a fitted green dress. She doesn't seem as excited about Mother as Elizabeth is.

Miss Hill, she says, extending her hand.

Pleasure to meet you, Mother says. *You're new to Chicago?*

No, we are new to this school.

Well, I welcome you officially, says Mother.

Thank you, Elizabeth's mother says without a smile. *We must get going.* As they walk away Elizabeth turns around and waves. I run to her and motion her to me, indicating I have a secret. She puts her ear close to my face.

We can only wear white socks, I whisper. Elizabeth looks down at her feet and then at mine.

Thank you, she says.

I pull the note out of my sleeve, give it to her, and run back to where Mother is waiting.

On the way home I tell Mother, *I think we are going to be friends. She's very smart. She does her times tables in a couple of minutes and her father is a teacher at the university. Something about boycotts? And when the boys say stuff about her being a Negro, she just sits there like she can't even hear them. Like she doesn't get her feelings hurt. I want to be like Elizabeth.*

Mother smiles at me and shakes her head. *This is the most you've talked after a day of school since you started.*

I tell her, *I don't have friends.*

Mother stops and looks down at me. *You don't?*

I shake my head, wishing I hadn't said that.

Why don't I know this? she asks.

I shrug.

We walk in silence after that and I worry she's deciding I don't belong with her, that we're nothing alike because everyone loves her and she's embarrassed because they don't love me.

I wish she would say something. I feel my chest start to tighten.

She stops again. *Well, if Elizabeth is so smart, perhaps she will see what an interesting girl you are. And friend.* Then she kisses the top of my head. *You're my best friend,* she says. *And I have excellent taste.*

I'm so relieved she's not mad at me that I throw my arms around her and start to cry. My nose runs. She holds me for a while, and then pulls us apart so she can look at me.

Heavens, child, she says. *What on earth is the matter?*

The sun is behind the buildings and the wind is blowing hard. It can seem to come from several directions, one after the other, so that it pushes you right then left and I feel like I could lose my balance.

Nothing, I say.

We start walking again and Mother says, *Oh, kitten, you feel so much. I'm afraid you are just like me.*

CHAPTER 10

WHEN WE GET home we stop at the front desk. *Sal, darling,* Mother says, *would you mind terribly having a coffee service sent up to the room?*

Right away, Miss Hill, says Sal.

It's not a fancy place. Jim calls it run-down. But when Mother's around, everyone acts like it's great here, or like it could be if we all just tried. Like Mother. I think they would do anything for her.

Oh, and maybe some sweets, says Mother.

Did you have something specific in mind, ma'am?

Surprise us, she says.

Sister loves sweets, she reminds me.

You do, too, I say.

Mother shakes her head, smiling at me. *You've got my number, don't you, darling?*

Rita is already there when we walk in. She has a pink-and-purple scarf on her head with her platinum waves coming out the bottom. I run to the couch and jump on her. She holds her cigarette way up in the air.

My caftan, darling! she says. *You're crushing my caftan!*

I squeeze her as hard as I can. When I release her she touches her hair with her free hand.

Your offspring is trying to kill me with love, she says to Mother.

Rita sucks the tip of her ivory cigarette holder and then gently sets it on the edge of the big blue ashtray. I put my hands out. She slowly takes off her rings, one at a time, and puts them on my fingers. I study them. She takes the scarf from her head and wraps it several times around mine.

My little gypsy, she says with her deep, smoky voice.

Sal rolls in an old, squeaky cart with coffee and sweets on a doily.

What's the occasion? says Rita

Can't I have my girlfriends over for coffee? says Mother.

Sister Eye comes in then and pulls off her ugly, brown nun shoes, leaving them at the door.

You don't have to take off your shoes, darling, says Mother.

Oh, yes she does, says Rita, scowling at Sister's shoes like they said a bad word.

Please tell me you remembered to pay the gas bill today, Sister says to Rita.

I did, of course I did. Naomi, darling, please get this woman a drink, says Rita.

I move quietly around the cart, taking a few butter cookies and two jam thumbprints. I love when we're all together.

Kitten, I wonder if you shouldn't go to your room and do your home-work? says Mother.

Sister Eye looks at Mother and then at me. *Maybe your math*, she says.

They want me out of the room, I can tell, so I pretend like doing math in my room is a great idea and leave.

When I get to my room I open and close my door. Then I crawl back down the hallway to listen.

I'm so glad you're here, Mother is saying. I hear her light a cigarette and inhale. *David has found me. His sister was in town and we got together and, well, she must have told him.*

You're kidding me, Sister says.

No, says Mother.

Oh, Lord Jesus, says Rita.

But listen, says Mother. *I think it's all going to be okay. I have a feeling.*

You have a feeling, Rita snarls. *Well, in that case.*

Didn't he marry that woman? The blonde? Isn't he married? Sister asks.

Well, yes, there's that. But I don't think it's working out, Mother says.

Not working out? says Sister. *Are we talking about a marriage? A sacrament?*

She's so VERY dramatic, says Rita. *You'd never know WE were the performers here.*

Rita and Mother try to hold back their laughter.

Sister is not amused. *Is he getting a divorce?*

It's such an ugly word, says Mother.

Because it's an ugly thing, says Sister.

Rita stands and I duck so she doesn't see me but her arms are out to her sides like she has an announcement. *That is not even the point.*

Darling, top me off, says Mother. *While you're up.*

Rita continues, *If you ask my opinion, this man can only complicate things, given your history. It seems to me your methods are perfectly sound as they are right now.*

My methods? says Mother. Ice clinks in the glasses.

You take a lover here, a lover there, as the need presents itself, and everyone is happy. No messy relations, no man to answer to. It seems to me an ideal arrangement, darling. Why dive in, hmm? Haven't you already swum in this pool?

But I like him, Mother says, her voice small. *We've known each other so long.*

Are you already seeing him? asks Sister Eye. *Is this whole . . . vulgar conversation moot?*

Mother looks embarrassed. *Once.*

Don't tell me, says Sister. *He said, "I'll come by later, or tomorrow," and you waited and waited and he never showed?*

It's complicated, says Mother.

Well, that is my point, says Rita. *Right there. There you go. Off chasing the rabbit. I'm already bored with this conversation and we've only begun.*

Mother turns to Rita. *Be happy for me.*

Your career needs your attention, darling. You are withering away at a low-level gig.

The Blue Angel is famous! says Mother.

Rita lowers herself into a chair. *It WAS famous. Now it is a relic. You are performing there because at the moment, Big Doug lacks a better option.*

Mother gasps. *What a terrible thing to say!* I hear her snap, snap, snap the big glass lighter. *Damn this thing.*

Sister says, *I might add* motherhood *here if we're discussing things that require your attention.*

Well, this afternoon is turning out to be a terrible disappointment, Mother says. *I invited my girlfriends over for drinks, to have a little fun.*

And talk about boys? Rita says. *Fix our nails and set our hair and talk about boys? Is that what you hoped for? So help me, Jesus.* She stands and begins pouring another drink.

Well, now I need one, too, says Sister.

Rita nods at her. *That's the spirit.*

There is a fast rap on the door then and Jim lets himself in. I wave at him and put my finger to my mouth.

I thought I was picking you up today, he says, blowing my cover.

Mom did, I say, following him to the living room.

I see that now. You need to communicate with me, he tells Mother. *How do you do, Sister? Miss Rita.*

I'm so sorry, Jimmy, Mother says, walking to him.

I was worried sick. I looked everywhere for her.

I know, I know. I'm sure. I'm terrible. I've just been so distracted.

Well, cut it out, he says.

It won't happen again. Don't be mad at me, darling. You know I can't bear it.

There's a new girl at school, I tell Jim. *Her name is Elizabeth. She's a Negro. The only one at the whole school!*

Well, it's about time, he says, but he's fixed on Mother, his face red.

I think we're going to be friends, I tell him.

Now Jim is listening. He squats down on his haunches and looks at me. *Good,* he says. *That's just fine.*

Rita beckons him to the couch. *Come join us, Jimmy. You've had such a trying day.*

Why the powwow? he asks, sitting next to Rita.

Mother bustles to the cart. *Let me make you a drink.* She moves fast when she's in the doghouse.

I sit on the floor next to the couch.

We're discussing Naomi's love life, says Rita, giving her cigarette holder a twist.

So it's a sleepover, then? he says. Rita laughs and gives him a little push.

Please let's not in front of the child, says Sister.

Kitten knows everything. Don't you, darling? Mother says.

I nod. *I have a notebook.*

Everyone laughs. I laugh, too, though I'm not sure why.

IS there anything you don't know, asks Sister, looking tired.

Is there anything we don't HAVE to know? says Jim.

Sister raises her glass. *Another toast. To music. And to motherhood. Which both demand your FULL attention. Salut?*

Mother blinks, already thinking about something else, and takes a tiny sip.

Jim stands up and walks over to the window. He turns around and looks over the room of women.

Sophia, you want to go shooting with me? he asks.

Who's getting the ax now? Rita asks.

A little old church on Belden. A beauty. They hired me to photograph it so they can raise money to have it rebuilt someday. Can you imagine? These people break my heart.

Rita shakes her head. I ask Mother if I can go and she waves at me.

Go change, says Jim. *Dress warm.*

I carry Jim's tripod down the street like I'm carrying a rifle. Sometimes I secretly aim it at someone and say *kapow.* We walk at a pretty good clip. I think I should settle on an enemy. All men in hats. *Kapow. Kapow. Kapow.* Ladies in any kind of fur—stole, hat, muff, coat. *Kapow. Kapow.* A woman notices me shooting her and scowls. Jim catches this.

What are you doing? he asks.

What? I'm just trying to keep up.

It's getting hard to shoot people because he's walking so fast.

Why the big hurry? I ask.

We're losing light.

I roll my eyes. We are always fighting the light.

When did you start rolling your eyes? he asks. *I don't like it.*

Why don't you just take pictures in the middle of the day? Then you could have all the time you like.

The light is flat then. I'm sure he's had to tell me this before.

Two men in hats walking with two ladies in fur. *Kapow-kapow-kapow-kapow.* I startle them. They actually stop walking and look at me, and then at Jim.

Sophia! says Jim.

Sorry.

I took her to see Cat Ballou *last week,* Jim tells the couples. *Guess it rubbed off on her.*

The couples smile and move along. I overhear one of the women say something like, *A little young for* Cat Ballou?

Where are we going? I ask.

Church of the Covenant. They're going to tear it down.

For progress?

He looks down at me and nods. *How'd you know?*

You told me already, I say.

The two things that upset Jim the most are progress and Mother.

Who's this David guy? I ask.

Jim takes out his pack and lights a cigarette.

I say, *Do you know you always light a cigarette when I ask you questions about Mother?*

No, I don't.

Yes, you do. It's okay if you don't know the answer.

Is that right? he says, stopping.

I stop, too, and look up at him.

Everything seems to be happening too fast these days, he says.

Yup, I say. *So do you know who David is?*

You met him. At the club.

Why are they having a meeting about him?

We turn onto Halsted and walk toward Belden.

What's a divorce? I ask.

It's when people who are married get unmarried.

We stop in front of the church.

I like this one, I decide, telling Jim.

Me, too.

Jim tries the door. We walk around to the side and find a smaller door that opens. He gives me the *be quiet* look as we step inside. An old man kneels in front of rows of small, red burning candles. It's only a little less cold inside the church. We put our gear down quietly, get on our knees, and bow our heads. Jim keeps an eye on the old man. I follow the planks of light coming in from the windows and landing on the pews or the floor, spotlights on empty spots where somebody stood once or prayed or knelt.

Once the man is gone we get to work. Jim shoots the main windows and the altar, the archways and the pillars, the sentences about God and the rows of candles where the old man prayed. The smell of the flash gets up in my nose, its white light hanging over my eyeballs long after it's done.

We are out before anyone else comes.

I try to imagine how you would knock down something so big, so solid. *When are they tearing it down?*

Any day now.

It's much colder with the sun down behind the buildings and I feel frightened by the idea of something just getting ripped down "any day now."

Can't you stop them?

Jim shakes his head. *I write letters practically every day. No one is listening. Remember when you were real little and I brought you to our protest? We all had signs? You had one, too?*

What did my sign say? I ask.

"Mayor Daley Save the Garrick."

Oh, yeah, I say. *I mostly remember Mother yelling at you.*

Me, too, says Jim.

I want to ask about David again but I can see that Jim's afraid I'm going to ask about David again.

I decide to ask Rita when we get home but all the ladies are dancing and drinking when we arrive. They've pushed the furniture to the edges of the room and Sam Cooke is singing "If I Had a Hammer" on the record player. They are clapping and snapping the fingers of their free hands. Jim takes a few photographs of them, mostly Mother, and then takes his camera off his neck so he can sing and clap along with Sam Cooke. *"I'd sing out danger! I'd sing out a warning!"*

Rita takes my hands and spins me around. When the song ends, Rita and Sister sit down and I squeeze between them. Sam Cooke starts to sing "When I Fall in Love" and Mother sways back and forth, singing along. She reaches her arm out to Jim. Jim shakes his head. She walks to him and takes his hand. He grabs her around the waist and pulls her close. They dance slowly, Mother singing lightly, her eyes closed.

Sister sighs. *She's not fair to him.*

He's a big boy, says Rita.

Still, says Sister. *Look at him.*

His face is against Mother's hair. His eyes are closed.

When that song is over, "Twistin' the Night Away" comes on. Mother grabs Sister and Rita and me from the love seat and we all twist together, bumping into one another. I don't realize until it's over that Jim has slipped out without even saying good-bye.

Naomi

CHAPTER 11

KANSAS, 1954

I WAS SEVENTEEN WHEN I graduated from school. Sister Idalia went to my parents and told them, *Naomi really ought to go to college.*

What's a woman do with a college education? Father said.

Sister Idalia gave them all kinds of ideas but they just stared at her like she was speaking Italian.

Father enjoyed listening to her talk about me, he did. But then he said, *We need her here. Or maybe she gets a job and helps out that way, Sister. College is not realistic. We have so many bank notes, they could get called any day.* He looked at his hands. Mother's face was blank. She got up from the kitchen table and floured a board. She had long since given up on thinking about anything but the next thing to be done.

I didn't stick around for the rest of the conversation.

That day, downtown Soldier was celebrating Eisenhower's visit. He wasn't even coming to our town but everyone cleaned up and decorated like he might drop by. It was a big deal that he had lived in Kansas and everyone was acting like he was their son. Laura and I sat at the soda shop. We were only apart when we had to be. Boys walked by us and said, *Hi, Laura.*

Miss Catherine is leaving, she said, trying to spoon the last bit of root-beer float from her glass. *She's marrying that man she's been going with. Maybe Daddy would take you on at the bank.*

Are you going steady with Alan? I asked.

Laura squinted at me. *What are you talking about?*

You do things with him.

Her eyes traced the long row of glasses behind the counter and she said, *We do spend an occasional excruciating evening together, it's true.*

Have you kissed him?

Don't you think I would have told you that?

I don't know. Do you want to?

Laura looked at me, vexed. *No. I don't. I wish I did,* she said to herself.

I'd been doing that a lot. Upsetting her like that. I kept trying to stop.

We were talking about getting you a job, she said.

I looked at my dress. *I wouldn't have anything to wear.*

Pfft, I have all kinds of old dresses you can have. Besides, with your shape, you could wear a flour sack and still look like Deborah Kerr. She put one palm against my waist and the other against the small of my back. I glanced around the soda shop. There was a feeling like a house of cards falling in my stomach.

That's settled. I'll talk to Dad tonight, she said.

Afterward we walked together to the edge of town. Fireworks popped randomly. *Look at it this way,* said Laura, *if you get a job at the bank, at least we'll be together.* She squeezed my shoulder and ran up the road to their big yellow house. Two dogs raced each other to reach her first, their tails whipping with happiness.

I took the long way home, past the schoolhouse. The sky was inflamed. Sister Idalia was playing *Ella Sings Gershwin*. I could hear it all the way from the road. She was lucky nobody lived nearby. Ella was singing, *"Gibraltar may tumble . . . but our love is here to stay."*

I found Sister sitting on an overturned pail outside her door, looking at the sky.

Hi, peanut, she said. I sat down in the grass next to her. *Don't be discouraged about today*, she said, smiling. *God's ways are mysterious. Where'd you disappear to?*

To meet Laura.

She looked at me a long time.

She's going to talk to her dad about getting me a job at the bank, I said.

Well, at least you'd be together, said Sister.

That's what Laura said.

Good, work is good. She looked at the sky. *You could save for college*, she said to herself.

We listened to Ella. Killdeer circled above a field in the distance. Their song frantic. *Kill-DEER. Kill-DEER.*

Don't you get lonely out here? I asked her.

Hmm, she said. *Yes. But loneliness is good. Loneliness usually means longing and longing's not so bad. Listen.* And Ella sang: *"They're writing songs of love, but not for me. A lucky star's above, but not for me."*

See? Sister said, like that explained everything.

Laura showed up at the farm the next morning before we'd even finished breakfast. Mama was still in her sleeping gown and embarrassed to be seen by her.

Don't worry, Miss Hutnik, it's just me! Laura said, but Mama was always embarrassed by her presence in our ramshackle house, we all were.

Laura swiped up a heel of bread left on the table and took a bite. *You make the best bread, Miss Hutnik, you do. But I'm here on business. I need to steal Naomi. My dad's agreed to give her an interview for Miss Catherine's old post at the bank and I've got to bring her up to speed. Do you mind?* she said to Mama, hooking her arm through mine.

Of course not, Mama said, her back to us.

Laura waited for something more and then said, *Well, all right, then. See you all later.*

We ran out of the house before Mama could change her mind.

I believe I just rescued you from a day of grim chores, said Laura. *So thanks are in order?*

I don't like you seeing how we live.

You've always been poor. The first time I saw you you were wearing shoes with buttons! Buttons! She tried to get me to laugh at this.

I think one day you're going to realize how different we are.

She took me by the shoulders. *We're alike in every way that matters. You hear me?* Then she kissed me hard and fast on the lips and we were off down the road, she talking about how her brother David was back from Kansas City, and how bad her mother's pie turned out the night before, on and on, and all I could think was, I have been kissed.

We got to her house and played with the dogs. Then Laura spotted her brother off in the scrub trees in the side yard. An old roadster was parked there, half covered with weeds. He had the trunk open and was bent over it.

Laura ran toward him. *Come on!*

What on earth are you looking for? she said, startling him.

He pulled out a plaid suitcase, smiling. *Just remembered where I put this.*

Laura's face pinched. *What would you want with that old thing?*

I'm sentimental, he said, glancing in my direction. David had become incredibly handsome but he still looked like him. He was wearing a striped suit and tie and cuff links. He was a man.

Who's your friend? he asked, not listening to her, just staring at me.

Oh, David, don't you remember Naomi? said Laura, presenting me with both arms.

Holy cripes! You were just a ragamuffin last time I saw you. Mean, if I remember. He leaned against the car. I didn't know what to do with my arms. I crossed them in front of my chest.

Still am, I said.

Laura laughed and squeezed my arm. *She is!* I looked over at the horizon like I had other things on my mind.

David reached into his pocket and pulled out a slim silver case. He popped it open. *Have a look here,* he said. He presented a small square of paper to Laura and took out another for me. It read: *David Miller, Proprietor, the Neon Parrot.*

What's a "proprietor" do? I asked.

He leaned down a bit to remind me I was smaller than he, and looked at me like there was nothing else in the world but me and his eyes on me. *Wouldn't you like to know?* he said.

I had hated boys for looking at Laura this way but I'd never been on the receiving end before.

Laura stared at David staring at me. Her eyes narrowed on him until he stood up straight and looked away.

It means he thinks he's Boss Pendergast or something, said Laura.

He put one hand on the roof of the car and his other hand on his hip. He was so long. I remembered him playing with us when we were little, how fun it was to try to run by him and not get caught.

You come visit me someday, I'll show you, he said with a grin.

She'll do no such thing, said Laura, hooking her arm in mine, her whole face smiling except for her eyes.

I stood there feeling like I'd walked into some kind of trouble, so I looked around to make as though I hadn't seen anything.

Where'd the dogs go? I asked.

Take care of my sister, ragamuffin. You hear? he said to me, tossing his plaid suitcase into the back and then lowering himself into the driver's seat of his pale blue convertible.

Seems like you're the one needs looking after, I said.

He leaned his arm on his window. *You got the devil in you, I swear to God.*

Maybe, I said, tilting up my chin so I could look down at him.

He laughed and slapped the window's frame. *Good-bye, ladies,* he said.

I followed Laura into the kitchen, where her mother and father sat, dressed, impeccably, reading the newspaper and drinking coffee from a full silver service.

Is he gone? Mr. Miller asked.

You remember Naomi, said Laura.

Hello, darling, said Mrs. Miller, standing and giving me a kiss on each cheek. She was statuesque in an emerald-green dress with an upright collar, a tiny waist, and a full skirt. Her black hair was twisted up and secured with a large brown comb. I would have been happy to inspect her, all of these details, for the rest of the morning.

Mr. Miller looked at me over the top of his paper. *You're going to come talk to me on Monday, I hear.*

Yes, sir.

I trust you've got your shenanigans out of your system?

Daddy! That was a hundred years ago, said Laura.

I have, sir, I said.

He shook his paper upright again. *Good to know.*

You'll stay for lunch? Mrs. Miller asked.

I shook my head. *I have chores. But thank you.*

Work ethic, said Mr. Miller to his paper.

Come on, said Laura, and I followed her up the staircase. The wall along the stairs was covered with family photographs. In the newer ones, I searched for Laura and David. They were so similar—their lines, their ease, the way they seemed to be daring you to forget yourself when they looked at you—and I longed to be one of them or between them or close enough to take on their ways.

In Laura's room, which was yellow and white—the walls, the bedspread, the furniture—she hauled out an armful of dresses from her closet and threw them on the bed like excess was a nuisance she had to deal with every day.

She picked up one dress after another, gripping the skirts, turning them this way and that, making piles. I didn't know what sort of science was going on but Laura was quite serious about it.

All right, she said, hands on her hips. *Let's try these first.* She held a dress up to me and tilted her head.

Well? she said.

I looked at her.

Your little smock?

I didn't move.

Oh, for heaven's sake, said Laura.

Turn around, I said.

I was frozen by my fear of her and by my desire, like I had to settle on one quick so I could proceed.

Laura dropped the dress on the pile and stood in front of me.

You've got to be kidding. You're shy? she said.

She unbuttoned my dress, pushed it off my shoulders. I pulled my arms out as fast as I could in order to cover my breasts.

Don't, she said, taking my wrists in her fingers and pulling my hands away. *Let me look at you.*

I felt like she was seeing me in an entirely new light because of how David had looked at me. I slowly let my arms fall to my sides.

Your brother was flirting with me.

Laura slid my dress over my hips and it dropped to the floor.

What does he know? she said. *I'm the one who knows you.*

Then she touched my ribs and looked me in the eyes. She tilted her head and held her hand underneath my breast, as though to gauge the weight of it. I squeezed my legs together, like I could contain my body, which seemed to be running out, emptying.

I'm sorry, she said, pulling her hand away suddenly and taking a step back.

I turned to face the bed and the dresses piled there, I touched them, lifted the skirts just to see what was underneath. Tried to breathe. To stop myself.

Laura stood beside me and our arms touched. I stepped behind her, putting my arms around her as she let her head fall back a little. I felt my breasts push against her back and pulled her tight to me. When I slid my hand up under her skirt, I heard her breath pull in like she might say something, but she didn't. Her hipbone moved under my forearm, the little adjustment she had to make so she could open her legs wider. Heat came through her dress and she made a sound like some small thing was stuck and she couldn't get it loose.

Mrs. Miller walked across the floor downstairs. Her heels banged the old wood floor. *Lunch, girls!* she yelled, and Laura spun around to face me, her face flushed, electric. I grabbed her jaw gently and held it until she finally took a normal breath. And then I kissed her.

Be right down, said Laura without taking her eyes off me.

She picked up the dress. Lavender with blue flowers. *Here.*

I held the dress and stared at her.

Step into it like this, she said, opening the dress for me like a ring. She zipped it up and arranged it on my body. I stood in front of the mirror and watched as she put her face in my hair.

You surprise me, she said.

At that, I ran out of her room, down the stairs, and out the front door, the soft cotton of that full skirt dancing around my legs. The dogs chased me as far as the main road and stopped, exactly sure of just how far they could go.

CHAPTER 12

SISTER IDALIA WAS not in her room when I went there. There was a man chopping a cottonwood down by the creek, so I sat on Sister's pail and watched him while I waited for her. When he started up the hill I realized it was Sister Idalia. She was wearing men's wool trousers, cinched at the waist with some rope, a flannel checked barn jacket, and was without her coif.

I couldn't speak. *Your hair.*

Oh, I didn't expect to be seen by anyone.

I threw my arms around her.

She pulled apart and looked at me. *What is it, peanut?*

I don't know what to do.

Then let's walk. We went down the hill to the creek. There was no haze, no dust in the sky, just fast, bulbous clouds. It was one of those days that is ninety-eight percent sky and two percent everything else under the sun.

We sat down by the water.

I'm someone else, I said.

Sister looked at the creek. She will sit here like this with me until the end of time, I thought.

It's Laura, I finally said.

Sister nodded like she already knew the whole story.

I love her, I whispered.

I know. She squinted at the creek.

I kissed her, I said, because I didn't think she understood.

Sister looked at me, smiled. *Oh, peanut.*

I know God is going to strike me down. I can feel it. Right here, I said, grabbing my stomach.

Oh, no, no, no, she said. *This is what God is. Love. See?*

I shook my head. *I don't know what to do.*

I don't either, said Sister.

Haven't you ever been in love? I asked.

Sister looked at me for a long time. *Once.*

What happened?

They separated us. Sent me here.

We looked at the river, listened to its movement.

I have to be with her, I said.

I know, she said, squeezing tears from her eyes with her thumb and middle finger. *Isn't it terrible?*

Yes, I said.

She pressed her hands into my cheeks. *I want to tell you to be careful but . . . It's what we say about love. Be careful. And it's, well, erroneous.*

I don't know that word.

It's wrong. Be bold instead. Love her. She had tears again. *Okay?*

Okay, I said.

Just then we heard, *Sister Idalia! Sister!* Laura was shouting up by the schoolhouse. *Sisterrrr!*

Sister pulled the string and key from around her neck and put it over mine.

Maybe Laura would like Dinah Washington, she said, looking at the creek. *I'm going to finish cutting that tree up. It will take me the better part of the afternoon, I expect.*

Laura called my name up on the hill. Creek water rushed around the larger stones. There was not enough time to think. I got on my knees and hugged Sister hard. *Thank you. Thank you thank you thank you.*

In the still, quiet air of Sister's room, I got to look at Laura the way I wanted. It made her shy.

How'd you know I'd come here? I asked.

You're always out here. You and Sister I are . . . friends, right?

I shrugged and looked around Sister's room until I felt infinitely guilty for shrugging. *Yes, we are friends.*

Like we are? asked Laura, fiddling with a pleat against my hip because she could, because we were alone and the dress was hers, after all.

No, I said.

Will you kiss me again? asked Laura.

I held her face and kissed her mouth and her chin. She looked at me like she was working out a math problem.

I have to get back, she said.

Okay, I said, believing the answer to her math problem was to leave.

I want to be alone with you, she said.

We are alone.

I want time, she said, looking at me again.

Then we'll get time, I told her, trying not to smile.

CHAPTER 13

ON MONDAY, I ironed the lavender dress and set my hair. I stuffed a bit of tissue paper into the toes of Mama's Sunday shoes and walked to town, into Miller's Bank and Trust, into Mr. Miller's big, carpeted office.

Mr. Miller said hello, how are you, how's the family, etc. And, *Now, how many of you are there?*

Seven, sir.

He leaned forward. *Is that a Polish imperative?*

He gave me a simple math test, looked it over, and threw it away. *Mostly, Miss Hutnik, I just need you to be pleasant and attractive and efficient. It would boil down to that,* he said. *Think you can manage?*

Yes, sir.

Well, then, let's start you today, he said, and it occurred to me that with love as my motivation, I might be capable of just about anything.

The work was easy. Math mostly. And writing numbers in tiny boxes.

Laura and I ate lunch together on the bench in the alleyway. Her mother packed her twice as much as she could eat and she shared with me.

She's trying to fatten me up for Alan Lawry, she said, handing me a piece of cold fried chicken. I took a bite.

She what?

Nothing.

I imagined Laura with Alan and had to force myself to chew the food in my mouth and swallow. It was all temporary—us, work—and would end as soon as some man came along and put us away in a little place in town or back on another farm. We were something to exchange hands, like cattle. I thought of Mother. I'd never seen her do anything but work and pause to catch her breath.

My Mother played the piano. When she was young. Back in Poland.

Your mother? said Laura. *She any good?*

I've never heard her. It's just a story now.

Well, that's terribly sad, said Laura.

We finished our lunch and leaned our backs against the building's warm bricks.

Sister I's brother sent her some new records, I said.

Laura looked straight ahead. *That so?*

She said we could listen to them if we wanted. Saturday.

Laura became very still. Then she ran back into the bank and came out with a sheet of stationery and a pencil. She tapped her pencil on the paper.

What are you doing? I asked.

A plan. If we're going to do this, we need a foolproof plan.

On Saturday, Laura and I prepared an elaborate lunch in the Miller kitchen. I had the plan fixed in my head and every move I made passed through it.

Mr. and Mrs. Miller sat at the table, he with the paper, she with the latest copy of *Look* magazine. "Margaret . . . the Girl and the Princess" was written across the cover below side-by-side images of Margaret the woman and Margaret the Princess. She was somehow entirely the same and entirely different and it gave me hope for myself.

Are you planning to feed the troops? asked Mrs. Miller, scanning the food on the counter.

No, said Laura. *Just us.* She lined a basket with a linen towel.

And Sister, I said.

Laura scowled at me.

Mrs. Miller bent to check her lipstick in the toaster. *I could've sworn Sister was going to Topeka for the day.*

No, said Laura.

And what is it you're doing? Mrs. Miller asked, folding wax paper around a sandwich.

We're helping her strip the desks. Horrible things written on them, horrible little pictures, said Laura with a shudder.

Seems like she could make the boys clean 'em up, said Mr. Miller, suddenly listening. *No doubt they did it. Unless it was Naomi,* he teased. Like I belonged to him, to them.

I told you, said Laura, *she's reformed.*

Bad girls don't reform, doll. They just get better at hiding. He stood up and stretched. *Isn't that right, sugar pie?* he asked his wife.

I'm not even listening, she said.

I'm off, then, he said.

On a Saturday? complained Mrs. Miller

Money doesn't know from Saturday, he said. And he kissed her.

Mrs. Miller strolled into the parlor with her cigarette case. *Everyone's leaving me.*

Mother, David said I could get something from his room before he left. May I?

Mrs. Miller glanced at her as she lit her cigarette. It was a look that said, *None of these matters interests me at all.*

We ran upstairs into David's old room. Black-and-white pictures of musicians that had been cut out of magazines were taped to the wall. Laura opened the third drawer of his bureau and pulled out a pack of cigarettes, tucking it in her shirt. Then she flipped through a stack of albums and took two. She hugged them to her as we ran down the stairs.

I followed her out the front door. As the screen door bounced in its frame she called, *Bye, Mother!*

Bye, Mrs. Miller, I said, and we raced the dogs to the road.

It was hot. My stomach leaped behind my ribs. I searched Laura's face but saw nothing to suggest nerves, guilt, fear.

What does David do in Kansas City?

Oh, let's see, gambling, women, jazz, whatever he wants. At least he lives far enough away to not be a COMPLETE embarrassment! Laura said, imitating her mother.

I laughed at her. She walked taller, having made me laugh.

The schoolhouse seemed a long way off. The heat's haze wiggled the lines of the road, of the fields, of the horizon. I thought of David. How different his world must look from this.

You should go visit him someday, she said.

Why don't you? I asked.

They would never let me. They watch me like a hawk, she said.

A truck went by us, the driver waved, and the draft of his passing knocked us into the weeds for a step or two.

But you could. Seems like no one watches you very carefully, she said.

They do, I said, though they didn't. They didn't watch me, they tolerated me.

Race you, said Laura, running up to the schoolhouse.

In Sister's room there were peonies in a glass jam jar. I unlocked the record player with the key around my neck and Laura pulled an album out of its sleeve. She handed the sleeve to me; there was a red saxophone with black wings on the cover, a sketch of a man, a black hand and an ivory trumpet, a finger on the valve slide. *Bird and Diz*, the album read. Short sweet words, words from another world. I had to hear them out loud. *Bird and Diz, Bird and Diz.*

The music bounced in my chest. It rose around us like a dark tent, shielding us from everything we knew, carving a space for us. The saxophone pierced me. Laura watched my face like she was putting me to a test. She turned up the volume carefully so as not to knock the needle.

We helped each other out of our clothes and I closed my eyes. There was just the music inside of me and Laura's hands and mouth, her weight. My mind was pulled here and there by her skin, her breath, to the river, to David and his women, his long hands, to touching myself in the bath while the others waited their turn. The music rushed this way and that, notes popping and fighting one another then flipping and tumbling down like playing cards whipped into the air.

I covered her with my mouth, felt all of her with the skin of my upper lip. She tried to stop me when I moved down her body and pushed open her legs with my elbows. *What are you doing?* she said, and I didn't really know; and I did.

We rested. I stared at her. Here was her face imagining things, here was her looking at me like she knew something I didn't. There was so much to this woman, so much to learn and memorize. Would there be enough time? Would I be allowed? She pulled the key and string from around my neck and put it over her head, resting the key between her breasts.

The music stopped and we lay there listening to the needle bump the center. She stood up, stepping over me to turn the record over. I studied her body as she bent to place the needle. Kneeling down behind her, I slid my hand up between her thighs. She reached back and braced her hands on my shoulders. I rested my cheek against her, touched her barely, and felt her swell. Then her legs started to tremble as I lowered her back to the floor so I could see her face, where she was going, her face without me.

While this was happening, while we were cutting ourselves loose from everything we'd known before, Mrs. Miller discovered the forgotten basket of food in the kitchen and maybe shook her head, saying, *oh, those girls*, and decided to walk it to us, because Mr. Miller had taken the car. So she wandered down the drive and up along the road and she probably thought it was hotter than she expected, like we did, was irritated and maybe thought about turning back but she didn't turn back. She looked for us in the empty schoolhouse, I imagine, before hearing the music and following the sound right to us, hot and naked, tangled on a blanket on the floor while Bird and Diz blew, pushed, pulled, fell down, flew up, notes shooting everywhere like the world would fall apart if they stopped. She dropped the basket in the doorway, her hand just opening on itself, and the glass pudding dish cracked inside.

She righted the basket before she turned and walked away.

Laura scurried like she was suddenly stuck under something heavy, and held her shirt to her chest as she ran out the door. I tried to stop her but she jerked her arm from me. When she caught up to her mother, who was walking stiffly down the road, her mother's voice flew out of her—a short wail like an animal snapped in a trap. Laura stopped. Stood in the road and watched her walk away. I was frozen and waited for her to turn around. I believed we could be okay if she would just turn around, come back to me. *Turn around, Laura. Just turn around.*

I stood absolutely still, staring at Laura's back. Her skin was ghostly in the afternoon sun, flushed in places, marked. The sound of her mother's shoes on the gravel road became faint. I begged Laura with my heart to turn around. I felt my bare feet on the rocks and promised to God I would take care of her. *Come to me.* She did turn around. And my breath fell out of my lungs and I smiled but she raised her hand to me like you would to stop a truck in the road.

She walked back to the schoolhouse, dragging her shirt in the dust, then dressed, collected her things, left. As she walked back down the road she pulled the key off her neck and dropped it in the weeds.

When I could no longer see her, I went slowly up the road and found the key. I lifted it from a shock of thistle and put it back around my neck.

Then I walked.

CHAPTER 14

DOWN THE HILL, past the copse of cottonwood, toward the creek. I stepped into the water and moved against the current, the silky mud sliding around my feet, small, moss-wrapped stones shifting, the water pushing and pulling my balance. Soldier Creek dumps into the Kansas River. All that rushing just to become something else. I felt its cold, cold water and the hot sun on my hair. I somehow knew, standing there, that my world was going to drop like a clean sheet slipping from the line and I was going to be all right.

When I got home I played with the little ones in the yard. I smelled their heads. My sisters huffed past me for being gone all day. A wet pile of laundry sat in a basket on the ground, so I strung it up.

I listened to my family talk during the meal, not eating. I watched them as though I'd never seen them before—the silverware tinking tin plates, the rush, the laughter, the freckles, the dirty nails. It was how I imagined the dead twin watched us when I was little, lingering, suspended. I put my fork down and stood at my place. Everyone looked. I started to sing. *"There is a balm in Gilead to make the wounded whole. There's power enough in heaven to heal the sin-sick soul."*

The little ones chewed their food. Murielle scowled. Mama cocked her head at me. *Where did you learn that?*

From Sister Idalia. A Negro woman taught her it.

Mama and Father looked at each other, and then down at their plates.

There's more to the song, I said.

I think we've heard enough, said Mama.

Dinner was over and I'd washed the last plate when Mr. Miller appeared at the back door. I stood in front of him, my heart pounding, and he looked through the screen door and through me. He came in without speaking and took off his hat and smoothed his hair. He was still in the suit he wore that morning when I cooked pudding in their kitchen and he teased me. I slipped out of the room and hid under the stairs and wondered how I might escape.

I heard Mama and Father rush to welcome him, offer him a seat, a drink. I peeked my head out and watched them through the balusters. He smiled at them but it didn't hide the fire in his skin. I thought about running down into the cellar and up out the cellar door but I was so afraid I couldn't think fast enough; I couldn't move.

I'll need to speak with Naomi, he said.

Of course, of course, Mama said, her brow pinched.

To Father he said, *Went in this morning and realized I'd not given her her first week's wages.* He held an envelope in the air. *New employees. It happens.* He slid it back into his coat pocket.

I stepped into the kitchen, my heart banging. A vein behind his collar twitched. *There she is,* he said. And then, to Mother and Father, *Do you mind? Business.*

Oh, my, yes, of course, said Mother, rushing Father back into the parlor and closing the kitchen door behind her.

Have a seat, he said.

I sat.

He breathed through his nose and stared. I squeezed my hands between my knees.

He took a deep breath and looked around the kitchen. *I hold the notes to this whole operation,* he said. *I own the dirt they're farming. Of course, you already know that.*

Yes, sir. The sound of my voice made him flinch.

It would take me but a few days to destroy it. Repossess. Auction. It would be real sad.

I nodded.

You know what happens to the kids? In situations like that? he asked.

No, sir.

Oh, they get separated and stuck in orphanages or put with other families.

My stomach squeezed into a small hard knot.

He set the envelope in front of me, pried it open like a mouth to reveal a small stack of bills, closed it. Then he leaned forward. *Now, what I want is for you to disappear. You will never come back. You will never, ever come near my daughter again, you sick little cunt.*

He stood, straightened his coat, and walked to the door. *What are you waiting for?* he said before he left.

Mama heard the door shut and peeked in. Seeing he'd gone, she rushed to the window and watched him walk to his car.

Did you offer him anything to drink?

I watched her mouth move.

Well?

He was in a hurry, I tried to say, but ran out of air.

Well, what did he want?

To give me my paycheck. I lifted the envelope in the air, my hand shaking.

Seems that could've waited till Monday, Mama said, pushing the chair

Mr. Miller sat in back against the table. *What will you do with a paycheck between now and Monday?*

I stood. *Sit down, Ma. Let me make you some tea.*

No, she said. *But thank you.* She wiped down the table again. I kissed her and told her good night.

She looked at me and moved a curl from where it hung in front of my eye. She never touched me. *Naomi*, she said.

I let myself feel her. The sound of my name in her voice, my longing for her, to be loved by her, adored, touched. Anything.

Your song, she said. *At the table tonight. It was . . .*

She twisted the rag in her hands. Night had blackened the windows. The kitchen clock clacked on the wall.

You go to bed now was all she could say.

I packed the lavender dress in my book satchel and stood for a moment in the room, listening to my siblings sleep. Murielle watched me as though this was not news, my leaving.

I'm sorry, I said.

She rolled over. *It's not fair*, she said into her pillow. *It's never been fair.*

The fields—high, black—seemed to breathe as I ran past them. I stumbled on rocks in the road. The wind started quietly in the distance and built up speed until I thought it would knock me over. I kept thinking I'd made a wrong turn and was lost. Nothing looked the same. I began to feel like I'd run forever.

When I finally saw the dim light outside the schoolhouse, I didn't believe my eyes, so I ran faster and fell, skinning my knee. The sting of it in the night air made me feel stronger. The truck was parked out front and Sister Idalia was rushing in and out of her room. I tried to catch my breath.

Naomi? What on earth, she said when she saw me.

Sister, I—

I can't talk now.

What are you doing? I asked.

She bent to lift the stereo. *Help me.*

I picked up the other end and we shuffled it into the truck bed. The moon was dim and I couldn't read her face.

What happened? I asked.

Mrs. Miller. Father Eugene. She stuffed her work clothes into a duffel bag. *I don't have to tell you, do I? Are you okay?*

You're going home?

Yes.

Are you in trouble?

She threw her bag into the truck.

I'm so sorry, I told her.

She put her stove in the truck, her bedroll, her blanket. *We are probably going to be in trouble much of the time. Women like us. For one reason or another.*

I'm scared.

What do you intend to do? she asked, looking at my bag.

I've never been away from here.

She looked at me. *Then get in.*

PART THREE

Come Rain or Come Shine

Sophia

CHAPTER 15

CHICAGO, 1965

JIM DROPS ME off at school and tells me he might be late picking me up, and I am under strict orders to stay with Sister Eye until he gets there.

I eat lunch with Elizabeth. The boys continue to say things to me and now to her, though their comments to her feel more frightening. Maybe it's because I'm used to them being mean to me. Sister says to the boys after recess, *I would like to spend some time with you gentlemen after school.* They make faces and kick at the ground but she just smiles and walks away.

I linger around Sister Eye after school. The boys sit at their desks with their hands crossed, quiet.

Sister Eye whispers to me, *Peanut, please wait in the hall.*

I wait outside the door.

I hear a big noise—something slamming against a desk. Then I hear a familiar noise, a sharp sliding sound I can almost place.

Do you see this? says Sister, her voice angrier than I've ever heard it. *Do you?* she says.

Yes, sir, the boys say together.

If you so much as look at Elizabeth again, or say a word to her, one single word that is not pure sweetness and light, I will cut your hands off. Then the sliding noise again. It's the giant paper cutter. I almost start to laugh when I figure it out.

Do you understand, gentlemen?

Yes, sir, the boys say, their voices shaking.

Sister raises and lowers the blade again with a slam. *Go home.* And the boys run by me. They see me but they don't even care.

Sister and I wait for Jim on the front steps. I can't stop staring at her.

Stop it, she says finally.

I start to laugh.

What is it you find so funny?

This makes me laugh even harder. *I can't believe you did that,* I'm finally able to say.

It's my job.

I know, I say. *Mom told me.*

Really. And what did she say?

That you protect the innocent, I tell her.

Sister laughs pretty loud for a minute and then she looks down at me. *Oh, peanut,* she says. *No one is innocent. Not even you.*

But you would still cut off the boys' hands for us? I ask.

She tucks a curl behind my ear and smiles at me. *I'm protecting them, too.*

Elizabeth and I eat lunch together all week and the boys don't come anywhere near us. On Friday she says, *My answer is yes.*

We are sitting at the craft desk in the back of the classroom. We don't play with the other kids and it's not clear to me if this is because we're not welcome or because we don't feel like it.

Yes, what?

Your note, she says. *You asked me if I would be your friend.*

I'd forgotten about the note. I had assumed the answer was yes because we'd been acting like friends all week.

I showed my father the note and he said you can't just say yes or no to friendship. He said you have to see how it goes.

A thin layer of clay is stuck to the table and I try to get it off with my thumbnail.

Do you want to come to my house tomorrow? I ask.

Don't you live at a motel?

Well, yes. It's still my home.

I would love to, she says, bending over the clay and helping me scrape it. I try to match her excitement, though the cup of worry in my stomach has already begun to fill.

I'll ask my mom after school but don't say anything, says Elizabeth. *Just let me talk to her.*

Okay, I say, though I can't imagine what I would say to Elizabeth's mother.

After school, Elizabeth's mother is waiting for her and Jim is on his knees toward the end of the block, taking a picture of the junker truck that has been parked there as long as I can remember. I pretend I don't see him.

Just go along with me, okay? says Elizabeth.

We approach her mother. I glance at Jim, who is stretching his body over the hood of the car so he can shoot the broken windshield.

Mama, says Elizabeth, *Sophia and me have a project to work on. Geography.*

Sophia and I, says Elizabeth's mother.

She said we could work on it at her house tomorrow, says Elizabeth.

I nod. Elizabeth's mother squints at me.

Jim yells, *Hey, my girl, come check this out!* But I pretend I don't know him.

I've spoken to Sister every day this week. She says you're doing fine, more than fine, says Elizabeth's mother.

Yes, but we took a pretest just this afternoon in geography and I missed half the capitals, says Elizabeth.

Probably more than half, I add.

Elizabeth makes a terrible face at me that lasts one second.

Jim walks up to us. *Hey, didn't you hear me? I want to show you something.*

Elizabeth's mother straightens her back. *And you are?* she says.

I'm Jim, he says, extending his hand.

My dad, I say.

He looks down at me.

Claire LaFontaine, says Elizabeth's mother.

You must be Elizabeth, says Jim. *I've heard a lot about you.* To me he says, *You should see this old car. I got some great shots, I think.* Then he turns to Mrs. LaFontaine. *I think there's something living in it. Seats all tore up.*

You don't say, says Elizabeth's mother. She often looks like she's smelling something foul.

Can Elizabeth come study with me tomorrow? I say. *At our house?*

Don't see why not, says Jim. *But I thought you were going to come shooting with me.*

Mrs. LaFontaine's eyebrow raises.

Photographs, says Jim, holding up his camera. *She carts my gear. Strong as an ox, really, for a kid.*

I could come! says Elizabeth. *I could help, too!*

Let's stick to our studies for now. All right, ladies? says Elizabeth's mother. *I have some business at church in the morning but my husband can bring Elizabeth by at, say, nine o'clock?* she says to Jim.

Jim's mustache twitches and he glances at me. *That'll be swell,* he says.

We all say good-bye.

Jim and I walk to his car. He puts his camera back in its bag and I open the glove box. I find a handful of root-beer barrels under the papers and empty cigarette packs. I pile them in my lap and unwrap one.

How come you said that back there? he asks.

Said what?

I stare at my pile of root-beer barrels. I've made a sling for them with my skirt. Some coffee nips are in there, too. I have to remember to add *hard candy* to my list. Jim keeps looking over at me. I don't know how to explain myself. Suddenly I don't want candy anymore.

It was a small lie, anyhow. Small lies are venial sins, not mortal. And besides, you are my dad. To me you are. I don't care what you think. I have to stop because my voice is breaking, so I cross my arms and look out the window.

Jim turns so he's facing me. *Hey, there, whoa.* He puts his hand on top of my head. *I'm not mad. Know what I really thought?*

What? I'm still looking out the window.

I thought, Wouldn't I be the luckiest guy in the world if this girl was my kid.

I don't look at him. I don't want him to see me smile.

He puts the key in the ignition. *I forgot to show you that car back there.*

I know.

He pulls out onto the street.

I would still like to help you tomorrow, I say.

It'll all work out, says Jim.

CHAPTER 16

MOTHER IS BEATING pillows, dusting and straightening knickknacks when we get home.

You having a party? says Jim.

She's wearing a tan dress, her hair down, no stockings yet. *No, silly. If I were having a party, you'd be the first to know.* She pats his chest. He stares at her with zero feelings on his face. *We just need a good sprucing up before the winter really hits us,* she says.

Jim mouths the words *Ask her.* I follow Mother into the bedroom. She opens a drawer and pulls out one stocking then another, holding them up. She runs her arm into one of them and spreads her fingers. *What is it, kitten?*

I told Elizabeth she could come over tomorrow. To do homework.

Sounds lovely. Good thing we cleaned up, huh?

Sometimes Mother talks to me like she talks to the crew. I start to leave.

What time? she asks.

Nine.

In the morning?

Is that okay? I say, watching her face, watching all the details get sorted, all the potential problems get visited. I'm tempted to say never mind, but I don't. I want her to figure it out herself.

Of course, she says, *why wouldn't it be?* She pulls a stocking over her foot and slides it on as she raises her leg. *We love company, you and me.* She snaps the elastic against her thigh. I leave the room.

Did she say yes? asks Jim, waving me to the kitchen table.

I nod.

Sit down, I'll make you a snack, he says. He puts a tub of oleo and the tin of saltines on the table and lights a cigarette. He mixes me some Ovaltine and pours himself a drink.

Did she say who's coming over? he asks.

No.

It's a new dress.

He butters five saltines and puts them on a plate in front of me.

Mother hums in the bathroom.

Quit worrying, says Jim.

This was a terrible idea.

It's going to be fine. I'll be here a little before nine.

I nod.

But you'll owe me, he says.

Okay, I say.

What are you scheming in here? says Mother, appearing in the kitchen, looking around.

You lose something? says Jim.

My cigarettes, she says.

Jim shakes a cigarette out of his pack and holds it out for her. *Keep this up and pretty soon you'll sound just like Louis Armstrong.*

He's famous, isn't he? she says, leaning over so Jim can give her a light. Then she spins around and sits down on his lap. *I feel so happy.*

When Mother is happy, I am happy. I don't even care if it has nothing to do with me. When it's just the three of us, everything is right.

Jim holds her around the waist and looks as though he's trying not to breathe.

Tomorrow will be fun, she says to me.

Who's coming over? I ask.

Your new friend! Elizabeth!

I mean tonight, I say.

Jim looks at me and Mother looks at me. She tilts her head a little bit. *Just an old friend. Nobody you know.*

David? I ask.

Mother concentrates very hard on putting out her cigarette, tamping and tamping until it breaks.

What's that? she finally says, hopping off Jim's lap.

Jim shakes his head.

Mother kisses my cheek. *I have to finish putting my face on.*

Jim follows her into the bathroom.

I'm not going to discuss this with you, she says.

We'll see about that, says Jim.

Mother sponges on makeup like he's not standing there.

Jim stares at her. *You only want him because you can't have him.*

How dare you, says Mother as best she can with her lips stretched over her teeth.

You can't resist a challenge.

That is simply not true! Mother says, trying to hold down her voice like it's a jack-in-the-box.

After Jim leaves, Mother and I go out to pick up groceries and booze.

Sing with me, Sophia, she says while we walk.

We sing a few bars of "Easter Parade" and a few bars of "I Found a Million Dollar Baby."

You have a lovely voice, baby, you do, she says. *It's like clean water.*

That's funny, I say, *I always say your voice sounds like* warm *water.*

You do? she says. *I never knew you thought that. Hunh.*

I'm a little out of breath trying to keep up with her.

Of course, don't think for a single minute I want you to be a singer, she says. *It is not an easy life. Boy, if you knew—I'll tell you someday, I will, and I won't mince words; I will tell you everything.*

Her coat is open and the wind blows it behind her like a cape she doesn't know she has.

You should button your coat.

Honestly, Sophia, she continues, *I don't care what you do, as long as you have passion.*

She holds my hand with both of hers now. *But, if you want to know the truth,* she says.

I do.

Passion will have you. Because you are just like me. Best to give in, sweetheart, let it take you where it will.

A cluster of men passes us on the street. They all look at Mother but she ignores them.

I wish you didn't worry so much. We're going to be just fine, don't you think?

I nod.

I think things are turning around. I have a good feeling, she says. *I need to tell you something.*

What? I say.

I'm quite certain I'm going to become famous. I can feel it. It's like it's happening already but I'm just not aware of it.

I try to imagine what this means but all I can see is even more people in love with Mother. Whole rooms of people looking at her, wanting her to notice them, and me disappearing in all the noise and bustle. Thinking about this makes me want to cry. I try to smile at her because she's so excited. About the future. But I can't. She's not really here any longer. She's walking down the street like it's standing in for another street. A future street full of people who can love her better than I.

Then the wind rises and whips at us. Mother tries to gather her hair, which blows around her head, and as she does, she finds a hairpin tangled in the back.

Oh, dear. Help me get this out, she says. *Guess I was in a hurry.*

She squats in front of me and I use both hands but still, when I finally get it, a few hairs come with it. *It's okay*, she says. *It didn't hurt. Thank you, darling. What would I do without you?*

I put the hairpin in my pocket.

We eat some dinner when we get home but I can tell that Mother is rushing, dialed to a higher setting.

I get out my homework and spread it on the coffee table.

Kitten, what are you doing?

Math, I say.

What child does math on a Friday night? She looks at her little wrist-watch. *And besides, it's almost your bedtime.*

I'm not tired, I tell her.

Let's look at your homework in your room. And get you changed into your pajamas.

I ignore her and focus on my nines. I feel like if I could just memorize my nines, I'd be okay.

Mother makes a drink, stares at me, waiting for me to move to my room. Eventually she leaves.

I can hear her in her room. After a while the apartment gets very quiet and I feel like I'm alone. All she wants is for me to be out of the way. I start to not care if I'm here or not. I pick up my books, go into my room, and think about Elizabeth. Maybe this is why Jim wanted me to make friends. Having a friend makes me want Mother less.

Eventually she comes into my room. *How are your numbers coming?*

Good, I say.

Can I help you get ready for bed?

I'm not a child.

You are, actually. Now put this on. She hands me my nightgown.

I don't want to, so I move as slowly as possible. I sit down on the floor, pull my sock off, and study it.

Oh, for Christ's sake, you test your poor mother's nerves.

I grab the nightgown from her. *I can dress myself!* I yell.

She takes a step backward.

I strip the rest of my clothes off, throwing everything this way and that. Then I pull my nightgown over my head and climb into bed.

Mother comes to the bed and tries to touch my hair but I flip over and face the wall, squeezing my eyes shut.

You'll feel better in the morning, darling. Everything's always better in the morning.

Mother opens the door and stands there a moment.

I'm here, aren't I? We're together, she says.

She shuts the door behind her. I open my eyes and look at the wall—playbills and flyers, photos of Mother, a few little newspaper clippings. Mother, Mother, Mother. I get on my knees and carefully peel off a page, then another and another until I'm just tearing it all down, not even caring that some of the pages rip as I do.

I listen to Mother in the main room, the clink of her glass on the liquor cart. I hear her cross the room—maybe to look out the window. She crosses the room again. She hums for a few seconds then stops. Crosses the room again. It makes me sleepy, the sound of her heels gently batting the floor like a heartbeat that stops, that can't keep going, that starts up again.

Something wakes me. I sit up and see all my memorabilia on the bed. I wonder if he's here. I sneak out my door and tiptoe down the hall. I hear something ticking. Mother is on the davenport. Her stockings and shoes are on the floor. On the record player the needle has come to the middle and is bumping against the last black ridge.

I walk in.

Oh, kitten, did I wake you? Come here. Come sit with me. She reaches with her arms and wiggles her fingers.

I get as close to her as I can and put my arms around her waist.

It's so late, she says.

Her body pulls a little so she can reach her drink and take a sip. *I'm sorry we fought.*

I don't say anything.

Sometimes I think we're just girlfriends. I forget you're a kid. You're so grown up. More than me, I think.

I listen to the needle for a long time until I finally get up and return the arm to its little fork.

Oh, no, let's have a listen, she says.

The album is called *Bird and Diz*. It's the one she always listens to when she's sad.

Thank you, kitten, she says, closing her eyes to the sound of the horns. *It's so beautiful, isn't it? And light?*

I start to pick up her stockings.

I used to be innocent, she says.

She raises her arm and waves me to her. *Leave that. Come back.*

I sit next to her again.

Do you remember the old place? With Sister and Rita?

Yes, I say.

We made a cradle for you out of an orange crate. We were so poor. Rita pulled the fringe off an old flapper number and put it around your crate.

I turn her bracelets around her wrist.

We had so much fun. Hilda made all your little dresses with the matching bloomers.

And the candles, I say, uncertain if I actually remember them or have absorbed the stories.

Oh, when the lights got shut off. Rita had a million candles, didn't she? And we sang. We sang to you and danced with you. You were a wonderful baby, she says.

The phone rings and Mother jumps, running over to it as fast as she can in the tight dress.

But once she gets there, she just stares at the phone, watching it ring.

Aren't you going to answer?

She picks up the receiver. *Hill residence.*

I watch her back. She takes a deep breath.

Oh, I didn't wait. I just got in, actually, she says. She listens a long time, her head tilted like it's heavy.

Let's just nip this in the bud, darling, she says. *I mean, how many times do we have to fail at his, huh? I love you. I'm saying good-bye now.* She sets the receiver down very carefully, then just stands there staring at it, one hand leaning slightly on the table, the other hand resting on top of the glass paperweight. And somehow, though she's not moving at all, it seems like there's a storm brewing inside her, like something is winding up tight. All of a sudden she lifts the glass paperweight and hurls it against the wall as hard as she can. I cover my head. She hits her fist into the wall several times and begins to cry. *Fuck you,* she is saying, over and over.

I feel I should stop her but don't know how. This one is new. Jim would know but he's not here. I think and think about what I can say or do that might help her, bring her back, but I know there's nothing to do but wait. Whatever could help Mother isn't inside of me. It's someplace else. I don't even know where.

She stops hitting eventually and presses her forehead against the wall. When she turns around and sees me, I see that she's forgotten I'm in the room.

Don't be afraid, darling, she says, bending over to collect her stockings and shoes.

I'm not, I say.

She just stands there holding her things, her stockings hanging down like streamers after a party.

Let's get you back to bed.

She climbs into bed with me and sings little made-up songs, her face close to my hair. *"The little sleep bug is on his way again, he's coming round the bend again. Just you wait and see. He's bringing sleep for you and me."* When she thinks I'm asleep she whispers, *I hope you have it easier, kitten. I did everything the hard way.*

Naomi

CHAPTER 17

KANSAS, 1954

THE NIGHT I ran away from home, Sister and I drove for hours. It was past midnight when we knocked on the front door of her convent but several nuns were awake and dressed, standing in the entry when we arrived as though they knew we were coming. They were clearly happy to see Idalia, some of them even cried a little. I realized they hadn't seen her in years. All of this they seemed to be trying to hide from their boss, the taller, sterner nun everyone kept an eye on.

Idalia put her hand on my back. *This is Naomi.*

Well, aren't you grown up, one of them said. I looked at her and slowly realized it was Sister Therese, the nun I'd been so terrible to.

Sister Therese, I said.

She frowned at me.

Long time no see, I said. Some of the nuns laughed while others scowled at the ones who were laughing.

The boss nun stepped forward, stilling the others.

I'm Sister Anne, Prioress here. Welcome.

Then she turned to Idalia and squeezed her shoulders. Idalia's head lowered a little, like she was sorry.

A tiny old nun stepped forward, reached up, and put her hands on my cheeks. *You're so tall!* she said.

This is Sister Regiswinda, said Sister Anne. *She'll show you to your room.*

Sister Regiswinda took my hand and we walked down the hall of the big old house.

Everyone calls me Sister Windy, she said, smiling, her round face squeezed by her coif.

She led me to a small bare room. *Are you hungry?* she asked.

The question reminded me of my body, the emptiness in my gut, which led me to think of Laura walking away from me, her back, her not turning around.

No, I said, looking at the floor.

Sister Windy took my hands in hers and patted them.

I wasn't sure if you'd let me in, I said. *It's my fault that Sister—*

Sister Windy shook her head no before I could finish my sentence. *That's unrelated.*

Beg your pardon?

It's our rule, she said. *All guests who present themselves are to be welcomed as Christ.* She touched my hand when she said the word *as*. She closed her eyes to finish . . . *for He Himself will say, "I was a stranger and you welcomed me."*

She let go of my hand and stooped to turn down the bed. *Others here might say we let you in because we're bored and courting trouble but they are sour old women.*

She looked around the room. *Prime is at six o'clock. I'll wake you.* On her way out she patted the two towels folded on a small wooden bench. *The bathroom is across the hall there. For you to wash up.* She didn't close the door all the way when she left.

If I were to wash I would wash away Laura and I'd never have her smell on me again. After settling myself in the hard, narrow bed, I brought my hair to my face to smell it, then my fingers. Lying down on the hard, narrow bed, I stared at the ceiling. I pulled the blanket tight around my body but it was too light. If only it were a heavier blanket, something to hold me down. The wind was windier here than at home, if that was possible, and rattled the small high window. A Johnny Mercer song played over and over in my head and I hummed it to myself, pausing between phrases out of worry that someone might hear me. But the nuns felt very far away. I had never in my life had a room to myself. Or a bed. It was nearly daylight when I finally fell asleep.

I woke again to Sister Windy shaking me lightly. I sat up and she handed me a small loaf of bread wrapped in a dish towel.

We're not supposed to eat before Holy Communion but you must be so hungry.

She left me to get ready and without my knowing it, took my dress to the wash. All I had left to wear was Laura's lavender dress. I put it on slowly, imagining the cotton was her skin as it slid over mine. When Windy returned she gasped and touched her fingers to my waist.

Oh, it's beautiful, she said, excited and worried.

It's all I have, I told her.

Oh, you have so much, she said, shaking her head, *so much more than you know.*

I sang prayers with the nuns in the small chapel that morning. Singing erased everything but what I was singing. No *Yesterday.* No *Later.* Sister Windy routinely pointed to where we were in the text. I nodded and watched Sister Idalia sing. She didn't have to read the text; she knew it all by heart. I wanted to talk to her afterward but she disappeared.

After breakfast, Sister Anne, the prioress, showed me around the grounds.

Sister Idalia wasn't at breakfast, I said.

Sister Anne observed something high up in a tree. *Sister Idalia needs some time to reflect.*

I need to speak with her.

Well, you may not.

What am I supposed to do? I asked.

Sister Anne began to walk and I followed. *You're pausing. Catching your breath. And since Sister Idalia was, in part, responsible for the events that led to your circumstances, we are letting you stay here. For a day or two.*

She took me into the church on campus. *St. Scholastica Chapel*, she said in a loud whisper. It was quiet and grand. Red pillars lined the sides. Just below the ceiling, stained glass handled the light like a sieve. Spears of red, blue, and green light pointed to empty spots on the pews, the walls. I wanted to stand in those colored lights. The image in the stained glass was a woman holding a small organ. Under her feet was a sword pointing at the ground.

Saint Cecelia, said Sister Anne. *Patron saint of music.*

I felt myself go hot, and wondered just how much she knew.

I would recommend that you spend a little time here in the chapel. Pray. Ask God for guidance.

As she spoke, it occurred to me that allowing others' opinions of me to strike me, to heat me up and shrink me, had to stop. Somehow. I had to be bigger.

You are so young. And though you may feel loss, you now have a chance to begin again. In any way you choose. Few women find themselves in such a position. Wouldn't you agree?

Everything she said felt like a test she believed I would fail. I glanced at the high, arched ceiling. I'd never seen anything like it, or heard so much quiet. It felt like we were standing at the bottom of a deep bowl of silence. Even the wind sounded very far away.

This is a gift. You would do well to acknowledge it as such, she said.

She looked at the watch around her neck. *I have meetings.* Then she left with a turn and a whoosh of fabric, the big door groaning as it opened and closed behind her.

The light that poured through the Saint Cecilia window lit the dust in the air. I sat in the last pew and thought about Laura. Her hair, her skin, her breath. I might never know her again.

I said hello to Saint Cecelia. I said hello to God, and asked aloud, *What is there to say? What can I tell You that You don't already know?* And nothing happened. I looked around to make sure no one else was there, and hummed a few notes. A little bit of the Attende Domine and then a little Johnny Mercer.

"Skylark, have you anything to say to me? Won't you tell me where my love can be?" I liked how it sounded in the big space. *"Is there a meadow in the mist?"* I'd never heard my voice like that. I listened to it come back to me and enter me. Me. My own voice. With my eyes closed, I imagined Mother and Father, Murielle and the little ones sitting all along the bench, even Laura, smiling at me. A voice in my head crept in and said, *They are not here. They will never be here again.* I thought I would explode at this thought, my insides shaking, so I stepped into the middle of the aisle, stood with my legs far apart so I could push the sound out louder, harder. I stretched my arms far out to my sides. *"And in your lonely flight."* The shape of the chapel or the silence made my voice sound so large. Fat. Fuller than it really was. I could make something bigger than I with just my body. *"Haven't you heard the music in the night?"* Somehow that sound came out of me and wrapped itself around me at the same time. It held me. And I believed I was going to be all right. *You're going to be just fine, all by yourself,* I said aloud. For Cecelia, God, Laura, my sweet family, and for Idalia, since none of them had a word to say.

I heard a sound, maybe a door closing somewhere, so I stopped. Then I whispered to Saint Cecelia, *Watch me.*

I ran on my tiptoes to the back of the chapel, raced to the convent, through the door, and down the hall to the little room until I was out of wind. I turned my bag upside down and out fluttered David's card, which I tucked in the envelope of money.

Sister Windy returned with my dress folded in her arms. I shoved the contents of my bag back inside it.

Sister Windy, I said. She handed me my dress. *I need to see Sister Idalia.* She shook her head no.

Sister, please. I must tell her good-bye and that I'm sorry and—

Sister Windy continued to shake her head no while saying, *All right. Follow me. And keep up. We don't have much time.*

I followed Windy through the building's maze. She was small and didn't seem capable of such speed. We came to the end of a long, dark hall and Windy knocked.

A chair creaked.

I'm to be left alone, Sister, said Sister Idalia.

I have the girl, said Windy.

Idalia opened the door and they smiled at each other. Windy rushed away, waving her hands in the air like she wanted nothing more to do with us.

Idalia's head was newly shaved. Her eyes looked large. *Hi, peanut.* I hugged her. She put me in her chair and sat down on her bed.

I'm going to Kansas City, I told her.

Idalia nodded and looked at the floor.

I'm going to find David. I would like to become a singer. And make records. He could help me, I think. And maybe he could help me talk to Laura, set things right.

Idalia looked at the wall above my head and then back at me. *That might not work.*

There was a small desk built into the wall of her room and on it was a stack of notebook paper and a pencil. Several pages were covered with Sister's writing. Next to that was a small plate with a piece of plain brown bread on it, untouched. I thought about my plan. I hadn't yet imagined the part about leaving Sister, setting out on my own, and the idea of it started to work into my bones like cold, damp air.

I can't stay here with you, can I? I asked.

No. Unless you're thinking about joining us.

I looked at her. *Become a nun?*

Eventually, yes. I don't suppose that's something you ever considered.

Murielle and I used to put dish towels on our heads and dip our fingers in the water cup in our bedroom before making the sign of the cross, I told her, the thought prying open the big tin of ache inside me.

Sister waited.

Aside from that, no. I don't want to be celibate. I looked at my shoes.

Sister rubbed her head. *Love is much bigger than what you've experienced in your young life. If anything, sex gets in the way.*

I tried to understand what she was talking about.

If you ask me, she added.

I still don't want to be celibate, I said, which made her laugh.

I know, peanut.

I looked at the piece of bread again, sure she wasn't eating.

Is this your punishment? I asked, looking around the room.

She looked at the floor. There was a scar on top of her head where hair didn't grow. *We punish ourselves,* she began, but then stopped and looked at the wall as if there was a window there.

You told me to love her, I said.

Idalia moved her head this way, then that. *I did.*

There was a clock on the small table, its ticking made extra loud by the emptiness of the room.

Idalia smiled. *Did you enjoy prayers this morning?*

I did.

She took a deep breath. *Some days I feel like the only way I can talk to God is to sing. The singing gets me out of the way.*

I know, I told her, *it feels like you're not you anymore but a thing that makes these sounds. I love that.*

I love it, too. She looked at the clock. *You must go,* she said, standing. *Sister Anne . . .*

I know. How would I tell her that I was sorry. It was so hard to make the words come out but I had to. I stood and said, *I'm so sorry about what I did.*

Idalia took my shoulders, shook her head. *I'm not.*

I love you. Thank you. I hugged her and turned to leave.

Peanut, she called after me. I turned around. *Sing well.*

I will, I said, and I gave her a little bow that made her laugh.

I left the convent and hitched a ride with a family, settling myself in the bed of their truck between a rusty wire cage holding three chickens and a herding dog who was missing hair in patches. A small boy turned around in the cab and watched me through the open space between the back windows. The wind whipped my hair and dress as he stared. I waved my hand in his direction like he was a fly and he blinked, hurt, before turning back around in his seat. There was a swirl cowlick on the back of his head, like God blew very hard on just that spot.

They took me as far as Platte City, where I found a Woolworth's and sat down for something to eat. A woman in a sky-blue uniform brought me a glass of water. *You all right?*

It's windy out there. I'd like a chocolate malted, if you please.

She pumped the metal canister up and down under the mint-green mixer with one hand while she took a drag of her cigarette with the other. All of her motions were like worn roads she drove by rote.

The drink's cold sweetness flew right down the middle of my body.

You don't slow down you'll give yourself a headache, said the man next to me. I never saw him sit down.

He smiled. His blond hair was thickly pomaded, and he had blue eyes that should have been beautiful for the color but wound up just looking cold. He wore a brown suit and tie.

Been out in the sun? A person with your coloring should always wear a hat. Otherwise, you just burn and burn. My sister's like that, he said. He picked up a chicken leg and pulled off most of the flesh with his teeth. I did not believe he had a sister.

You from here? he asked with his mouth full.

I shook my head.

Yup, me neither, he said. *Passing through. Where you headed?*

Kansas City.

Ah, me, too. The city has it, he said, pouring salt over his coleslaw. *You driving? Alone?*

No, I got a ride. This far.

I can take you the rest of the way. He crunched his slaw.

I'd appreciate it, I said. *Thank you.*

The waitress tore off my ticket and handed it to me. Blue ink on soft, gray paper. It was mine, that ticket, for what I had. I wanted to save it. I pulled Mr. Miller's envelope from my bag, opened it, and closed it without removing a bill, thinking: Once I use this money, Mr. Miller has won, he's bought me.

I can spot you if you're short, said the man.

I'm not.

We better hit the road, then.

I felt his eyes look me over as we left and walked to his car.

He drove slowly down the highway. The wheat fields seemed to move entirely in one direction and then entirely in another.

So what's in Kansas City? he said. *A fella?*

Yes.

Lucky fella.

We drove in silence but not. He hardly moved. The way a dog on the end of a taut leash hardly moves. After some time, he put his hand on my thigh. I didn't do anything but I knew I was in trouble. Had I made some deal with him? He agrees to drive me and I agree to—? My heart banged. There was sweat on his forehead.

When we reached Kansas City, he needed both hands to navigate traffic, so he pulled it away. I'd never seen so many cars, people.

You can just leave me anywhere.

This isn't some one-horse town. Tell me where to go, he said.

I pulled out David's card. *Here. The Neon Parrot.*

I know the place. He looked at me again, differently, then turned into an alleyway and threw the car into park. I reached for my door handle but he snagged my arms, turned me, pushed my back against the door. He pulled me toward him by my leg and I kicked. He struck my face, a sudden hot burn near my eye, then he hooked an arm around my hip and pulled me under him. I twisted and bucked under his weight until I was against the door. When I got it open, I fell out backward on to the concrete.

I scrambled to my feet and ran until I was sure he was gone. Folks on the street stared at my face and I stopped a few to ask where the Neon Parrot was but they rushed away from me. Finally a Negro man with a guitar case pointed the way, saying, *Hope you got a friend there. 'Cuz you look a mess.*

CHAPTER 18

The NEON PARROT was a small storefront, its name written in unlit neon above the door with a green parrot about to land on the *P*. The door was propped open with a brick. I walked in and tried to adjust my eyes to the stale darkness.

Ain't open, said a woman's singsongy voice in the back.

The lights clicked on. A Negro woman in a blue dress approached me. *We ain't open for hours.*

The door was open, I said.

On account of this place stinks. Now go on. We'll see you later. She shooed me like a chicken as she headed for the back of the bar. When she walked, her hips said *look-at-me, look-at-me, look-at-me.* I told myself to practice walking like that someday.

I'm here to see David.

She looked at my dress. *You a friend a Davie's?*

Yes, I said, but she noticed my head.

You bleeding! she said, more disgusted than concerned.

I touched my finger to where it burned. *I fell.*

She walked around to the back of the bar. *Off the turnip truck*, she said under her breath.

I just stood there with my arms at my sides. Because that was it for me. I couldn't go on and couldn't go back. I was at the end of the line and I would stand there all night if I had to.

Come sit down, she said, shaking her head like now she's got *another* chore.

She dabbed my cut with a damp rag. I held my arms in close to my body, trying to keep my smell from escaping. The aqua sleeves of her dress floated over her skin and she smelled like a gardenia. Her beauty made it hard to breathe like a normal person. She caught me staring at her. *You ever seen a Negro before?*

Yes, I said.

Where? I could feel her pulling little hairs out of the cut.

Berry Street, I said. *About five minutes ago.*

She laughed out loud with her perfect teeth. *Oh, brother.* Then, as she tried to move some curls off my forehead, *Ain't nobody teach you how to handle this hair?* she asked sweetly.

I shook my head no.

You got more freckles than I ever seen on a woman, she said.

She put a Band-Aid on my head and touched her finger lightly beneath my eye. I winced. As she stood she continued to inspect me. *Some fall*, she said, squinting.

I looked down.

You gonna lie, you ought to improve your skills.

I looked up at her. *A man offered me a ride in. From the country.*

The country, she said, raising an eyebrow. *I had no idea.*

I didn't want to go on, so I looked at the bar, damp still from being wiped down.

I'm sorry, sugar. So what happened? He just go after you like some dog?

I nodded. She sighed through her nose.

You want a drink, she asked, *while I'm back here? Fixing to make me one.*

I'll have what you have, I said.

Of course you will.

She dropped ice cubes into two short fat glasses, filled them with a slow-moving brown liquid, and watched me drink. It tasted like fire. I tried to hide the surprise, the burn in my throat, the terrible taste.

She held her glass with one hand and smoothed the hair at the back of her neck with the other. I had a feeling that was what she did when she was thinking.

You'll learn to sort them out, she said. *Soon enough.*

Sort what?

The men. The dogs, she said. *They show you what they are first thing they do if you know how to look.*

Okay.

Okay, she said, mimicking me a little. *How old are you? And please don't make me watch you trying to lie again.*

Seventeen.

Oh, brother.

And then a sudden shadow at the door. David.

What do we have here? he said.

See for yourself, said the woman.

I got up and faced him, tried to stand straight and to breathe, but I felt strange, like I was standing on a stage and the curtains began to close.

Ragamuffin? he said. The last thing I remember was him walking toward me as the curtains closed all the way.

A few minutes later I opened my eyes to find myself looking up at David and the beautiful woman, both squatting beside me.

Don't know exactly what happened . . . the woman was saying.

My first thought was, What happened?, and my second thought was, David doesn't know yet. About Laura. About home. I sat up. Why would he?

Take it easy there, doll, he said.

I'm okay.

He kept his arm around me. *So what are you doing on my floor?*

It's a long story, I told him.

Would you mind taking her upstairs, Miss Elaine? Give her something to eat, set her up on the davenport?

They helped me to my feet. I followed Miss Elaine. She stopped, turned around, and said to David, *So how'd we do last night?*

David shook his head, like last night was bad news.

God damn it, she said to herself as we climbed a dark narrow staircase near the back of the bar.

The door at the top of the stairs opened to a long room with windows on either end. A woman in a silk robe was pinning dollar bills to a laundry line strung from one end of the apartment to the other. The room smelled of mildew and smoke. The woman took the cigarette out of her mouth and said, *What on earth?! Elaine!*

Don't shoot the messenger, Elaine said, her hands raised. *She's some friend of Davie's. And she needs a little rest. Sit down here, sugar,* she said, patting the davenport. I sat.

She's all yours, Elaine said, walking to the door.

The blonde walked to me, her heels tapping. She studied me, held her cigarette close to her red lips as she brushed a wave of long hair away from her face.

You from Soldier?

Yes, ma'am, I said.

Ooooh. Not that. Name's Caroline, she said, extending her hand, her red nails pointing at me.

Naomi. I couldn't help but glance at the dollar bills drying on the line and the old plaid suitcase sitting on the card table.

This is . . . she began, pointing at the bills and tilting her head. *This can be explained. You hungry?*

I nodded again. She went to the little kitchen area, took a few dinner rolls out of the bread box, and brought them to me with a glass of water before she sat beside me.

Honey, let's cut to the chase, shall we? I need to ask you something and you'll go on and tell me the truth. Are you and David . . . She looked at me, expecting me to fill in the sentence on my own.

No. Oh, heavens no, I said with my mouth full.

She leaned back. *I didn't think so,* she said, waving her fingers once over my dress. *But God knows with that man.*

I felt my face redden, flattered that she might see me as an actual grown love interest, as a woman at all. David walked in then and sat in front of me, folding his long fingers prayerlike. Caroline went back to the money.

So what are you doing here? he asked.

You said we could come visit anytime, I told him. *Laura and I. That day at the house? Remember?*

Caroline looked over her shoulder at us, grinned, and clipped another dollar bill.

David leaned back in his chair. *Well, sure, kid, yeah, a fella says "come on by" but then to just show up out of the blue, well . . .*

I thought he was going to ask me to leave the way he was staring at me, waiting for me to say something that might make sense.

Something happened, I said.

Caroline stopped with the money and turned to look at me with her hand on her hip.

I need to tell you privately, I said, glancing at Caroline.

I'll go help Elaine, she said, irritated.

I told David almost everything. That we borrowed his records. That we were just going to listen to music and then—I watched his face change as the story went on. He winced at the part about his mother.

Laura. The perfect child. He shook his head and leaned forward. *Our pretty little goddamned saint. Christ.*

I would like to talk to her.

Why? he said. *Honestly.*

I looked at the ceiling. Because I loved her. And because I needed her to either come to me or tell me she didn't love me. Once I was certain, I could proceed with becoming someone new.

To make it right.

He shook his head. *Now, kid, this is a mess here. And Pop? He means business. You don't want to test him. I sure as hell don't. I mean, what was your plan, doll?*

I felt my stomach quiver. Be bigger, I told myself.

What about your folks? They know where you are, even?

It had only been a few days and I was trying not to let the sight of them enter my mind, the thought of Papa's coffee cup, Murielle's freckled forearms, the quilt on our bed. It was all too much.

I straightened my back but it didn't work. My throat tightened and the tears came up.

He moved next to me and put his arm around me. I cried on the shoulder of his navy suit. The more I tried not to cry, the more I cried. With my face against his lapel, I realized I'd never been this close to a man before and breathed in deep, trying to identify the smells—smoke and women's perfume, starch and sweat, and something else, something entirely his. His smell was like wind in the house, throwing one door open and slamming another.

Maybe you help me out downstairs. A few weeks tops. You can stay up here. Make a buck or two.

That would be real nice of you, I said.

And you gotta call your folks, let them know you're safe.

I nodded.

But you can't stay here forever. You got to move on. All right?

I know.

Got enough stray cats around here, he said, pinching my chin, trying to make me smile.

And you'll help me talk to Laura? I asked. *Maybe you call home, get her on the line, and I could talk to her?*

He let go of my chin and stood up, shaking his head. *And then what?*

Maybe she could come here, too? We could . . . I tried to imagine her here with me but I could only see her back home. She was stitched into the fabric of Soldier. She could not be cut out.

There are things I need to know, I told him.

He smiled weakly. *Well, sometimes there are things we don't get to know.*

I looked at the money hanging on the line, at the makeshift curtain—a square blue tablecloth with cherries on it tacked over the window—and something inside me shifted. Like when Sister and I would be listening to music and the music, all the parts of it, suddenly moved as a whole. She would say, *Did you hear that? It's called a key change.* In that moment, I felt a key change inside me.

PART FOUR

Stormy Weather

Sophia

CHAPTER 19

CHICAGO, 1965

IT'S CLOUDY THE morning Elizabeth is to visit and I wake up late. I run into the kitchen to see what time it is. Eight. I run down the hall to wake Mother but she's not there. Her bed and floor are covered with clothes and the drawers of her bureau are open. I open the bathroom door—nothing. So I call Jim's apartment. No answer. I put my shoes on, pull my coat over my nightgown, and head for the elevator.

I find Jim with Mother in the lobby. Sal stands near them, his back extra straight, and Jim is talking to Mother on a small settee. She has changed into the blue dress and half of her hair has fallen out of its twist. When she stands up she wavers. Jim reaches for her but she weaves out of his reach and steps onto the end table by the settee.

A little song for my friends, she says. Then she sees me and clasps her hands together. *Kitten! You came! I was just about to sing!* Jim reaches for her. She swipes at him and he ducks. He lifts her by the waist and she struggles on her way down, kicking so we can all see the tops of her stockings and that she's not wearing panties.

Come on, says Jim, forcing her to walk with him toward the elevator. *Peanut*, he says to me, and points to the floor by the couch. *Box of donuts. Grab them, will you?*

I pick up the box, telling myself not to look at any of the people standing around, but then I do. I can't help it and I wish I hadn't.

Mother and Jim get in the elevator and the door begins to close. Jim stops it with his hand and I slip in fast. I'm always afraid the doors are going to close on me, today especially.

In the elevator, Mother leans on Jim. *The thing is*, she says. *I do love you. I really, really do. I sometimes think we'll end up together. You know, once I get better.*

Jim watches the elevator dial arch from left to right. *Get better how? What's that supposed to mean?*

Someday I'll stop wanting what I can't have. You're right what you said.

She tries to hold herself up and pitches a little. *Got any tips?* she asks. *'Cuz I'm all ears. Wait, don't tell me. Pick the good guy. Pick Jim.*

She reaches for Jim, takes his face like she might kiss him. He turns his head. The door opens and he ushers us both out.

You're no fun, she says.

You have enough fun for all of us, says Jim.

He takes her back to her bedroom. To me he says, *Why don't you red up the place.*

I straighten up the living room and wish I had never invited Elizabeth. Mother and Jim walk from the bedroom to the bathroom, where he runs a bath. In the kitchen he starts coffee and puts the donuts on a plate. When he comes into the living room, he takes the bottles and clothes from my hands. *Go get dressed*, he says, and then, *Hey, everything's going to be fine.*

I run into my room to change. I wish he hadn't said that because now I want to cry. The mess I made covers my floor still, so I shove it all under my bed and then put on the cleanest clothes I can find.

Jim takes a coffee to Mother in the bath. When he comes back, I catch him looking at the clock. We can hear Mother singing in the bathroom, her voice sounds tired. Jim puts the donuts on a tray and sets out a pitcher of juice.

I head for the bathroom. *C'mon, doll, let's just leave her be*, he calls after me.

I open the door. Mother is in the bath, her eyes closed, singing to herself. Usually, her beauty interrupts what I feel, but not today.

Please don't ruin this, I say. *She's my only friend.*

She lifts her head from the edge of the tub and looks at me for what seems like a long time. *Your eyes get so green when you're mad*, she says.

I leave. She calls out behind me, *I'll be good, kitten. Good!*

Sal stops Elizabeth and her father in the lobby. He rings the apartment and Jim answers the phone with a happy hello. But then his voice lowers into a quiet shout as he says, *He said they are here to see us, they are here to see us!* And then he snaps again—*I don't think careful is what you're being.*

Jim apologizes to Mr. LaFontaine as he answers the door. Mr. La-Fontaine says, *You must know that being Negro is reason enough to be stopped in a motel lobby. Anywhere, for that matter.* He is short with a graying beard and a happy face. Jim apologizes again as he welcomes them, offering donuts, coffee, and juice. They talk while I show Elizabeth our home, especially my window seat and the little kitchen.

Mother comes down the hall in the white dress with apples on it, an apron, her hair up, only the slightest hint around her eyes of having been up all night, of not yet being entirely collected.

Eugene LaFontaine, says Elizabeth's father, standing and offering his hand. *If you don't mind my saying, I am a fan. It's an honor, Miss Hill.*

Mind? Why, don't stop! Welcome to our home. Mother shakes his hand and then sits down quickly. She's pale and sweating a little bit. *I met Mrs. LaFontaine at school. She strikes me as a woman who runs a tight ship.*

Mr. LaFontaine laughs. *Oh my. And how. You have an artist's intuition, I can see that.*

Jim refills Mother's coffee and brings it to her.

Mr. LaFontaine says, *I was going to bring your album. To have you sign it. But my bride asked me not to embarrass myself. Where would I be without her?*

The people who love us, Mother says, sighing and shaking her head.

Elizabeth whispers to me, *Will you show me the hotel?*

In a minute. I so want to run off with her but I'm afraid to leave Mother. As though me watching her is making her behave.

Sister told me you were involved with the boycotts? She tells me the school conditions in your part of town are frightful. So was your boycott successful? You'll have to forgive me for not being up on the news.

Elizabeth's father laughs. *Well, if you WERE the news, you would probably be very interested.*

Well, now, that is the God's truth, says Mother.

I'm afraid so, he says, and they laugh.

Is it true you're the first Negro to receive tenure at the university? Mother asks.

Jim and Mr. LaFontaine look startled. Even Elizabeth is suddenly listening.

She continues. *Your people must be enormously proud.*

Perhaps. My people, he says in a funny way, *are many things right now.*

I came here from Kansas City. I sang there. Whites and Negroes alike in the joint. We all just got on swimmingly. Of course we all loved the same thing—music—and dancing. And gin, she says, winking.

Humans do tend to love the same things, which suggests we are more alike than not, says Mr. LaFontaine. *Of course this idea is troublesome to some.*

White people, says Mother. *The stiff ones at least.*

Perhaps, says Elizabeth's father.

Mother sighs. *Whatsoever will we do?*

Make the kids do their homework, for starters, says Jim.

Your husband has the right idea, says Mr. LaFontaine.

Mother tilts her head. *I beg your pardon?*

What time will you be back? asks Jim.

One o'clock? says Mr. LaFontaine.

Perfect, says Jim. *We'll be right here.*

Elizabeth and I go to my room. We sit down on my floor and Elizabeth flips through my records. When she comes upon Mother's record, she smiles. *When Mama and Papa were fighting about me coming over here, my mama called her "provocative,"* says Elizabeth, studying Mother's face.

I don't know what that means.

Me neither, she says. *I asked Papa and he said, "Look it up." Look it up, look it up, look it up. It's all he ever says.*

Why were they fighting? I ask, suddenly back in touch with the pit in my stomach.

Mama doesn't think we should be mixing so much. Papa does. He thinks it's the answer.

The answer to what? I ask.

How am I supposed to know? she says.

I open my tablet and add *record player* to the list.

Hey, what's that? says Elizabeth, sidling up to me.

Nothing, I say, closing the tablet.

Is it your diary? she says, excited. *Because I have a diary. It's dark green with a lock on it and my grandmam gave it to me. She said I was supposed to write down everything I could about the places I've been, because she's never even once been out of Georgia, and she wants me to come back and share the world with her, that's what she said.*

So what do you write in your diary? I ask.

Names of places I've been to. What's in yours?

Promise not to tell, I say.

Is it about your mother?

Not this first part, I say. *You didn't promise.*

I promise!

You know the civil defense drills at school?

Yes, says Elizabeth, frowning.

Paul says that if a nuclear bomb hits us, everything will be destroyed. I wait for her to understand what this means.

I don't get it, she says.

Everything will have to be invented all over again. I show her the list. *I mean, this isn't everything, it's just a start.*

Elizabeth looks at the list and starts to laugh. *Yeah, there's lots of stuff missing here.*

She studies the list, flicking her barrette with her fingernail.

Do you understand that if everything gets destroyed, YOU get destroyed, too? she says.

I put my hand on her shoulder to calm her down. *No, listen. This hotel burned down once a really, really long time ago and the men who re-built it built it so good that nothing could ever, ever destroy it. Plus there are secret passages underground.*

Who told you this?

Sal, I tell her.

Who the heck is Sal?

The manager.

Oh, says Elizabeth, *The guy downstairs who tried to make us leave.*

I nod. Suddenly wondering if I want to believe what Sal says anymore.

We hear Jim and Mother having words in the living room and trying to keep it down. Elizabeth looks at me.

Does everybody have a bee in their bonnet today? she asks.

Jim knocks on the door. *Can I come in?* He opens it. *I'm going to go take some photos. You be okay for a bit?*

I jump up. *Take us with you!*

Yeah, take us with you, says Elizabeth.

Not today, he says, heading for the kitchen.

Please! Please! we say, following him.

You're supposed to be studying.

The capitals, says Elizabeth, putting her hands on her hips.

The capitals are important, says Jim as he opens the fridge and pulls out several boxes of film.

Name a state, says Elizabeth.

Jim shoves the film in his pockets. *North Dakota.*

Bismarck, says Elizabeth.

Florida.

Tallahassee.

The phone rings.

West Virginia, says Jim.

Charleston, says Elizabeth.

Jim points at her. *Delaware.*

Dover, she says. *Easy.*

I'll have to ask your mother, he says to me.

Mother is sitting in a chair, talking on the phone. She holds the receiver like it's a little kitten and says, *Now is good. Come over now.*

Jim looks at us. *Fine. But we need to hustle. Get your coats on. And hats. I want you both in hats and I'm not going to argue about it.*

I show Elizabeth my two hats and let her choose one.

Jim tells Mother that he's taking us to the record store.

She nods, uninterested. *Have fun, darlings.*

We drive to the Armory on South Michigan. It looks like an old castle or a fort. Jim parks in the lot and stares at it.

What is this place? says Elizabeth.

CHEVROLET is painted across the front of the building and down the belvederes.

It looks kind of run-down, she says.

You have to imagine it without all the signs, the way it was once, says Jim. *She's still a beauty.*

Hmm, says Elizabeth, looking at me with her eyebrows raised.

Jim gets out of the car.

Are we going in that place? she asks.

That's the idea, says Jim.

It's probably pretty neat inside, I tell her, but she doesn't seem convinced.

Elizabeth takes my hand. It makes me feel useful. I vow right then and there to protect her.

I like those, I say, pointing at the belvederes.

She agrees, *They remind me of* "Rapunzel."

I imagine being trapped in one and waiting for rescue but nobody comes. So I'm forced to jump and wind up with many broken bones. Everyone comes to visit me in the hospital with flowers and candy and Mother stays by my side day and night in her ugly brown sweater.

Sophia? says Elizabeth. *Hello? Anybody home?*

It's only a matter of time, you know, says Jim, studying the armory.

After we help him unload his gear from the trunk, we walk to the building and Jim looks for a way in. He gets a crowbar out of his trunk, looks around, and looks at us. Then he pries several boards off one of the doors and we climb carefully through its broken glass.

You okay? he asks us. We nod.

The room is big, rising two floors into a domed ceiling where light is pouring in. Its perimeter is rimmed with two levels of railed walkway, across which are strung several rows of cord and hanging lamps. There is junk everywhere on the floor and the gray sunlight reveals the filth covering everything.

This place is huge, says Elizabeth, smiling.

We pick through junk on the floor as Jim takes pictures. It feels very important, what he's doing, and we whisper, trying to see what he's seeing when he takes each one. My favorite part is when he stands and stares for a little while before choosing his shot. It's the same look he gets on his face when he looks at Mother.

Jim climbs a set of stairs and sets up his tripod on the second level. The sound of his shutter rings in the big room. We look up at him and wave.

Take a picture of us! says Elizabeth.

He takes several pictures. Then he tells us to stop looking at him so he can do his work.

We peer into a recessed area that is dark.

Let's see what's in there, I say.

Elizabeth takes my hand and we bend over to peek. Jim's shutter snaps. We discover a box of roller skates and send them flying across the floor, crashing them into beams and piles of trash. I pick up a little bottle opener, blow on it, and rub it on my coat. It says "Schlitz" on it. I put it in my pocket and Elizabeth looks at me.

It's not stealing if nobody knows it's here, I tell her. *Plus it'll just get buried when they knock this down.*

She nods like she agrees but I don't think she does.

A shadow passes the front door, Jim scurries to collect his gear and get downstairs to grab us. We hide in one of the recessed areas and wait. We don't hear anything. When Jim says *okay* we laugh uncontrollably.

You two would make the worst spies ever, I should tell you, he says.

We laugh even harder.

Let's get out of here, he says.

As we drive away, Jim says, *I think it would be best if we didn't tell anyone about our work today, don't you?*

Elizabeth makes the zip-lip gesture and I mimic her.

Back home, Jim moves fast through the lobby. People stare at us and Elizabeth looks nervous, so I take her hand and she smiles. I begin to realize that even though she and I live in the same state, the same town, go to the same school, and are, right now, standing in almost the exact same spot, we live in different worlds.

Quit staring at me, says Elizabeth.

I'm sorry.

This elevator is so slow, she says.

You can say that again, says Jim.

Mother and David are sitting close on the settee when we open the door, which prompts Mother to stand, straighten her skirt, and touch her hair.

Welcome home, darlings. She kisses my cheek, then Elizabeth's, then she pats Jim's arm. *Look who stopped by. You remember my friend David.*

I don't look at David.

He says, *I better scoot. Leave you to your day.* He has the kind of voice you can feel under your skin. Elizabeth stares at him as he says good-bye and heads for the door.

He looks like a movie star, she whispers.

See you tonight, says David.

Mother follows him into the hallway, closing the door behind her.

When we are alone in my room, I say to Elizabeth, *I have to tell you something.*

What? she says, interested.

Jim is not really my dad.

Elizabeth says, *No duh.*

I think that man might be. David.

Why do you think that?

It's the way he looks at me, I tell her.

Maybe that's just how his face is? Mama says a lot of white people are born with mean faces and we should pity them and pray for them. Maybe that man just has a dad face.

Maybe, I say but I don't really believe it.

Ladies! yells Mother. *Elizabeth! Your father is here!*

We don't respond right away.

I wish I could stay longer, she says.

Me, too.

CHAPTER 20

Tʜᴀᴛ ɴɪɢʜᴛ ᴀᴛ the club, Jim opens the door to Mother's dressing room, knocking on it at the same time.

Can I come in? He walks in and slides a chair into the middle of the room.

Mother spins a bit of hair with her forefingers and pins it against her temple. *You're ahead of yourself, darling*, she says.

You'll never believe what happened this afternoon.

What? I ask.

So I walk into the Sun-Times *a couple days ago*, he begins.

Mother's shoulders drop. *Oh, Jimmy*, she says.

Wait, wait; hold on, now.

Mother is working herself up. *Darling, you know they don't understand your . . . your love of architecture, and besides, the* Sun-Times *is getting more conservative by the minute. Everybody knows that. They're not going to write any stories about your old buildings.*

Jim says, *Well, you're probably right but there's a new reporter there. Green as they come. I tell him the whole story of Chicago wrecking all its best buildings. I'm talking about Adler and Sullivan, Frank Lloyd Wright, Burnham and Root. They're the ones put Chicago on the map, I say to the kid. Then I pull out my pictures of the Armory and he's sold. He called me just this afternoon and said they're going to run a story and want to use one of my pictures.*

Mother has turned in her seat to face him. *Well, this is wonderful news, Jimmy. Delicious.*

But that's not all. This kid has a friend at Look *magazine. They might be interested in a story on Chicago and he's going to introduce us.* Look *magazine! Can you believe the luck!*

I hug him. It's the happiest I've ever seen him.

When does your photo run? asks Mother. She's gone back to her eyelashes. *Tomorrow*, says Jim. *If you can believe it.*

Of course I can.

Jim shares his good news with the crew during the show. They shake his hand and say things like *Go get 'em!*

Jim and Steve chat by the control board while they watch Mother.

Steve says to Jim, *On fire tonight.* And I see Jim look for David in the crowd. He's there at his table. It seems as though the whole show is between Mother and David.

After I finish my homework in the greenroom, Jim takes me home early and puts me to bed.

Nothing wakes me up until I hear Jim tapping lightly on the front door. There is a certain way he knocks so that I can hear it, but not Mother.

I open the door. *What time is it?*

Six thirty, he says. He looks around. I look where he looks. A suit coat is draped over a chair. He lifts it, unfolds it, studies it, and puts it back the way it was.

You want to get pancakes? See if the papers are out yet?

I almost ask him why I would care if the papers are out but I remember in the nick of time.

I'll go get dressed, I tell him. He pokes around the living room, investigating.

Think your ma would want to come?

I look at him like he is completely crazy.

He crosses his arms and taps his foot like he came in here with some kind of plan that he can't make happen. Like when I think of the terrible things I'm going to say back to the mean boys at school but then I can't.

I stand in front of him. *I'm ready.*

He leans around me and looks down the hall, like her door might open just then. *Don't you want to put on a hat?*

Nope, I say. We walk to the door and Jim stops at the little silver bowl in the entryway. He lifts a set of keys, holding them in his hand for a moment. I open the door. *I'm leaving.*

It's a bright, cool morning. Jim doesn't hold my hand. We stop at the magazine stand and he buys the paper, folds it in half, and tucks it under his arm.

Once we sit down in a booth, he starts to open the paper but refolds it again, putting it beside him on the seat.

Jim! I say. *Come on, let's see.*

He brings it out again. *I'm nervous.*

I get up on my knees in the booth so I can reach him across the table. I put my hand on his arm. *It's okay. I'm nervous all the time.*

He takes a deep breath and opens it, turns the page. *Get a load of that! Page two!*

There is his photo under the headline THE HIGH PRICE OF PROGRESS. It's Elizabeth and me, picking through some junk. We are very small. The Armory looks like a giant skeleton around us. Like it's the whale, and we are little Jonahs.

Hey, it's us, I say.

I know. It really gives you a feel for the size of the place, doesn't it? Two little people.

I smile at him. We read the article together and Jim nods.

It's pretty good, he says.

I think so, too, I say, though I don't know many of the words.

Jim sits there smiling for a while.

What? I ask.

I don't know, he says, *you sometimes get a day where what you do matters. I just wish your ma was here right now. To see it.*

I am.

And you're number one, don't get me wrong. Your ma, she's just spare change. Hell, you're the one in the papers! He opens it facing me.

Let's get you some pancakes, he says. *As many as we can eat.*

When we get back to the hotel, Jim walks into the lobby with me but I stop him. *I don't think you should come up. Not right now.*

I know. I was just walking you to the elevator. I wasn't planning to come up, he says, giving me a hug.

He smells like cigarettes and Jim, which is the smell of cold air, soap, and the chemicals he uses in the darkroom—vinegary, metallic. Jim is my favorite smell.

The apartment is quiet. Sometimes, if you stand in a place and you feel carefully enough, you can tell what's going on there. All the rooms are still. All I hear are the sounds of traffic on Monroe, of the El on a curve in the distance.

I walk straight down the hall and open Mother's door. She sits on the edge of the bed, the sheet covering her lap but not the rest of her, with her face in her hands. She lifts her head and smiles.

Hi, kitten.

David is standing on the other side of the bed threading his belt through the loops in his trousers. He tucks in his shirt as he turns around. His shirtsleeves hang open.

Mornin', he says, like I'm always here, like he's always here. He leans into Mother's chaise while he puts on his socks. I don't know how Mother can keep from watching him get dressed. I can't stop staring at him.

Do you want coffee? I ask.

Yes, baby, she says. I look at him once again. He leans over in front of Mother's vanity and slides little tabs into the underside of his collar.

I walk back to the kitchen, wobbly. Mostly I think of us as living in a bubble, being tumbled around by it gently, lit by its shiny lavender light. But every now and then I just have to give the wall a kick, to change the shape, to test its elasticity, and make a little more room.

I pick up the coffeepot, pull the lid off, turn on the water, and fill it. David walks in. I light the stove, set the pot on the flame, and dump some coffee in the basket. I can feel him watching and I try very hard to appear competent. As I slide the basket back on the rod and shove the lid on, I realize I need to add *percolator* to the list.

Guess you know your way around a kitchen, he says. I turn to face him. He smiles and stares. *You've got your mother's hair*, he says.

No, I don't.

You do. Trust me.

He sits. The little chair is too small for him. He watches me. I try to invent things to do—thread the dish towel through the icebox handle, slide the spilled grounds off the counter and into the sink.

Why don't you take a load off.

I sit down and look at the table, brush some of the ashes into my hand, and dump them back in the ashtray, then wipe my hands on my jeans.

You remember who I am? he says.

I know. I met you two times now. I know I sound mad.

You remember, he says, leaning on his elbows.

And then his closeness, his eyes on me, change me, make me feel like I'm floating. He seems like an important person. And he's talking to me like nobody else exists.

Jim had a picture in the paper today, I say. I squish a crumb with my thumb. *You'll probably see it.*

Well, good for Jim.

He's basically my dad. He's been around my whole entire life. I look up at David as I say this. His face becomes serious for a little while. One of his eyes squints at me. I don't look away.

He breathes in through his nose and smiles. *Good fella, Jim.*

Yup.

We listen to Mother move from the bedroom to the bathroom, close the door, and start the bath.

I look at the square glass bubble on the top of the coffeepot.

I love your mother, he says.

I laugh.

That funny?

Kind of, I say.

We stare at each other. He is so tall and so calm. Like he already knows how everything works.

I know things, too, I tell him.

He leans back and sets his big hands on his thighs. *I'd wager you know all kinds of things.*

I know you don't come when you say you're going to, I tell him.

The coffee starts pushing up into the bubble, pale at first and slowly growing darker.

It's more complicated than it looks, he says. *I want to be with your mother. You can only see one side of this.*

I stare at him. He watches me. I get up, pour her coffee, and take it to the bathroom.

Mother's head is on the narrow back ledge of the tub and her eyes are closed. Her face is damp, flushed and clean, her hair is wet. I set the cup on the side of the tub.

Thank you, baby, she says, touching the side of my head with a dripping hand. I wipe a line of water off my cheek. She takes a sip of coffee and sets it down carefully.

Has he gone?

He's in the kitchen. I close the lid of the toilet and sit on it. *Is he going to leave?*

Probably, she says. I pull my legs up and wrap my arms around them, putting my chin on my knees.

Is this confusing? says Mother.

I pick at a piece of thread hanging from the hem of my pants.

Mother leans forward so she can reach me.

I don't want anything to mess us up, she says as she runs a wet thumb along my eyebrow. *We have a good gig, don't you think?*

I stare at her for a minute. She wants me to believe that she's protecting us but I don't. There's more. There always is. I rest my forehead on my knees. She always does this—makes me believe she's telling me everything and leaves out all the secrets, all the important bits.

My jeans smell like the diner—cigarette smoke, grease, and syrup. I start to cry. Mom rests her hand on my feet.

The door opens. David hovers in the doorway for a minute, then sits on the tile floor across from me, propping his elbow on the edge of the tub.

I peek at him through my arms, at his striped suit pants and dress shirt with the cuffs still open, at how he hardly fits on the floor he's so long.

This a . . . it's a small bathroom, he says.

Mother covers as much of her breasts as she can by crossing her arms. She looks at him with one eyebrow arched. *If you're uncomfortable, go sit someplace else.*

So he stands, unfolding himself like a jackknife, and steps into the tub, shoes and all.

Don't mind if I do, he says as he lowers his body into the water with Mother.

David Augustine Miller! she yells, laughing and pulling her legs up out of the way. I don't even know I'm laughing because of how her face looks. Because for a moment, I feel like I'm seeing her real face, her real self. I can even see myself in her. The freckles, the hair starting to tighten into little curls around her wet forehead. The water overflows, splashes or the floor.

Well, now we've got a real mess on our hands, says Mother.

I should say, says David. They look at each other. *I could stick around. Help you clean it up. If you'd reconsider.*

Mother produces a washcloth from the bathwater and gently wipes the makeup from under her eyes. It's what she does when she needs to think—tends to her beauty. She could solve nearly any dilemma in the time it takes to apply lipstick, blot, and apply again.

I rest my chin on my arms and watch them.

How long? she says. There's the face again. Her genuine face. It's like a girl almost.

I have to be with you, says David.

Hmm, she says.

David watches her as she thinks hard, as various expressions pass swiftly across her face.

Don't do that, he says.

She looks like she's been reprimanded for the twentieth time for the same thing. *Well, what we've been doing isn't working, is it?*

David sees hope in this. He slides his arms into the water, slowly lifts her heels, and rests her feet against his chest. He holds her feet flat against his chest like he wants to protect them.

They look at each other and quietly reach some sort of decision.

Then she seems to remember I'm there. *Kitten, remove this man from my bath, will you?*

It's clear by David's face that he's won. I pretend to lift him out of the tub and the water runs off him, filling the rug, and I don't want to laugh but it is funny. Funnier, somehow, because I can imagine telling Elizabeth at school tomorrow, because I have someone to tell stories to now.

Then David begins to unbutton his wet shirt, so I leave.

CHAPTER 21

DAVID IS MAKING breakfast when Annie from housekeeping arrives to collect his suit.

He hands her some folded money. Annie doesn't raise an eyebrow. *Thank you, ma'am*, he says as he stands there barefoot in Mother's pink makeup smock. It's just long enough to cover his undershorts. His legs are long and strong and hairy like some sort of animal.

An hour later there's a knock at the door. *Must be my suit*, David says as he jumps up to answer it. *That was fast*. I look down at my paper, determined to finish the problem before he comes back.

Beg your pardon, I hear David say. *I thought you were someone else.*

And who might you be? says a woman's voice. I listen, think. As soon as I realize it's Mrs. LaFontaine, I run to the door.

I'm a friend of Miss Hill's, says David.

Mrs. LaFontaine looks him up and down. *Is that so?*

Mother comes out of the kitchen in her long peach robe, braless still, smoking. *Mrs. LaFontaine!* she says, rushing to close her robe around her.

Mrs. LaFontaine marches past David and holds a newspaper up in the air. *You better explain this!*

I don't know what you're talking about, says Mother.

A photograph of my child in the Sun-Times, *playing in a building that is CONDEMNED. THAT is what I'm talking about.* She shakes the paper at Mother. *I entrusted her to your care.*

It was my idea, I say, stepping in front of Mrs. LaFontaine. *Mother didn't even know.*

Mrs. LaFontaine looks at me like she pities me. *You are a child,* she says, moving her eyes slowly to Mother. *You didn't know?*

It's not like that, says Mother.

David steps forward. *Why don't we simmer down a bit and have a seat. Talk this through.*

Mrs. LaFontaine says to David, *The man in a housedress wants me to simmer down.*

I assure you I can explain, says Mother. *Jim, my Jim, is very capable. He took the girls on a little field trip—*

Mrs. LaFontaine puts her hand on her hip. *The man you pretend is your husband? About whom your child lies?*

Mother glances at me and says gently to her, *Can we please sort this out? Over some coffee? I believe we can sort this out.*

Mrs. LaFontaine straightens and her face softens. She says calmly, *I am not going to sit in this place and be party to the . . . loose operation you are running. Nor is my daughter. Ever again.*

She looks down at me. *Sophia, my dear, I am sorry.* To Mother she says, *Good day, Miss Hill.* David nods at her and she makes a barely perceptible click with her mouth.

I stare at them both with their robes on, their startled looks.

Mother turns to me, her face a caricature of surprise.

I hate you, I say, barely able to get the words out, and walk to my room. Her disbelief is hot as the sun on my back.

I open my music box and take out the Schlitz bottle opener I stole from the Armory. Mother's record sits on top of the stack and I pull it out so I can drag the bottle opener straight across the black vinyl. Then I write David's name in the back of my notebook. It used to be a list of people Mother loved but now I think it's a list of people she's going to leave.

An hour later, when I hear the door, I leave my room to open it. I am sure it's Jim. I feel my anger has pulled him here. But it's Annie.

Like new, she says, handing me the suit, looking at me the way Mrs. LaFontaine looked at me.

David comes up behind me and thanks her. He carries the suit to Mother's bedroom. While he's dressing, Mother moves around the living room in such a way that each wall seems to appear sooner than she'd expected. It's not hard to see that she hasn't given a second thought to me, to what I said. She pours herself a drink and arranges herself on the chaise.

Back in his suit, David quickens. He bends over Mother.

It might be late, he says.

Mother gives a light smile, a shrug.

He squats in front of me.

Where you going? I ask.

To take care of a few things, he says.

He leans forward to kiss my head but I move out of the way. Mother studies the ceiling as he leaves.

Is he coming back? I ask. She doesn't answer.

Where are you going? she says as I turn to leave.

Back to my room.

She reaches her hand toward me. *No, no, don't,* she says. *Stay with me.*

I go into my room and shut the door.

I don't know what to do when I get to school but keep my head down and pretend to be working on my numbers. The boys say something to me that I don't hear. Looks from the other students tell me it was something particularly rough. But all I can think about is Elizabeth. I put my head down and let her come to me.

The bell is going to ring any second and she's still not here. I prop my desk lid with my ruler and rearrange my desk, making a pile of papers on the floor—math homework I couldn't finish and never turned in, drawings I started and hated, penmanship practice pages.

Paul says, *Maybe she's a little doggy. The papers are in case she pees.*

I gather the papers in my arms and take them to the wastepaper basket.

Just then Elizabeth walks in the door, a little breathless. She hugs me and we walk arm in arm back to our desks. The students look away from us.

We take our seats and Elizabeth scooches her desk closer to mine.

Ladies, no moving desks, says Sister Marie.

Elizabeth wiggles her desk a bit, making a little noise on the floor, but she doesn't actually move it back to where it was.

Was my ma terrible? she whispers, her eyes big.

She was so mad. I didn't think I would ever see you again.

Well, I'm not supposed to be talking to you, she says.

What about your dad?

He's a little mad but he never said I shouldn't be your friend. He says that's up to me.

Ladies. I don't want to have to separate you, says Sister.

Elizabeth looks straight ahead. I stare at her profile. Nothing is certain. When Sister's back is turned, Elizabeth mouths, *Write me a note.*

Sister begins with division and I look at the board while I'm writing Elizabeth her note. I imagine her mother finding it in the pocket of her cardigan, so I set out to explain Jim, the photos, the importance. I try to sound worried, like Jim, about the future, telling her things like *Progress is a bulldozer,* and how I hope we can be friends again.

At recess, she says, *We'll just be secret friends,* shrugging, like she does this all the time.

Okay. We walk to our tree.

So who was the man wearing a pink dress? says Elizabeth.

It was a smock, I tell her.

A woman's smock.

Mother's, I say.

Why was he wearing your mother's smock? She's smiling and holding her arms way out from her sides, like Jesus.

Because he got in the tub, I begin.

What?

With his clothes on.

He WHAT? she says, laughing and covering her mouth.

He loves my mother.

And he's crazy? she asks.

Yes. I pull out a piece of brown crabgrass and pretend to smoke it. *He borrowed the smock while his suit got laundered.*

Are they going to get married?

I don't know. I never thought of that.

Well, do you like him?

I think of David. Of the others. It doesn't occur to me to like them or not like them. *They usually don't last very long.*

I wish my life was interesting, she says.

Jim picks me up after school. I watch Elizabeth run to her mother, and when her mother looks both ways before they cross the street, she sneaks me a wave. In the car Jim asks if he's still in the doghouse. I don't answer. He says that he, Sister Eye, and Miss Rita talked about throwing me a birthday party, and I get so excited I almost speak to him. Instead I press my teeth together, but then I start to worry. Who would come?

Something small, he says, as though he read my mind.

But I would want Elizabeth to come and we're not even supposed to be friends anymore. We have to be secret friends. I don't want a party if she can't come. Because then it would just be all the grown-ups talking about things

I don't understand like every other day of my whole entire life, I say in one breath.

Easy, there, girl. I'm working on it. I'm going to make it right.

He puts his hand on my head and I say, *Don't mess up my hair,* which is kind of our private joke.

Being secret friends is easy enough. Elizabeth and I sneak each other notes and talk all we want at school and sometimes, when her mother is at church or at the neighbors', her dad lets her call me. One day after school, Jim and Mr. LaFontaine are talking when we come out.

Mr. LaFontaine says to me, *Miss Hill, we were wondering if you'd like to come to the university with us. I have some work to do and you could explore the library with Elizabeth. You are infamous explorers after all. Well documented,* he says with a glance to Jim.

Can I go? I ask Jim. He nods. Elizabeth and I try to conceal our excitement.

When we get to the library, Elizabeth rushes ahead. She looks at the labels on the ends of the stacks, eventually stops, and turns into an aisle.

Look! she says.

A whole shelf of books on modern inventions and inventors.

If you read all these books, you'll be able to reinvent everything on your list! After the bomb! she says, excited.

Holy cow, I say. Elizabeth wanders off but I stay.

I study pictures of turbine engines and gyroscopes, and try to understand what on earth they are. It's all more complicated than I'd imagined and I wonder if Elizabeth understands this stuff. I find her in another aisle, sitting on the floor with a giant book open in her lap.

You won't believe this, she says, wincing.

We study a black-and-white plate of a man with a growth on his neck the size of his head. And another one of two children sitting side by side, their faces odd. Like birds. But then you realize they are sitting in someone's hands. They are miniature children. We look at a picture of two babies with their bellies joined together.

How would you even put clothes on them? I ask.

You'd have to have them made special.

We spy on a man and woman who are sitting across from each other at a table, fighting while trying to keep their voices down.

I'm never going to have a boyfriend, I say to Elizabeth.

It seems to involve a lot of fighting, she says.

Does your mother know we're together?

She slowly shakes her head no.

Will she find out?

No, she says, *but—*

But what? I ask.

It seems like I always think she's not going to find out things and she finds out. I don't know how. Does your ma find out things?

I think about this. *She's not really paying attention.*

Lucky, says Elizabeth, and then the couple catches her eye. *Look!* she says.

The woman stands. *Go to hell!* she shouts, and walks off mad, throwing her bag over her shoulder. Her dress is short and she wears a belt around her hips.

Elizabeth saunters down the aisle, moving her hips back and forth. *Go to hell!* she whispers. I imitate her, pretend to throw my hair over my shoulder. *Go to hell!* I tell Elizabeth. She crosses her arms and scowls.

Girls! says Mr. LaFontaine, who has appeared at the end of the aisle. *This is a library!* he whispers loudly. We try to stop laughing but laugh all the way to the car.

Eventually we are able to settle down.

Do you go to the university every day? I ask Elizabeth's father as he starts the car.

I do.

Do you stay late? I ask.

No, I'm always home in time for dinner, he says. *Why do you ask?*

So Mama doesn't say, "Go to hell!" says Elizabeth, under her breath, and we are hysterical again.

CHAPTER 22

I RUN THROUGH THE lobby and take the stairs up to our floor. Mother is on the settee and the lights are off. Sometimes it's hard to know whether to go to her or pretend to be invisible but there's happiness in me still, so I try not to care.

It's nice to watch the sky get dark, isn't it? she says. *And the lights come up.*

She's not wearing any makeup and hasn't fixed her hair.

Did David come today? I ask. *He said he was going to stay. In the bathroom. Remember?*

Make me a drink, will you, darling? She holds out her glass.

I went to the library at the university. With Elizabeth. We looked at all kinds of books and spied on people and laughed in the car the whole way home.

Mother is still holding her glass out. I don't know if she hears me, so I continue. *I'll probably go to the university someday. Maybe I'll be a teacher or something. Elizabeth is going to be a doctor. She's practically an expert on deformed people.*

Mother looks at me.

I have homework. I'm going to go to my room, I say.

She remains there, alone, as the room goes dark.

I get out my math homework and hear a knock on the door but ignore it. So does Mother. The knocking continues. My little clock says six. Mother shouldn't be here still. There are ten long-division problems on the page and the blue ink of the mimeograph looks like a bruise.

It's Jim. He yells. She talks back quiet and high, asks him not to be mean. *Don't be so mean, Jimmy.*

I try to remember eight times nine. I rub the ink on the page and it smears.

Eventually, and not because I care anymore, I move to the hall and watch Jim and Mother in the bathroom, her on a stool in front of the mirror. Together they re-create her, him moving fast with the bobby pins, pancake makeup, and rouge, and her moving slow, touching up the edges of his work.

He dots a lighter color foundation under her eyes.

Jim? I say.

What?

How'd you learn to do all that? I ask.

He squeezes a line of glue onto an eyelash and hands it to her. *Go lay out some clothes for your mother,* he answers.

I know as soon as I hear the knocking that it's David, that he's come back. I open the door and he's standing there with his bags.

Your suitcases match, I say.

He looks down at them. *They do.*

His hair is a little messy and his eyes look rubbed red.

Jim steps out of the bathroom and sees David. *Jesus Christ,* he says.

Hello, Jim.

Sophia, put on coffee, says Jim. *Make it strong.*

David sets his bags down quietly. I watch him.

Sophia, now! Jim says.

I want to obey but I can't.

Mother comes out of the bathroom and stands in the hall. She and David look at each other like they're on opposite ends of something—a teeter-totter, a balance beam. He goes to her slowly like she might startle, like she's a bird or a squirrel, and gets down on his knees in front of her, wrapping his arms around her, pressing his face into the middle of her body.

It's over, he says. *I'm all yours.*

Mother just stands there with her arms down at her sides, caught. She looks at the suitcases, then down at David's head. She looks at Jim. She looks at me and smiles like she feels sorry for me as she wraps her arms around his head.

We don't have time for this, Jim says, looking away from them.

I'm here now, says David, standing up and facing Jim. *I'll take it from here.*

Jim moves his jaw. He shifts his weight back and forth a few times. *You'll take it from here? What the fuck do you know?*

Men, Mother begins.

Jim tosses his handful of hairpins into the bathroom and begins to leave. *Be my guest,* he tells David. *Just a few things. She's drunk. You'll need to make a set list because she likes a new one every night. Of course she can't make one right now, can she?*

Jim, there's no need, David says, but Jim walks right past him to Mother, who has her back against the wall and is rubbing her forehead. He faces her.

So is this it? Is this your guy? The one?

Jim—

Do you love him? Or should I say, do you still want him now that he's gone and left his wife for you?

That is not—

Are you even capable of loving someone who's here for you?

You chose to be here. It has always been your choice, she shouts.

Jim backs away from her and starts to laugh. *It has. Because I think one of these days you're going to come around, you're going to grow up. Break a leg tonight.*

He turns away.

Mother follows him. *Please don't.*

You're covered.

I'm not. Jimmy, I'm not. I need you. You know that.

No, I don't. He moves for the door, I follow him and grab his leg. *Please, don't go. Please.*

He takes my hands in his. *I'm not leaving you. Your mother pisses me off, that's all. It doesn't change a thing here,* he says, pointing back and forth between us. *Got that?*

I nod. He looks over at Mother and back down at me, shaking his head. *You've got your work cut out for you tonight.*

I have to get ready, Mother says to David, who has been standing all the while with his arms crossed like we are a zoo exhibit. *This is not a good time.* She steadies herself against the wall and slowly slides down it until she is sitting cross-legged on the floor.

David looks at me. *I don't know what to do here.*

I turn back to Jim but he's already gone.

I go to Mother's desk and try to find some old set lists. There are three, and I choose the one that looks the easiest—nothing that's going to make her voice, or her brain, work too hard.

In the bedroom, David tries to get Mother dressed. He won't be able to dress her without me.

I don't want to sing tonight. Let's just stay in. She looks down and pulls at his belt. He is gently pushing her away by the shoulders when he sees me.

Please help me, he says.

I stand in the doorway, wish the whole thing would just come crashing down.

Sophia? says David.

I slowly gather her clothes and undergarments and lay them out on the bed.

Now put those on, says David. He turns her to face the bed. She drops her robe to the floor and tries to dress herself. David stands behind her, holding her by the hips to help her balance. I watch them with my arms crossed until I remember that she probably needs coffee.

Mother drinks her coffee while we walk to the club. It makes her walk more slowly but she seems to think it's fun.

The cool air feels nice, doesn't it? she asks.

Yes, it sure does, says David. I look at his face when he says this. It is half trying to talk to Mother and half worrying about how to handle her.

At the Blue Angel, I leave them to get the set list to Steve. He looks at me when I hand it to him.

She had a bad day? he says.

I shrug and go to the dressing room, where David is trying to get her gown on, which Mother also thinks is fun. I pull her merry widow from a basket and hand it to him. *This goes on first. She can't wear that without this*, I tell him.

He opens it and looks closely at its clasp.

Just sit down, I tell David. He sits, watches me unhook the back of the dress, wrap the merry widow around Mother's waist, and fasten it. *Bend over*, I tell her so her breasts can fall where they're supposed to. She stands so I can fasten the dress and in the mirror I see a cloud come over her face.

Jim comes back then. *I left some stuff here*, he says, pointing to his light meter on the counter.

Does Steve have a set list yet? he asks me.

Yup, I say, trying not to smile. I knew he wouldn't leave me alone.

After much rushing around, everyone but Mother caught up in that backstage panic, which is kind of real but also kind of acting, Mother walks onto the stage. Her heels on the old wood boards sound like the second hand of a giant clock. The lights and the applause connect to her like puppet strings, holding her up. She is suddenly taller, composed, power in her arms and neck, something about her chin seeming to say, *I know what I'm doing.*

Jim, David, and I stand backstage and watch. I sit down on my *X*. David and Jim don't say a word to each other until David says, *I know what I'm getting into.*

Jim snorts. *The very fact that you would say that, that you think people ever know what they're getting into, means you have NO idea what you're getting into.*

Steve makes a short hiss at them and frowns.

You're being too loud, I say.

Jim and David laugh at me and in that very small moment where they seem to be getting along, David says*, Well, now that everything seems to be under control here, I need to go take care of some things. Business*, he says.

I don't care where you go, says Jim.

CHAPTER 23

THE NEXT MORNING Mother feels terrible. David talks quietly and sweetly to her, brings things to her room—coffee, water, magazines, scrambled eggs.

In the afternoon, Rita appears.

Well, where is he? she asks when I open the door.

In the kitchen.

Rita glides past me, her back extra straight, one arm already out to the side as though getting ready to gesture broadly. I follow.

Well, look who's back, she says.

David faces Rita. *Have we met?*

Oh, yes, you probably don't remember it was so long ago. You stormed into my bar like some sort of two-bit gangster demanding to see Naomi. Ring a bell? Name's Rita, she says.

I remember now, says David. *Been awhile.*

Rita sits down and looks around the kitchen. *What are we making?*
I'm putting on a stew for later.

Charming, says Rita.

You like a drink? says David.

Do I look like I need a drink?

Yes, ma'am.

Prosecco, then, she says.

He takes a deep breath as he passes me and fetches a drink from the liquor cart in the main room.

Rita looks at me. *Where's Mama?*

Asleep.

You can say that again, says Rita, watching David return with her drink. *You look, I don't know, more manly than I recall.*

David goes back to peeling a head of garlic. *And you look more like a woman.*

Rita tilts her glass. *Hmm. All of the glamour, none of the bullshit.* She empties her glass and sets it down on the table. Standing, she steps up behind David, rests her hand on his arm, and leans into his ear. *I'm watching you.* They are almost the same height.

I walk down the hallway with her to Mother's room. She sits down on the bed and pulls Mother's scarf from her eyes.

Wait, says Rita, pretending to think, *Greta Garbo. Camille. 1937. No. '36.*

Hello, Mother says, and the sound of her voice makes my teeth clench.

Some night last night, says Rita.

Was I awful?

No, not awful, says Rita. *But Big Doug rang me this morning, a courtesy call. Told me to have a word with you. Who knows. Maybe you'll get a bigger crowd after this. Folks wanting to see the wreck for themselves. If that's how this is headed.*

Oh, Rita, don't start. Not today.

And you know what my first thought was? When I heard? Rita sits down on the bed. *I thought, It's that man. The boy from back home she couldn't WAIT to get all tangled up with again. SO disappointing.*

This has nothing to do with him, whispers Mother.

Rita leans her back against the headboard and looks around the room. *I've been thinking.* She lifts a hairbrush from the nightstand and tugs the hair out of it. *Look that way*, she says. Mother looks away from her and Rita begins to work on the swirl of tangles at the back of her head.

Darling, Rita says as she works. *I've never known anyone who wants fame more than you. It was this . . . engine humming in you the day we met. I thought, This kid has it. But then you began to realize how hard it is to get there. How relentless it is, the work. You thought once you put yourself on any little stage, the whole world would pound down your door and you're mad now because it hasn't happened. Your feelings are hurt. Like a little child wondering why she's not in the popular group.*

Rita, stop—

Not done. So the beautiful unavailable man wanders back into your life and you jump at the opportunity. You drop everything, happily, for the distraction. Wait by the phone, buy a new dress, cry to your girlfriends, get too drunk. Look at you. Aren't you just the most normal girl now, pining over her man. Ambition? What ambition?

Mother reaches behind her. *Stop, leave it be. No more*, she says.

Rita stands. She's like a pitcher winding up.

Did the distraction work? Is the disappointment gone now? The pain of your only dream dying on the vine? Is it gone? Are we all better now that the boy's here?

Stop this right now! shouts Mother.

You will leave him, he will leave you, you will stay together forever, whatever way you slice this, your hunger will haunt you, rot in you. It will never leave you be. It is what you are.

The hell is going on back here? says David, standing in the doorway.

Get out, yells Mother.

He shakes his head and shuts the door behind him.

What would you like to happen here? Do you hope to marry him? says Rita. *Would that do the trick?*

People marry all the time.

Girls who have no other options, who have no imagination, yes. But you? You have everything. You marry him and you will disappear. It WILL be the final blow.

Mother kneels on the bed and points at Rita. *You're jealous. You're jealous because this will NEVER be an option for you.*

Rita pauses and tilts her head. *What? To be some nameless, faceless wife shuffling around in a little house, asking herself,* Meat loaf tonight? *Or* casserole. Hmm.

Mother looks over at me sitting on the floor. Like this conversation suddenly involves me. I am frozen. Mother and Rita fight but it's often about hairstyles or shoes.

Rita studies herself in the vanity mirror. Slowly she collects herself, calms until she is as smooth as she was when she walked in here. I have seen Mother do this a thousand times. *I don't mean to be cruel, darling, but please take in what I say. Please know that it comes from my love for you. My adoration. Now you need to get a compress for those eyes. You look like hell.*

There's something I can do, I think. *Make a compress.* I go into the kitchen and David and I stand beside each other, he cooking, me filling the blue bag with ice and screwing the lid on.

Mother doesn't know what she wants, I say. *I heard her with my own ears.*

He grins at me. *Ain't a woman alive knows what she wants. That's how come you have to show them what they want.*

After Rita is gone and Mother is cleaned up, she says to David and me, *Darlings, would you mind giving me some time? I feel I ought to be alone for a little while, maybe work on the songs a bit.*

We stare at her.

She glides over to the cupboard and gets a glass, filling it with water. *They get so old, the songs, I have to confess. Can you imagine singing the same ones over and over, night after night?* She turns around to face us, exasperated by the idea.

David approaches her and she puts her hand on his face. *Would you mind?* she says.

I've got some things to deal with.

You can take her with you, she says, dropping an Alka-Seltzer in her glass.

I think she's a little young, says David.

Oh, but she's not. She's actually quite old, aren't you, kitten? Older than you and me, she says as she passes David with her hissing glass.

We drive to a fancy hotel and get out of the car. David hands his keys to a man in a long coat and we go in. Soft music plays inside and the carpet is thick with huge green leaves all over it. I try to step only on the leaves. David doesn't scold me for this even though I know it slows him down.

We go down some stairs, down a long hallway, down another set of stairs.

Are we going to the bomb shelter?

Sure looks that way, don't it?

Inside there are lots of people. David sits down at a big round table and I sit at the bar.

The Negro man behind the bar pours something in a glass and adds some red liquid and a cherry on a toothpick. *This here is a Shirley Temple. You like Shirley Temple?*

I nod and tell him, *Thank you.*

Your dad always bring you to games? asks the bartender.

I start to say he's not my dad but I stop. I look over at David and stare. Then it's like he feels my eyes on him and he turns to look at me, nods and smiles. Right then I know he's my father. Everybody knows. I know I'm supposed to love him and he's supposed to love me. But I love Jim. Jim and I are on the same team. The men around the table study their cards and one another, back and forth. They sweat and smoke cigarettes or sweet-smelling cigars.

When the game is done we leave. David walks fast because he is happier than when he came in.

Did you win? I ask him once we're in the car.

Yes, ma'am, I did.

Are you the best at that game?

I'm the best at reading people. It's all about having an eye for the tell.

What's the tell?

You got any secrets? he asks.

I don't answer.

Do you? he says.

Maybe, I say.

Of course you do. Everybody does. You look carefully enough, you can see everyone's secrets. Right there in front of you, on their face, how they move their hands.

I do that with Mother, I say.

She's a tough read.

No, she's not.

I get her wrong an awful lot, he says.

I know your secrets, too, I say.

Really, he says, pulling the car over in front of our place. *Shoot,* he says.

We stare at each other. *You're married to another lady.*

He crosses his hands over his knee. *Anything else?*

You're my father.

He itches his nose. *She told you?*

Nobody told me anything, I say.

He looks out the windshield and sighs through his nose. He presses his thumb against a small, star-shaped crack in the glass then rests his hand on the steering wheel and wiggles it back and forth. *I don't know what to say.*

Me neither.

You'd be awful good at poker, I'll tell you that. If you ever want me to teach you.

I would, I say.

Mother has the vaporizer going when we get upstairs. The apartment is warm and damp. She is pacing the rooms with her arms crossed doing lips trills.

What's going on here? says David.

Warming up, I say.

Already?

Mother waves her hand at David as though to say, *Not now.*

Sometimes she thinks her voice is gone, I tell him.

David frowns. *Laryngitis?*

She thinks it's been taken.

Taken? says David.

Jim shows up then and Mother looks so relieved.

He shakes his head. *I've got something for the kid. Only reason I'm here.*

Mother opens her mouth, pushes, and a little squeak comes out.

Well, you pushed it really hard last night, says Jim.

Punishment, whispers Mother.

Probably, says Jim. *Get some honey and tea.*

She sounded fine this morning, says David.

That was her speaking voice, I say.

Jim hands me a package. It's a record.

What is it? I ask.

It's a cat, he says.

I pull it out. *Skeeter Davis Sings The End of the World.*

Thought you might have something in common, says Jim.

Mother takes it from my hands and looks at it.

This is not music, she whispers.

It's not for you, Jim whispers back.

So will she iron out this voice problem? David asks.

She'll be fine, says Jim. *The problem is here.* He points to his head. *You two smell like you've been sitting in a tavern all day.*

Thanks for the record, I tell him. *I'm going to go listen to it right now.*

Jim follows. *I think you're going to like her,* he says as we sit on my floor in front of my record player.

I hold the record.

What you waiting for?

I know about David. I know he's my father.

Jim takes a deep breath.

He is, right?

Jim nods and looks at his shoes. I wonder just how many secrets there are.

Why didn't you tell me? Why would you let me feel stupid?

I thought you might be too young for that conversation.

Sister Eye says family is who you choose to love, I tell him, trying to keep my voice in order. *You chose me. You said you did. I chose you.*

He smiles at me and nods.

Not David. Mother can choose him but I don't have to if I don't want.

You're right about that. He looks uncomfortable sitting on my floor.

I pull the plastic off the record. *I wish she could be happy with just us.*

Jim nods. *Me, too, kid. Go on, now. Put that sad goddamned record on already.*

CHAPTER 24

AFTER JIM LEAVES Mother finds me in my room. *How was your outing?* she asks.

Fine.

Do you get along, you two?

I nod.

I'm glad. I really am keen on him. Did you do something fun?

Poker, I say.

Very funny, she says.

David appears in my doorway.

Will you be staying here tonight? she asks me.

I study her for a clue as to what I should say.

I'd like to keep her in, says David. *A normal night at home. You know, dinner.* My Favorite Martian. *Popcorn. Bed by nine. You've probably read about it in the magazines.*

A flash of disgust passes over Mother's face, but she asks, *You all right with this plan, baby?*

I don't care, I say, and turn the volume up on my record player.

David follows her out the door.

I might be late, I hear her say.

Why's that? says David.

I don't hear anything by way of an answer.

Just come on home, doll, I hear him say before the door closes behind her.

We make grilled cheese and popcorn for dinner. David spills more popcorn than he eats while he stares at the television. It seems to be a problem of him always grabbing more than he can hold. He tries to think of things to say to me—do I like cats, have I ever seen *King Kong*—but I don't say much back. Finally he sighs and says, *I think you don't want to get close to me because you think your ma and I aren't going to work out.*

Probably, I say, as nicely as I can.

Why is that?

Because it never works. With her. Not once in my whole life.

David looks at me and thinks.

It's after ten o'clock when he says, *Should I tuck you in or read to you or something?*

I'm not a baby, I say. Back in my bedroom, I write *television* and *Jiffy Pop* in my notebook.

My clock says three A.M. when I wake up to the sound of something crashing, laughter, and then David coming out of Mother's bedroom.

Hi there, Mother calls to him.

I get out of bed and peek out my door. Mother and the brown-eyed woman from a few months back are in the living room.

Darling, this is Margaret. My friend, Mother says to David.

He says, *I thought I asked you to come straight home.*

You DID, darling, says Mother. *That is precisely what you said.* And she and Margaret laugh at that or something else, I'm not sure.

It's late, says David.

Is it? Shhh, she says to Margaret, who is bending over, trying to pick up something from the floor.

Won't you join us?

No, I won't. He seems angry and walks away.

Not on these terms, right, darling? On your terms, yes, let's have a ball, she says with her arms up. *But not these, not mine.*

David slams the bedroom door.

Go back to bed now, kitten, she says when she spots me by my door.

When I'm back in my room, I sit on the floor and open my notebook. Margaret is her name, I remember. I manage to stay awake until the apartment is quiet. Eventually, I go out and wake her up.

You should go, I say to Margaret.

Her eyes open and settle on me. *I should.*

She fastens her pants and puts on her shirt. I notice that she doesn't wear a bra. Then she puts her hand on my head. *I'm sorry we kept you up. I really am.*

Do you love her? I ask.

While she is thinking about this, she finally starts buttoning her shirt. *Sometimes you take what you can get.*

I understand. It would be better to be with Mother just a little bit than not at all. Margaret puts me back in bed, tucking the blanket very tight around my body and under my feet. *You're very strong*, I tell her.

She crosses her arms and looks down at me. *You're pretty tough yourself.*

Naomi

CHAPTER 25

KANSAS CITY, 1955

I'D SLEPT ON the couch of the little apartment above the Neon Parrot for several days. I read a worn, old copy of *Cosmopolitan* magazine while Caroline and Elaine got ready to go downstairs. Marilyn Monroe was on the cover. It was hard to tell whether she was pulling the black lace dress off her shoulder or trying to keep it from falling. *Oh, this silly dress*, her face seemed to say. "Why Men Pick the Wrong Women" was the sentence next to her head and where her hips would be it read, "Hollywood's Most Valuable Property."

I longed to be beautiful, to be someone's valuable property.

The noise below us swelled until the voices and the music rattled the apartment. Caroline and Elaine moved from bathroom to bedroom to kitchen, quickening, giggling, saying *he* this and *she* that and *did you ever*. Caroline was wearing a black half-slip and pink bra, the hair around her face wound and pinned into perfect circles. She had two cigarettes going in different ashtrays. Elaine came in and out of the bedroom in various dresses, finally settling on a tight black shift. She pulled a scarf off the lamp, shook it once, and wrapped it around her hips, tying it to the side.

What do you think? she asked, posing.

I think you could wear anything, I said.

She cocked an eyebrow at me and said to Caroline, *I kind of like the country girl.*

Let's not jump to conclusions, said Caroline, perching next to me on the davenport with a haze of perfume and hairspray. She began to deftly roll a stocking in her hands and pull it on, starting at her toes, straightening it along her leg, and fastening it to her garters. Her legs were fine, not strong like a country girl's but long and bony like a colt's. She quickly did the same with the other stocking and hopped up.

Am I straight? she asked, facing her back to me. I reached down and pressed my thumb along the seam of her stocking at her calf, to straighten it.

Thanks, doll, she said.

They grabbed their cigarette cases and were out the door, their heels rapid-firing down the stairwell.

The dollar bills waved in their wake like sad little flags. Smoke slowed and hovered under the ceiling. A breeze pushed out the table-cloth curtain like a blue belly and then pulled it empty again. It was suddenly so still.

I went to the phone and dialed home. Mother answered. I didn't speak at first. *Hello?* she said. *Hello? Naomi? Is that you?*

Yes.

O mój Boże, o Boże ("Oh my God, oh God"). *Where are you?*

I tried to breathe because her voice made me cry instantly.

Are you there? Please don't hang up, she said.

I'm in Atchison. At the convent. I'm safe, I told her. *But you can't call. They're strict. I have to go. Tell everyone I . . . I have to go.*

I hung up, sat down, and cried for a long time, until I couldn't anymore, until I could see that all the sadness in me didn't change anything. There was the breeze coming in, there was the lamp, there was the same stillness the girls left behind when they ran downstairs.

A nearly whole cigarette teetered in the dip of the ashtray's edge. I picked it up and relit it, coughed and breathed enough to clear my lungs, then tried again. It was awful and hurt in a way that moved me, burned something in me that wanted to be burned.

The door opened and I smashed the cigarette in the ashtray, coughing again. David saw me and said, *Oh, for Christ's sake.* He went to a low cupboard under the bar and pulled out a gun, popped open the cylinder, and clicked it back in place before tucking it in the back of his pants. *Help yourself to whatever,* he said, gesturing at the kitchenette.

Where you off to? I asked.

A game.

You need that gun for a game?

It's not just any game, doll, he said, heading for the door.

I could come watch.

Nobody watches, he said.

I paced around the little apartment, opened the cupboards and the fridge, looked at the booze on the little liquor cart. I opened things and smelled them, poured myself a glass of brown liquor. It was awful, just like the drink Elaine gave me, but I felt like it was cleaning me somehow.

Elaine threw open the door then and the room filled with sounds from the club.

Did he leave? she asked.

Yes.

Good, then. Just needed to be sure.

What kind of game did David go to?

Cards, Elaine said, checking herself in the little mirror by the door.

Does he play for money?

Elaine faced me. *You think Daddy bought him this club?*

I shook my head no.

And don't drink that stuff, she said, pointing to the glass I was trying to hide. *It ain't gonna help one thing.* Then she left.

The girls' room was a terrible mess. I put away the stockings and slips, panties and bras, tried on the shoes, and walked all over the apartment. The heels made me feel very serious, like I was standing on the tip of something, walking along the very edge of myself.

I lay on my back and listened to the crowd downstairs, the bubbling and billowing of sound like water boiling, and then a woman's voice sang out, loud and plaintive, calming down the boil. I sat straight up. The sound of her made me ache and I put my hand between my legs—let it just rest there—and I realized that I wanted her, the woman who was making these sounds, or I wanted to be her. I lay back down with my hand still resting, letting the longing course through me and through me, never moving my hand, never doing a thing to stop it, to let it go.

CHAPTER 26

WHEN ELAINE AND Caroline woke up the next morning, they ignored me half the day as punishment for touching their things. But then I heard Elaine say to Caroline, *It DOES look better in here.*

Finally Caroline said to me, *If cleaning is so fun for you, why don't you march downstairs and put the club back together?*

Yes, ma'am, I said.

What did I tell you about calling me ma'am? she said.

Miss Caroline, I said.

I'm a young woman, she told Elaine. Then they turned their backs and walked away from me, Elaine telling Caroline she had the most famous legs this side of the Mississippi and Caroline returning the kindness by saying Elaine's skin could make a peach feel ugly. All this to make up for the word *ma'am.*

I cleaned the club every day, and every night I fell asleep on the couch or in the stairwell, listening to Elaine sing. She danced with her voice in a way I couldn't imitate. She hopped it up and down her throat and into her head and way down in her chest like she was skipping a stone. I worked and worked on that while I was alone, scrubbing floors and washing glasses. My hands got rough as Mama's. With my sweat and my muscles, I believed I was clearing the slate, killing off the weakness in me, the childish needs. I dug my nails into the bar's crevices where booze had spilled and crusted; I would leave nothing untouched.

David played poker constantly. He and Caroline either loved each other or hated each other, I could barely keep up. I watched, listened, and learned, and tried to stay out of the way. In my daily letters to Sister Idalia, I asked her about her life, wrote down all the memories I had of learning music and listening to records and of the other kids at school. I wrote of the creek, her truck, the sky. I didn't want her to forget all that. And I told her I was working all the time and learning to sing, both of which were somewhat true.

One afternoon I finished my work and the apartment was empty, so I ran myself a bath. I picked up the phone to call home but then put it back down. What was there to say? While I was in the tub, David and Caroline returned. I heard them talking quietly in the main room but soon their voices got louder and louder until Caroline was shouting, *You promised!*

And I'll make good, said David. *Just not now.*

It's never going to be now with you. Never, said Caroline. *I could go someplace else.*

Yes, you could.

Other people think I've got something really special, she said. *They do.*

I agree, he said.

Then feature me tonight. You know I'm good.

You are good. And Elaine is better. It's her they're coming to see.

Fuck you, boss, said Caroline, storming across the floor and down the stairs. I waited for David to leave the main room but he didn't. The bathwater got cold. I sat there shivering.

David tapped on the door. *Kid? You in there?*

Yes? I set a washcloth on my breasts like he could see through the door.

You about done?

I scrambled to get out of the tub. *Yes, hold on.* I dried my body fast and pulled on my dress, which was still wet in the armpits where I had washed it. It stuck to me, and when I reached up to pull my hair back, I noticed there was still soap in it. I opened the door and moved past David quickly, apologizing, and waited outside for him to finish.

He peed with the door open and I turned my back. After washing his hands, he said, *Come back in here.*

I went.

Let me help you, he said, pointing to my hair. He slid off his jacket and hung it on the door. Then he draped a towel over the edge of the sink and told me to bend over it. After pulling up his sleeves, he slowly poured warm water over my head with a cup, running his hands through my hair as he rinsed. All of a sudden there seemed to be a thousand invisible threads connecting the side of my body to the front of his where he was almost touching me. I wanted to lean into him like I used to lean into the wind. He squeezed the water out with a towel and said, *Sit down here.*

I sat on the toilet seat and he took his comb from the shaving kit he kept on the shelf.

That's not going to be easy, I told him, pointing at my head.

I can see that. But still he took a small handful of my hair in his fist and began to comb it out, starting at the bottom. His face was close to mine but he was focused on my hair, so he didn't see me staring. I wanted to feel his bristly cheek with my lips.

Am I hurting you? he asked, looking me in the eyes. His eyes crashed on me and I suddenly didn't feel like a ghost anymore, a cat trying to be quiet. I felt some part of me catch up to myself, like it had been dragging behind me for days, miles. Then all the parts were together again. I felt this especially under my dress and hoped he couldn't see what was happening to me—and I hoped he could.

No, I said finally, *you're not hurting me.*

Let me know, he said, working his way around my head, the tangles, knots made up of other knots. It took a long time. We were both quiet and tired by the end, from the work of my knots or from the invisible threads or both. I thanked him and left, wishing I had someplace to hide, to be alone. I looked at the clock; six P.M. The apartment would be empty soon. Just hold on, I told myself.

Elaine arrived and talked to David in the kitchen.

You're set up to play with Sandy and his crew at the Continental tomorrow night, she said.

You kidding me? said David.

Wish I was, she said. *You gonna be in over your head down there. Sandy will be by tonight to collect your buy-in.* She walked with purpose into the main room and stopped in front of me. *Where is Caroline?*

Not here, I said.

I can see that.

I'm making you a sandwich, Elaine, yelled David. *You're not drinking on an empty stomach.*

Davie, look at this dress. Do I look like I have room for a sandwich? She posed and I felt like she'd given us permission to look hard at her and I looked hard. She was so perfectly designed. If the magazines allowed Negro women, she'd be in them.

She hid the sandwich in a drawer, giving me a look that said, *Don't you even.*

Davie, where's Caroline? she yelled.

Stepped out.

Ah, shit, said Elaine. *You fighting?*

Where's your sandwich? said David.

Tell me how I'm supposed to work the room and be your canary at the same time. Do you see two of me here?

Easy now, he said.

Elaine crossed her arms. *Don't you "easy" me.*

We'll have Miss Naomi cover for her, he said.

Elaine dropped her arms and looked at me. I knew what she saw, a country girl in the wet dress she'd been wearing for a week, pale red hair combed straight and just starting to frizz up at the ends. Never even shaved her legs. Freckles. Bare feet. I knew what she saw.

She crossed her arms again. *Let me know when you think up a Plan B.*

No Plan B, David said, his patience done. *Help her. Fix her up and do whatever you do. Put her in one of Caroline's dresses.*

Do you think this, she said, gesturing at herself, the final product that was Elaine, *is just some lipstick and a dress?*

No, no, I do not. Improvise, Elaine, he said, walking away. *This is jazz, remember? Pull out the fake book.*

He left.

Elaine looked at me like I was covered in pig shit, sighed through her nose, and lifted up a bit of my hair to look at it. *This part I can handle at least. As for the rest of you—*

She turned on the little fan on the table, walked to me, and spun around.

Unzip me, she said.

I moved the zipper down the length of her back slowly and carefully.

She stepped out of her dress, laid it out flat on the bed, and stood looking at me in her peach slip, hands on hips.

Sit down, then, she said.

On the vanity was a container of some thick substance, like lard, which she scooped with her fingers and worked into my hair. Then she wrapped sections around big green rollers and secured them with pins she opened with her teeth.

What's a fake book? I asked.

All the players have the fake book. It's got all the most popular songs, chords, changes, and whatnot written down so even if you don't have the full sheet music for a tune, you can fake it.

I kept my chin tilted upward as she put makeup on me—pancake, shadow, liner, mascara, lipstick, rouge, powder. As she worked she slowly forgot she was mad. When the makeup was done, she studied me, then picked up a silver gadget, turned it on, and blew heat on my face and hair. She spent a little time on each roller, sometimes so long my head felt like it was burning. When she was done, she said, *Hmm. Get up now.*

I stood while she looked me over, turned me this way and that. She put her hands around my waist, rested them on top of my hips, put her fingers on my shoulders, all the while doing some sort of calculation in her head. *M-kay,* she said as she pulled a green dress from the closet and brought it to me. I thought of Laura and the pile of dresses and the kiss, but it felt far away by then, like a song I heard once.

This is the one, she said. She got out a slip and told me to put it on but gasped when she saw my bra.

I haven't seen something like that for twenty years, she said. *This could be tricky.* She fished out several bras from Caroline's dresser and fiddled with them. *Take that thing off and try this.*

I turned my back to her and tried to get my breasts into the complicated cups of the bra. It squished them. Elaine turned me around.

You've got to reach in and sort of get them centered in there, she said. *Bend over like this.*

I was so embarrassed handling myself in front of Elaine but I had to get my breasts sorted out if I was ever going to get clothes back on.

Not bad, she said when I finished, and handed me the dress. I put it over my head and felt around for the zipper, found it along the left side of my ribs and pulled it up. It was tight but I was relieved that it fit. I tried to pull my ribs together to make a little room.

Let me look at you, said Elaine.

I stepped back.

Hmm, she said, nodding with approval.

She sat me down and unrolled my hair, turning pieces this way and that and pinning them. Then she found a fake pink flower and pinned it above my right ear and brought me a pair of shoes that were snug but I didn't care.

Stand up, she said.

I stood, wobbled, caught myself. I put my hand on my hip because I didn't know what to do with my arms.

Elaine made a clicking sound with her mouth. *I have skills*, she said. *Terrible skills.*

She brought me to the full-length mirror that leaned against the wall. *Allow me to introduce you to Miss Naomi*, she said.

I was shocked by the sight of myself, I looked like another person. Like a painted photograph of myself. I moved a little and tried to get used to it. It was what I wanted after all. I practiced walking around the room. *Thank you, Miss Elaine.*

You still walk like a hired hand but nothing to do about that now, she said.

CHAPTER 27

AS I FOLLOWED her through the apartment and down the stairs, I was aware that nearly every inch of my body felt altered—covered, slicked, pinned, tucked, bound, painted, fastened, powdered, squished, pushed— but again, it was a pleasant sort of pain. It reminded me how much of me needed to be controlled and if you worked really hard, you could.

Hobbling down the stairs, I thought: There's no way I can get through the whole night in this getup. I felt like my body would explode out of the dress and shoes at any moment.

We walked into the club, which was empty except for a lone man sitting at a table and David, who was behind the bar. He took his gun out of his pants and tucked it under the bar before noticing us.

Elaine said to me, *You've got to stand like there's a rope attached to the top of your head and it's pulling. That's how you walk.*

I straightened my body as much as I could, and the taller I got, the easier the dress was on me. David came out from behind the bar. I made a face that I hoped said, *What do you want?*

I'll be goddamned, he said.

I stared at him. In heels, I could nearly look him in the eyes.

Put your tongue back and sit down, said Elaine. *We don't need you bothering us.*

He joined the man at the table and Elaine followed him, saying, *And let's try to remember ourselves, shall we?*

Elaine showed me the whole system, described how Caroline worked the room, how to be efficient, how to deal with this sort and that sort. It didn't sound so different from managing my siblings—everyone wanting something different, fighting for your attention. Tom, the barkeep with the round face, said not to worry.

It was easy at first. I smiled, took orders, told the orders to Tom, delivered the drinks, trying to bend in a way that would keep the dress from splitting. I never knew a dress could give orders to a body, make me move like a whole different person, and my breasts were so out there that I could see them in my peripheral vision. I even looked right down at them once to see if I was imagining it. All night I looked forward to going upstairs and unhinging myself like a jack-in-the-box.

There were Negro folks and white folks in the club. Talking to one another and mingling like the world outside wasn't cut clean in two. David visited with everyone and every few minutes, all night long, glanced at the door.

Finally a short man, Negro with light skin, strolled in and looked around. David wandered over to him and they stood side by side, chatting, surveying the room like it was the High Plains. Eventually David handed him an envelope and the man left.

He caught me watching and approached me.

Naomi, I didn't say earlier because, well, you took me by surprise. But, you're beautiful. I mean, you look beautiful.

I looked him in the eyes. *Well, if you didn't find me beautiful before, you shouldn't now. It's all make-believe*, I said, tugging at my skirt.

I did, he said.

What?

Find you beautiful before.

I tried to manage my face, to hold back whatever it was that made my cheeks twitch.

A man at a table raised his empty glass and jiggled the ice in it.

Excuse me, I said, and pretended to not notice my skirt brushing David's body as I passed him.

The club filled and I ran myself ragged trying to take care of everybody. There was a man at the bar holding something in his arms, but I was too busy to be concerned. Then I came close to him to drop off a tray of glasses, and when he turned to look at me, I recognized him as the man who drove me to the club. It was my bag in his arms. Suddenly I couldn't breathe.

You work here? he asked me.

I unloaded the glasses from my tray. He hadn't recognized me. My arms felt like they were filled with ice.

You know a girl by the name of Naomi? he continued.

I asked Tom for three gin and tonics.

Well, he said, *this belongs to her.* He set my bag on the bar and put his hand on it.

Hold on, I'll go get her, I said.

Much obliged, he said, and then turned in his seat a little so he could see the stage.

I walked quickly along the bar and around it. Tom was at the other end talking to a girl, so, at first, he didn't notice when I pulled out David's gun and pointed it at the man's head.

Get the fuck out and don't come back, I said.

The girl talking to Tom gasped and he rushed to me, saying, *What the hell, Naomi?* And then David ran to the bar as the man scooted out the front door. I put the gun back and brushed off my skirt where it had gotten wet from the ice bin.

I picked up my bag. *Mind if I leave this back here?* I said to Tom, tossing my bag on the floor beside a box of wine and grabbing my tray.

She's from the Wild West, this one, David announced. *She gets home-sick*, and the people laughed as I took the gin and tonics to a table by the stage.

When the band started warming up, there was a sudden eruption of applause, the sound of folks shifting their chairs for a better view.

I looked around for Elaine, letting my eyes land on her and sink into her as she walked up the three little stairs, holding her skirt and moving her hips demurely back and forth as she did. I put all my attention on her until my heart settled down.

Let's not waste any more of my time, she said into the mike, provoking whistles and hollers from the crowd. After a few measures, she opened her hands and her mouth and there she was, Elaine in her glory. I sat down in an empty chair by the bar and everything but her fell away. I traced her notes inside my chest and throat, imagined exactly where the sounds were formed and pushed and held. In that moment, I knew that I was going to do that someday. No question in my mind. I thought, If Mr. Miller's dirty money is still in my bag, I will buy my own damn dress. I will wear my own dress on my own stage. Mark my words.

CHAPTER 28

I LAY ON MY back on the couch that night and arranged the flat pillow just so under my neck in order to preserve my hair. The bones in my feet ached, my back and arms, too, even my face. I wondered where David was and couldn't sleep. There was little noise on the street except for a dog now and then, or a horn, and I was so happy to be alone for once. I slid my hand under my slip and touched myself. My head flooded with people, with the memories of anyone who'd ever touched me. Ever. David combing my hair, Laura's pale weight, Elaine turning me this way and that, handling me. I made myself come quickly, it had been so long with so much piling up.

I drifted off listening for the bell on the downstairs door and woke to the sound of a body falling on the stairs, and jumped to my feet. I looked around for something to use as a weapon, and then grabbed a plate, holding it in the air as David stumbled through the door. He had trouble climbing to his feet.

Don't plate me, whatever you do. Please don't plate me, he said, laughing and coughing, wiping some spit and blood from his mouth. I helped him to his feet. He smelled of booze and maybe urine.

If you're gonna pick a fight with your girl's boyfriend and you're not afraid because you're heavy, he said, miming placing a gun in his waistband, *you should be CERtain you've actually got your piece.*

It's under the bar, I said, trying to lift him to his feet.

I remembered that. Round about the time the fucker finished beating me and took a piss on me. In front of my girl. In front of Caroline. Fuck, he said, trying to get up.

I ran a bath and helped him to the bathroom. He steadied himself on the sink while I unbuttoned his shirt. My fingers touched his chest. I slid his arms out of the sleeves. His eyes were closed as I unfastened his belt and pants, and they dropped to the floor. I slid off his shorts without looking and helped him into the tub. His whole suit sat in a pile on the floor, so I gathered it in my arms and began to leave.

Naomi, he said. *Don't let me drown.*

I won't.

Look at you. You're a woman. It happens so fast, he said. *Doesn't it, doll?*

I nodded.

He shut his eyes, leaning his head against the back of the tub.

I tried to leave again but his voice stopped me. *Can you just set here with me for a while?*

I closed the toilet lid and sat on it with my back straight, holding his suit on my lap and staring at the door. I wanted to look at his body but I wouldn't let myself.

I have an idea, he said.

What's that?

Tomorrow we just start fresh.

Fine.

Got any ideas about that? he asked.

I'd like to buy a dress.

All right, then, he said. *Tomorrow we go to the dress shop. Good. Tomorrow we buy you a dress. And I'm going to win a game. That's what I'm gonna do.*

I have my own money.

Excellent, he said, drifting off.

He was way too tall for that tub. I looked at his penis. I'd never seen a grown man's penis before. It reminded me of an animal, something just born. It seemed to be made of entirely different material than the rest of him, which was solid, rough, covered in dark curly hair.

When he woke up and lifted his head, he suddenly seemed more sober. *It's late,* he said, looking over at me. I put a folded towel on the edge of the tub and went back to the couch.

He walked to the bedroom and shut the door behind him. I smelled him smoking and told myself to lie still. The cords connecting us were getting stronger. They stretched all the way through the walls now. I ached in my skin. Stay, Naomi, I told myself. Try to stay.

I started a letter to Laura, told her I was with her brother, told her that he reminds me of her—his easy smile and laugh, the way everyone likes him. Except he doesn't seem like the type to walk away. In fact, I wrote, he's willing to fight for somebody he loves, but I crossed out all of these sentences and put the notepad back under the davenport.

I wrote to Sister instead: *Kansas City is swell. I miss you and wonder if you are all right there at the Mount. I hope you did not get fired. Can sisters get fired? I am sorry for making such a mess of things. I truly am. Are they giving you enough to eat? I don't like to think of you in that horrible, little room. Maybe I can come there. Would they allow me to come back?*

I am working at David's club. I have to ask you something. I feel love for David. I also often feel I could love Elaine, a singer who works here. And none of this takes away from my love for Laura, even though she's finished with me. Do not worry. I am keeping to myself. But I feel there is something terribly wrong with me. About love, that is. I think I could divide my love over and over and still have so much left. I feel I am made wrong where love is concerned and it sits inside me, this worry, like I ate something bad.

The only relief I feel is to think of your face. Because you know me. This is the only time I do not feel like someone capable of all sorts of destruction.

Write soon. Please tell me what exactly I can do about this.

PART FIVE

My Foolish Heart

Sophia

CHAPTER 29

CHICAGO, 1965

MARGARET IS NOT the only lady who sleeps over. There are others. But David stops getting mad. Mother watches him like she's waiting for him to burst out and yell at her, but he never does.

How come you don't get mad? I finally ask him when Mother is in another room.

It's not her fault, he says. *She's just rebelling. It's okay.*

He's studying a ledger book that is full of numbers, making little notes and marks.

I understand her, you see, he says. *She's afraid of being trapped. Pretty soon she'll settle down.*

She's never going to be normal, I tell him.

We'll see, he says.

Mother walks past the kitchen like a nervous bird, looking for something she lost, and pokes her head in. *Kitten, are you coming to my fitting with me?*

I look at David, who is whisking something in a bowl.

I would very much like your opinion on this dress, she says.

Okay, I say.

This will be ready when you come back, says David.

Mother looks at his back like she doesn't understand something. *Fine*, she says.

Hilda is taking in some of Mother's dresses.

Miss Hilda? I say.

Yes, dziecinka.

Have you ever made clothes for babies who are joined together?

She looks at Mother and turns her palms to the ceiling. *What is this question?* she asks.

Or people with growths? Or hats for those people with really, really giant heads?

Darling, says Mother, *Hilda is trying to concentrate. Let's ask her questions later.*

Hilda scowls at me and shakes her head. *She's not a normal child*, she says, trying to be quiet.

She's not normal, says Mother. I look at her, wondering if I've heard her right. *She's exceptional. Like her mother.*

Hilda shakes her head. *Turn around now, angel*, she says gently. She is being very kind to Mother today. I don't know why.

You have to eat. I know you. Your black moods, says Hilda.

I need to work harder, Mother says. *Or for my luck to change.*

How much more luck do you need? says Hilda. *You have beauty, you have lovely strange little child, you have good job.*

I want to be known. I have to be known. She touches Hilda's cheek. *Do you hear me?*

Relax your face, says Hilda. *You're getting wrinkles thinking like this, and too skinny. You want your* piersi *to become two little sacs?* She points at Mother's breasts with her piece of chalk.

I would like shoes to match. What do you think of that?
It is wonderful idea, says Hilda. *Perfect.*

W*here are we going?* I ask Mother when we leave.

To look in on the girls. Should we bring them something? she asks.

I nod.

We buy magazines at a small bookstore. *Vogue* for Rita and *National Geographic* for Sister. I hold them. There is a man on Sister's magazine with black fabric wrapped around his head and the bottom half of his face. He looks like the Aladdin at Riverview Park but he's a real man. I stare at him while we walk.

Please watch where you're going, kitten, snaps Mother. She moves like a small animal today: quick, nervous.

I tuck the magazines under my arm and watch where I'm going.

When we arrive, Rita and Sister's apartment calms me down. The scarves on the lamps, tapestries, stacks of books, plants, plants, plants. I feel like I can breathe there because everything is kind of a mess.

Rita sits me down at her vanity, looking at me in the mirror. *Just have fun*, she says. *A girl should be allowed to experiment.* Then she goes into the kitchen to talk to Mother and Sister.

I lean in close to the mirror and put on some lipstick but I look like a clown, so I wipe it off. The women are keeping their voices down and for some reason I don't feel like spying on them. I guess I don't really want to know, but then I hear Mother say, *This is the ONLY thing I know how to do!*

I walk into the kitchen to listen.

We were just discussing your party! says Mother.

No, you weren't.

Sister looks at Mother and shakes her head.

Rita is going to make a cake! Mother says.

Have you lost your mind? Rita asks her, then turns to me. *I have no such inclinations, my darling. I will BUY you a cake. Now, what kind would you like?*

They all look at me. *I don't care*, I say. *No one will come.*

Sister looks at me with concern. *We'll all be there, Sophia.*

But not kids, I tell her. *Not Elizabeth.*

I'm working on that, Mother says. She tries to take my hand on the way home but I move away from her. We walk faster. *What were all those questions back there? At Hilda's? About deformed children?* she snaps.

Just curious.

But why? Why are these things in your head?

I don't know.

Mother looks perplexed.

You're not the only thing in my life, I tell her.

She raises an eyebrow at me.

You don't tell me everything, I add.

Mother walks on, looking straight ahead. Sometimes, for some reason, she listens to me. When we get near the park she asks if I would like to sit with her for a little bit. We find a bench and sit quietly for a few minutes, watching the people go by.

This is nice, isn't it? she says.

I nod.

It's not easy for me to appreciate the little things in life, she says. *It never has been.*

She presses her palms against her lap and takes a deep breath. *The thing is, kitten, Big Doug.* She looks at me. *Well, I'm just not pulling in the kind of crowds he needs. And, I seem to be on a downswing. They're looking for someone new. Modern.* She smiles at me, but I can tell she's sad and maybe even afraid.

Then what? I ask.

He's going to let me go.

She watches a man and his very small dog move briskly down the walk and stares at him like she knows him.

What will we do?

I try to imagine not performing, kitten. Just leaving it all behind and getting a nice little job somewhere. Maybe at the Merchandise Mart. Settling down.

With David?

Maybe.

I know he's my dad.

She takes a deep breath. The sun moves behind a building and we can feel its sudden absence. We're both looking up now as if it might change its mind and come back out. *Do you have any questions about that?*

How come you didn't stay with him?

I chose to come to Chicago. I chose my career. Some women do, she says. *It's not unheard of. And I kept you, I did that at least. I didn't get rid of you.* She stops suddenly.

Get rid of me?

She looks at me like she has so many things to say but nothing comes out. She finally just says, *Oh, darling, it's been a long day. Let's go home.*

CHAPTER 30

JIM IS SITTING in the lobby reading a paper when we get home. He stands and hustles toward us when we enter.

Boy, have I got news, he says.

Is that so? Mother says.

I talked to an editor from Look *magazine today and he wants to do a whole story on Chicago.*

A fellow admirer of buildings, says Mother.

Actually, he was very interested in the pictures of you, of the scene here.

We have a scene? says Mother.

It's not clear just what he has in mind but he's interested, that's for sure.

Whatever I can do to help. I have always wanted to be in magazines, she says, a bit of breathlessness in her voice, posing for someone I can't see.

This could be big, says Jim, *for both of us.*

Well, I need my luck to turn. We make a good team, Jimmy.

She puts her hands on his face and he stands there letting her like he's stuck in time.

I've got my work cut out for me, he says, breaking the spell. *I must have six rolls to process of you alone.*

No bad pictures, says Mother. *You know the rules.*

Jim shrugs and flips through the little notepad he keeps. *I can't make any promises, doll.*

I mean it, Jim.

Me, too, he says, tucking his notebook back in his pocket and grabbing my shoulder. *I'm going to shoot the Stock Exchange now. You wanna come?* he asks me. *I think you should. It's not going to be standing much longer. Time is running out.*

Go ahead, says Mother. Then she says, *Hey, Jimmy. I miss you. I wish you'd come around more.* He squints behind his glasses like what she's saying hurts.

When we start walking to his car, Jim says, *I hear someone's going to have a fancy birthday party.*

It's no big deal, I tell him.

It's a big deal to turn eleven. Although . . .

What? I ask.

I wouldn't be eleven again for all the tea in China.

I lean Jim's tripod against my other shoulder and think I must look like a toy soldier.

How's it going at home? With David and all, he asks.

I can't really tell, I say. *He's in love with Mother.*

I'm sure, says Jim, scratching his mustache. *And she loves him?*

She acts like she does.

Does that mean she does?

How am I supposed to know? I say.

I don't know, says Jim.

Are you coming to the party?

Are you kidding me? I wouldn't miss it for the world.

We stop in front of the building. I look up and try to count the floors, but I lose track. There is a crane parked in the street and a ball hanging from it, which is almost as big as Jim's car. All the entrances are blocked.

You want to go in there? I ask.

Do you know who did this one?

I have no idea. *Just let me think.*

He's my favorite, says Jim.

I know this. Jim gave me a sentence for remembering. Try not to sully the van, whatever that means.

Sullivan.

You're so smart, he says.

Jim turns his back to the building and watches the street, then all of a sudden says, *Follow me. Quick.*

He slides open a small panel covering an open space in the wall and we climb in. It's dark and dirty and the floor is covered with piles of stone, glass, and wire, piles much taller than I. But the railings and columns are beautiful, smooth, and black with very small engravings all over. I try to get the dust out of all the small places with my fingers.

We climb the stairs, up and up, until my legs burn. When we can't go any farther, we step into a room with an open place in the ceiling. Wires and beams hang, some of them move in the wind.

I don't want to be here, I tell Jim. All the other buildings we've been in feel like they'd stand up through anything—storms, wind, bombs. But not this one. This one feels loose.

A few shots and we're out, he says.

Something falls. I jump and knock over the tripod.

It's okay, says Jim. *I wasn't screwed in yet.*

Can't you just hold your camera? I say, watching him slowly turn the screw into the bottom of his camera.

It's too dark in here, he says. *I'll be fast.*

I think I hear something move, but when I look at Jim, he doesn't seem to have heard it. There's so much dust in the air I can push my hand through it. I want to leave, I want to be home in my room on the floor with my notebook. This is what it will look like, I think, after the bomb falls. Everything will be like this.

I look up at a hole in the ceiling. Through it I can see the clouds fly by so fast, unbelievably fast. It makes me feel like I'm spinning and I start to run. I've got to get out. As I fly down the stairs, my hands collecting dust from the rail, I hear Jim yell, *I'm right behind you, kid.*

When we get out Jim sets down his gear and hugs me.

I'm so sorry, he says. *I didn't mean to scare you.*

I know.

She's just so beautiful, though, isn't she?

I nod.

I wanted you to see it before she's gone.

I thought it was going to fall on us, I say, and then I start crying.

Oh, doll, she's been standing here nearly a hundred years. She's not going down without a fight.

I put my hands in my pockets and can taste the dust in my mouth.

We're okay, he says. *We're okay,* and we head back home.

CHAPTER 31

THE NEXT MORNING, David wakes me up so early it feels like the middle of the night. Right away I think something is wrong.

Is she okay? I ask him as soon as I sit up.

David shakes his head no and waves his hand. *We have to run an errand. Top secret.*

I climb out of bed and stand in front of him. *You have to leave so I can change,* I tell him.

Yeah, right, he says as he goes into the hallway. I close the door behind him and wish I were back in bed.

When we get in his car, there's dew on the windshield. It's chilly and nobody is out on the streets except for some trucks.

Thanks for coming, he says. *I needed a sidekick this morning.*

I cross my arms and look out the window.

We stop in front of a small florist shop. A thin man in a white apron stands in the door holding a cigarette with one hand and rubbing his eyebrows with the other.

They shake hands and we follow him inside. He gives us several large trash bags that weigh almost nothing. David fishes some cash out of his pocket and the thin man is clearly happy with how much is there.

Pleasure doing business, says the man. David tips his hat and we throw the bags in the backseat. As we drive, a pale, sweet smell fills the car. I take deep breaths through my nose with my eyes closed, and think I can almost feel the smell behind my eyes.

David sees me and laughs. I look at him. *Pretty swell, huh?* he says.

I nod.

He pulls over by a small park not too far from the hotel and turns off the engine. I say, *Wait.*

Leaning back, he rests his hands on his thighs. He has such big hands, kind of hairy, and the cuffs of his shirts are always perfectly white. I wonder if he knows the first thing about surviving a bomb.

Finally he says, *What we waiting for?*

I don't want to leave this smell, I tell him.

Let me see, says David, closing his eyes. I hear him take a deep long breath.

We sit there smelling the air for a few minutes, and once I feel like I've memorized the smell, like I'll never ever forget it, I tell David, *Okay, I'm ready now.*

We get out of the car, he grabs a bag, and I do the same. There is a bench near a cluster of trees where Mother likes to sit sometimes and I follow David to it.

He opens up his bag and turns it over, dumping flower petals all over the ground and the bench. They are pink and red and white and some yellow. I open my bag and scoop the petals out with my hand, feeling them, feeling how I can hardly feel them they're so soft and light. Sticking my head down into the bag, I take a very long breath.

Enough already, he says. *Just dump her.*

I turn the bag over and the petals fall, some of them lifting up on the wind to drop here and there.

What's this all about? I ask.

What's this all about, says David. *You sound like Jim. You're a little Jim.*

So what's it all about? I ask, mad that he's talking about Jim like he knows him.

Cool your jets, Jim, he says. *You'll see soon enough.*

You think I'm supposed to be all excited about you because you're my dad. I don't have to get excited if I don't want.

David stops and kneels down in front of me. *I know. You're absolutely right. But you gotta give me a shot. Give me a break, here, kid.*

And if you think you can get her to love you, you're stupid. I take a deep breath then. I feel like I can't stop myself.

And? he says.

That's all.

He reaches out his hand for me to take it. I don't.

I want something better. For all of us, he says, looking around. *This is no place for you. Out in the suburbs, they got swimming pools, places to ride your bike.*

I don't have a bike, I say.

A little wind kicks up. We both look over the petals. They stir a little and fall, not far from where they were.

We gotta get back. He puts his hand out again. This time I take it because now I feel a little sorry for him.

When we get back home, we stop at the front desk and Sal looks like he's been standing there all night.

I'll take that package now, says David.

Yes, sir, Sal says. He disappears and returns carrying a large wrapped box with a seal that says, "Evans."

Thank you, says David.

Good luck.

David looks at him and wrinkles his forehead like he's missed something.

We slip quietly into the apartment. I put my nightgown back on and get in bed, but I can't fall asleep. Instead, I lie there, listen, and wait.

Finally I hear Mother in the kitchen, humming like she does, like there's a song running in her head. Every now and then a note accidently escapes. I lie there on my back trying to figure out what song it is. It's like the word game at school where Sister gives us one or two letters and we have to guess the rest.

I tiptoe into the kitchen and watch her fill the percolator. She sways a little bit, her long gown moving back and forth like it's trying to sweep the floor. David comes down the hall with the box. Mother whips around and looks at us, perplexed.

What on earth, she says.

Pull up a seat, he says.

She lowers herself into a kitchen chair and crosses her arms. David presents the big box to her. The ribbon pops off easily as she wiggles the lid loose, gently tugging the tissue paper apart, her mouth opening as she does.

Good heavens, she says, and David smiles.

She stands so she can lift the coat from its box and it rises like the ghost of an animal, a bear maybe, something large and dark and fierce. I take a few steps back so that it doesn't touch me.

David, it's exquisite, she says, stroking it like it's alive.

Try it on, he says, taking the coat and opening it for her.

She tries to put her arm in but the sleeves of her robe are too voluminous, so she backs up and unties it, saying, *Nobody look.*

Underneath her robe is a nightgown sheer enough to show her nipples and the shape of her legs. I look away. She puts on the coat and hugs it around her, turning the collar up around her face.

It feels delicious.

Let's take her for a spin, says David.

What are you talking about? Mother asks him, putting her arms around his neck, the coat opening as if to let him in.

I don't know. Let's go for a walk, see if it works.

Don't be ridiculous. I haven't even had my coffee.

David crouches in front of the low cupboard and grabs a green thermos. *I'll take care of that while you get dressed.*

Mother smiles at him like he's telling a great story and does as she's told.

You, too, he says, and I go to my room.

As we walk toward the park, David carries the thermos and mugs and Mother walks like the coat is perched on her, like it might fly off. We pick up a little bag of pastries I can't wait to eat. I look at Mother and at David and everyone seems happy. I want to be happy but there's this hole in my stomach, a jittery thing around my heart.

When we get in the park, I can feel David's excitement, the difficulty he has walking slow, like he just wants to run as fast as he can to the petals, to everything finally being okay, to the future.

We approach the clearing and Mother notices the ground, walking a bit ahead of us to investigate. She walks faster now and looks back, then she waves for us to catch up and we are all there in the petals, walking in them, them moving and lifting around us with the wind.

David puts the coffee, cups, and pastries on the bench, and says to Mother, *Sit down.* Then he kneels down in front and rests his forearms on her legs, squeezing her thighs with his hands.

What are you doing? she says.

He pulls a ring box out of his coat pocket and holds it in front of her, taking a deep breath.

Naomi Hill. I've known you since you was just a skinny troublemaker and I'm the only one who knows you like that. I'd like you to marry me. Because nobody but me can put up with your shenanigans.

Mother is shaking her head, putting her hand in front of her mouth, and maybe her eyes are tearing up from happiness or from fear, I can't tell. But the wind blows and the petals swirl and the hairs on her new coat lift and drop, lift and drop.

He puts the ring on her and she stares at it, watches it like it's going to start talking.

Let's be a family, a proper family, he says. He waves me to him and grabs me close so that we're both facing Mother, like we're both asking her. I've wanted to have a normal family all my life and now that it's here, I don't want it. At all. I just stand there silent and wish he'd let go of me.

It's a swell idea, she says, putting her arms around us, the fur touching my mouth. I turn my head from it.

Is that a yes? says David.

Yes! Yes, why not! she says, with the littlest bit of stage voice, but not enough for David to hear.

David is so happy he jumps to his feet and into the air, hugging me and Mother, saying, *It's just the thing. I'm sure of it. It's just the thing we need, doll. To make it all right.*

He reaches his hand to her, she takes it, and for a moment they look like a photograph until the wind gusts and the petals blow away and Mother takes her hand back, to close the coat around her, to protect herself.

CHAPTER 32

Rita buys me a dress for my birthday party. It is long with many colors, like a quilt, like a gypsy, she says. The party is held in Rita's office, in the back of a club on Division where she works. Its walls are lined floor to ceiling with shelves of wine bottles—all shapes and sizes, each little label like a small painting. There is a long, rectangular table with a red-and-white-checked tablecloth and short fat wine bottles with candles stuck in them. When Jim and Mother and Sister and I sit down at it, the table seems particularly large.

I like to get to a party early, says Mother, stretching her arms along the table like she's trying to take up more space.

Rita comes in then wearing a very tight dress with very high heels, so she has to take very small steps. She has an apron on and looks hot.

Why, you look like you've been cooking, says Sister, jumping up to help Rita with a stack of plates.

That's the idea, says Rita. *But don't worry.*

She hugs and kisses me. *My girl. Another birthday. Time is escaping me.*

Hi, Miss Rita, I say.

Do you still love pizza? she asks.

She's eleven, says Jim. *She hasn't lost her marbles.*

Mother looks at the door and at the tiny little watch she sometimes wears, then smiles at me. I don't think Elizabeth is going to come.

Look at us, says Sister. *Like the old days. The original gang.*

I try to smile at her.

Then Rita's head tilts like a squirrel and she runs out of the room. My stomach flutters.

Willkommen! Willkommen! Rita is saying, and Jim shoots me a worried look.

C'mon, he says. *I think they're here.*

The LaFontaines are standing in the main room of the club staring at the walls, which are covered with photographs of tall glamorous women like Rita, posing in front of the giant silver star on the back of the stage. Without the stage lights on, the star looks to be made of tinfoil. Elizabeth runs to me, we hug, and I tell her I didn't think she would come and she says, *Me neither. We've been sitting in the car out front for fifteen minutes.*

Why?

Fighting, she says, wiggling her finger back and forth at her parents.

Jim ushers everybody into the back room, making a lot of noise about pizza! And cake! Mother is standing next to the table, her hand resting on the back of the chair. When the LaFontaines enter she extends her arms.

Our friends, she says in her stage voice. Mr. LaFontaine is jovial. Mrs. LaFontaine nods hello and looks around, her lips squeezed.

Why, you look absolutely lovely, Mother says to her, and Mrs. LaFontaine tries to smile.

Hi, sir! Elizabeth yells to Sister.

Mrs. LaFontaine says, *Elizabeth!*

All the kids call us "sir," says Sister. *We find it amusing. Well, most of us.*

Everybody sit now! I do not want my gourmet dinner getting cold! Rita wiggles out of the room, returning with a stack of pizza boxes and two bottles of wine in one hand.

As we examine the different pies, Mrs. LaFontaine looks around and says, *A most interesting choice for a child's birthday party.*

I look to Mother, watch her wheels spin fast.

She finally says, *Isn't it just dreadful?* Then she leans forward on the table. *Oh, well, I may as well tell you. The girls here gave me my first break. Put me on that sad little stage there when I was just a timid young thing. This is where it all started for me.* She leans back, gestures at the room, and shrugs. *But I believe we should never forget where we came from, I do. And how far we've come. Don't you agree?*

Mrs. LaFontaine looks at her like she's just been beat at jacks and takes a deep breath in through her nose. She is about to say something when Mr. LaFontaine jumps in.

A valid position, he says, and raises the glass of red wine Rita has poured him. *Here's to humble beginnings!*

With all due respect, Mrs. LaFontaine says to Mother quietly, *I do not believe you have the vaguest idea what humble beginnings truly look like.*

Here here! says Mr. LaFontaine.

Here here! says Jim.

Rita sets two beautiful Shirley Temples down in front of us.

Elizabeth says, *What are these?*

They're called Shirley Temples! I exclaim. *I had one at a poker game.*

Mrs. LaFontaine shoots a look at me and I realize I shouldn't have said that.

Sister and Mr. LaFontaine sit across from each other and talk like they're old friends. Then they start to talk about the war.

What are these drinks you've given them? Mrs. LaFontaine asks Rita.

Well, cocktails, darling, says Rita. *What else?* She taps Mrs. LaFontaine's arm with the back of her hand and Mrs. LaFontaine straightens.

Oh, for Pete's sake, says Rita. *They're pretend.*

Pretend, says Mrs. LaFontaine, squinting up at Rita. *There's a great deal of pretending that goes on around here, I gather, Miss.* She hisses when she says *Miss.*

Jim takes a picture of them.

The room goes quiet suddenly as everyone listens to Sister and Mr. LaFontaine's conversation.

I just don't think six hundred dead Vietcong is cause for celebration, says Sister.

Jim looks up from his plate.

Mr. LaFontaine cocks his head. *No, of course not. I'm only suggesting that profound changes are bound to come from this, some of them of great interest to me, to us.*

Sister nods, considering what he says.

Mrs. LaFontaine looks at me. Her face softens some. *Miss Sophia, you look lovely in your birthday dress. Is it new?*

I nod.

I rather like these new hippie fashions, she says, like she never got mad at anyone in her life. *I can certainly see the appeal.*

Can I have a dress like that? asks Elizabeth.

We'll see.

Mother looks at her watch and at the door.

So how is the performing life? Mrs. LaFontaine asks Mother.

Oh, you know, it's a living. Have you been to the Blue Angel? she asks.

Mrs. LaFontaine looks at her for a moment. *Do you see many Negroes at the Blue Angel?*

Mother laughs. *Well, of course! Why, Dizzy Gillespie played there. Etta James?*

Onstage, says Mrs. LaFontaine. *Do you see them in the audience?*

I suppose I hadn't noticed.

You don't have to notice, Mrs. LaFontaine says sternly.

Well, Mother says. *These things have to change sooner or later, right?*

How do you figure? says Mrs. LaFontaine.

Mother opens the clutch on her lap and takes out an envelope.

I know it's Sophia's special day, but this is just a little something to say thank you, for your friendship and your understanding. She hands the envelope to Mr. LaFontaine. He opens it; he smiles.

I've reserved the best tables in the house for you. And your friends. It's going to be my last show there, she says. *It's time for me to move on.*

Mr. LaFontaine thanks her. Elizabeth says, *Do I get to go, too?*

Her father says, *Of course.* And her mother says, *We'll see.*

Everyone at the table seems very excited about this except for Mrs. LaFontaine. I can't tell what she feels.

I eat my way along my pizza to the edge of the crust, leaving the crust on my plate. Mother is still glancing at the door and at her watch.

Sophia, do you know the history of your name? asks Mrs. LaFontaine.

This feels like a pop quiz.

Sister looks at me and nods as if to say, *You know the answer to this.*

My mother and Rita and Sister gave it to me when I was born, I tell her.

Mrs. LaFontaine smiles. *Yes, of course, but do you also know that Sophia appears in the Bible many times. She is wisdom. Your name means "wisdom."*

I know, I tell her. *Sister told me. I forgot.*

Don't ever forget, says Mrs. LaFontaine.

Mother takes little bites of pizza quietly, like she's been punished.

Aren't we missing someone? says Mrs. LaFontaine, looking around the table. *Yes. The man in the housedress?*

Elizabeth bursts out laughing. Rita glares at Mother.

David, says Mother. *He's running a bit late.*

Can Sophia open my present? asks Elizabeth.

Jim says, *I don't see why not.*

Elizabeth hands me what is surely a book wrapped in shiny silver paper. *You probably already know what it is.*

Not EXACTLY, I say, pulling open the paper.

Show us! Show us! says Mother. I turn the book to face them.

I can't see what it is! says Mother, delighted. She glances at Mrs. La-

Fontaine but Mrs. LaFontaine shrugs as though she knows nothing about the gift.

I read them the title. *Fallout Protection: Understanding and Surviving Nuclear Attack.*

I smile. The adults look at one another with stunned faces.

What on earth? says Rita.

How did you even get this? I ask Elizabeth, throwing my arms around her.

My dad helped, she says.

Mr. LaFontaine nods and smiles at us. The adults look at him and they try to smile, too.

And another one, says Jim, pulling his present out of a bag. One long box is stacked on a square one and they are individually wrapped.

Did you wrap those yourself? asks Mr. LaFontaine.

Of course.

He's very good at that sort of thing. Our Jim, Mother says to Mrs. La-Fontaine.

I open the small one first and study the sketch on the box. *Soldering iron?* I ask.

Soldering, Jim says, leaving out the *l* sound.

What does it do? I ask.

Open the other one, he says.

The other box is plain cardboard with the word *Heathkit* written on the corner and on the bottom it says "Heathkit 6 Transistor Radio."

You can make your own radio. We'll do it together. He helps me open the box and pulls out the instruction manual. A drawing of a man and his son is on the cover. *See. It tells you exactly how to do it, start to finish.*

I hold the instruction book and study it—numbers, colors, sentences—and I think of all the things on my list, wishing I had an instruction book for everything. It's quiet in the room. Everybody is watching me like I'm supposed to say something.

You'll need a radio if you survive a nuclear explosion, says Mr. LaFontaine. Jim and Elizabeth nod. The mothers scowl and shake their heads.

I begin to feel like everything might be okay. I put my arm around Elizabeth and she puts her arm around me.

Then David appears in the doorway, exclaiming, *Where's the birth-day girl? Sorry I'm late. I was at the airport.*

Mother moves toward him. *Whatever for?* she says, like he's so silly.

A woman comes in behind him. It's the airline stewardess who gave me the trouble dolls. She's got her uniform on and her little hat.

Hello, everyone, she says.

Mother stares and the woman stares back.

David introduces everyone to his sister, Laura.

Jim moves the chairs around, telling everybody to sit down and eat more. *Look at all this pizza,* he says, taking more pictures. Mother scooches closer to me and Laura sits down on the other side of her.

What on earth, Mother whispers to Laura.

Davie said we were going to a club, says Laura, smiling. *I'm as surprised as you are.*

Son of a bitch, whispers Mother, shaking her head and lighting a cigarette.

Is that for me? Laura says to her. She passes the cigarette to Laura. *He's always up to something, our David. Isn't he?*

Mother says to Rita, *Darling, I think we could use a good deal more wine, don't you?*

You read my mind, says Rita.

David eats a few bites of pizza and drinks some wine. He wipes his mouth with a napkin and stands up with his glass.

We're not just celebrating Miss Sophia's birthday tonight, he says. *We've got other news.*

Mother interrupts, *David, darling—*

I've asked Naomi to marry me and she said yes.

Oh, my goodness! says Mrs. LaFontaine. Rita's mouth hangs open as she looks from David to Mother. Jim shakes his head and the look he gives Mother makes me forget to breathe for a second.

Mr. LaFontaine says, *Ah, marriage,* and raises his glass.

David looks at Laura. *See why I wanted you here? For this!*

She looks at him like he's just said something very mean to her.

Mrs. LaFontaine says, *Congratulations to you both.*

Sister studies the base of her wineglass.

Elizabeth leans in close. *Are you happy?*

I look at Jim, who is staring at the table like his spirit left the room. Looking at him makes me want to cry.

They toast. Mother is so flustered she drinks all the wine in her glass while the others just take a sip.

What a terrible, terrible surprise, says Rita to no one in particular.

Mrs. LaFontaine looks over at Laura, who appears to be frozen. *Where are you from, Laura?*

It takes Laura awhile to answer. *Kansas originally,* she says, clearing her throat. *Same as David. And Naomi.*

Everyone has gotten very quiet with their forks and glasses, like if they move too fast, something might explode.

Whereabouts? asks Mr. LaFontaine.

Soldier, says Laura. *You've never heard of it, I'm sure.*

I ask, *You knew Mother when she was little?*

Yes, I did, says Laura. *Naomi was my best friend.*

It was another lifetime, though, wasn't it, sis? Hell, I can hardly remember, says David.

I remember, Mother says, staring at David. Her jawbones move under her skin.

David stands again. *Well, that's all ancient history. I've got another surprise!* He fishes around in his inside pocket, pulling out one little box and then another. He places one in front of me and one in front of Mother.

Mother says, *It's not my birthday.*

Now, says David, *you brought Sophia into this world, so it's a happy day for you, too. Go on, open them up.*

Mother and I look at each other, and then we untie the yellow ribbons. I take off the lid and there is a key on a piece of red ribbon. I pull it out and look over at Mother. She is looking at her key but doesn't touch it.

What's it for? I ask.

It's for our new house, doll. I bought us a house. He glances at Mother and then says to Mr. LaFontaine, *Three bedrooms, two baths, a great big yard.*

He says to me, *You could have a swing set. Hell, maybe even a dog.*

I don't move. It seems like nobody in the room moves.

A dog! says Elizabeth, clapping her hands. *What will we name it?*

Mother finally says, smiling, *Where is this house, darling?*

Naperville. Just west of the city.

How far? I ask.

Oh, a few dozen miles is all, says David.

Elizabeth looks at me. *Will we see each other?*

Of course, says David. *You can come out anytime.*

Mr. and Mrs. LaFontaine look at each other and seem to have a little conversation with their eyes. Elizabeth notices this and frowns. She leans in close. *I don't think they allow Negroes out there.* We stare in each other's eyes, our fears wrapping around each other.

An unbelievably bold move, says Jim. David frowns at him and Jim raises his glass like in a toast, but he's not smiling.

Rita enters with the cake, candles flickering. *Kick us off, Miss Hill,* she says.

Mother clears her throat.

Before I catch fire, says Rita.

Mother begins to sing "Happy Birthday" and everyone joins in. It is weak and out of tune.

That was perfectly terrible, Rita says to me. *Make a wish, baby.*

I look around at the table and try to think of a wish. I look at Mother but she's not paying attention, she's looking at the key. And I know it's not going to work—our love, everybody in this room—it's not going to be enough for her. I start to feel like I'm going to cry with everyone looking at me. I just want us to be okay but I know, somehow, that we won't be. That it's going to be like Mother says, *Sometimes things just come crashing down.* I blow out the candles as hard as I can without even making a wish. The others clap.

CHAPTER 33

DAVID SAYS SOMETHING about going out to the bar to make some real drinks and Rita follows.

Laura watches her brother leave. *Always full of surprises*, she says, looking at Mother. *Is this what you want?* Everyone looks at her and at Mother.

It is so generous, isn't it? says Mother, smiling at the others. She takes a little bite of cake and seems to hold it in her mouth like she can't swallow it.

Everyone starts eating cake. They say, *Yum* and *Good stuff* and try to talk to one another, try to leave Mother and Laura to their conversation, but they can't help themselves. They have to listen in.

Laura doesn't eat. *Are you done?* she says to Mother.

Done what?

Singing. This will be the end of that, she says, pointing at the box.

Don't you start, says Mother.

I know you, says Laura, sitting up tall and straightening her little uniform jacket.

Maybe I am done, says Mother, her voice tight like she's going to cry. *Let's be honest. It's not really going as planned, is it?*

What do you mean? says Laura.

I'm soon to be out of a job, she says.

I can feel her sliding into that place, the place you can't get her out of, but she catches herself and looks hard at Laura.

A woman has to know when to stop. Before she becomes embarrassing.

You're being dramatic, says Laura.

Sister says, *Girls! Honestly.*

It's getting late, says Mrs. LaFontaine. *We ought to be going. Happy birthday, Sophia. Bee, say good-bye.*

Elizabeth hugs me. *Happy birthday*, she says, and they head into the main room. I follow them all the way out into the street. The rain has stopped and the streets are wet. I watch them climb into their car. Elizabeth waves from the back window. *Thank you for the book*, I call out but I don't think she hears me.

Jim walks out of the club and Laura follows behind. *Come away from the street*, he says to me.

He offers Laura a cigarette and she stares at him, then slowly takes it from his hand.

I know who you are, he says, lighting her cigarette.

Really? says Laura.

Her first love.

Laura looks down the street. *Looks like we both lost.* She smiles a little. *David hated our father but they're the same. Isn't that funny? They just get what they want. One way or another.*

I head back inside, not wanting to hear.

Where you going? says Jim.

To get my presents, I say.

Rita is behind the bar when I walk back in, wiping the counter and straightening the bottles. The stage lights are on now and the big silver star shines like it has just woken up from a nap.

I walk toward the back room but stop when I hear shouting.

What in God's name are you thinking? bursts Mother. *What the FUCK is wrong with you?*

Rita looks over at me and turns on a faucet, shaking her head.

We're going to be together, says David. *It's what we both wanted.*

This is not a game. I am not one of your games! Mother shouts.

David's voice is calm. *I won't have my child raised in a hotel. Surrounded by—*

By what? says Mother.

You're not getting any younger. This life you've chosen isn't going to hold up much longer. Let's be realistic.

And what do you get out of this deal? she says.

I can't quit you. You can't quit me. What else is there?

You want to stop me, says Mother, her voice quieter now and low. *It's what men do. You STOP us. You fuck us and knock us up and tuck us away so we never become anything. ANYthing.*

Rita rushes toward me, saying, *Baby, let's go wait outside,* but just then Mother comes blazing out of the room and runs right into me.

What are you doing here? she shouts. *WHAT? Why are you always creeping around, spying on me? I'm sick of it, Sophia. STOP looking at me. Stop watching me. I am NOT your business. Get your own. Leave me alone, Sophia.*

She yells so much it seems like it's not going to stop. I back up, into the side of the little stage to try to get out of her way, and can feel the heat of a footlight next to my leg as I watch Mother cross the room and walk out the door. Then the heat seems to hit my skin and I smell something burning. It has burned a hole in my birthday dress.

David comes out and sees me. I am crying now and he's on his knees in front of me lifting the side of my skirt, holding my leg tight. *Jesus,* he says, leaning his face close to my leg. *You're okay.*

My dress, I say.

Jim opens the outside door and says, *Sophia, your mother wants me to take you both home.*

Now, hold on, says David, letting go of me and walking toward Jim.

Jim moves around him. *Back off. Just leave her alone, all right?*

And where am I supposed to go? asks David.

I'm sure you'll figure something out. Come on, Sophia. I reach up for him to hug me. He pauses and then puts his arms around me to lift me up off the ground. He holds me like that for a long time, then sets me down carefully and takes both my hands in his. *Let's go, kid. You're okay.*

Outside, Laura and Mother stand close to each other, Mother holding Laura's arm like she does to me when she's mad. Laura gently pulls out of Mother's grip.

This is madness, says Laura. Then they see us and stop talking and Laura turns away, walking down the street.

Mother calls after her, but Laura doesn't turn around. She just waves her hand above her head.

It's quiet in the car on the drive home. Jim smokes and Mother keeps twisting a lock of hair on top of her head like she's fighting it, like it just won't do what she wants.

Who does he think he is? Mother asks herself.

Jim looks at her and sighs.

What? What do you have to say? she yells.

How did you think this would go? says Jim.

Mother crosses her arms. Sometimes I think I can imagine exactly what she was like as a child.

My dress has a hole in it, I say. *My new dress.*

Mother turns her head to her left like she can't hear me. *What are you talking about?*

My dress, I say.

Yes, I heard that. What are you talking about a hole? she snaps.

I stepped too close to a footlight, near that little stage. When you were shouting at me, I add. My heart pounds. *And my leg stings.*

You were shouting at Sophia? asks Jim.

I was not.

Then why would she say that?

She's making it up. She's always making things up.

I am not! I say.

She says, *If I lost my temper, you deserved it.*

I didn't even do anything, I shout back.

Mother says calmly, *No you didn't, darling. You never do anything. You just follow me around, lurking. You have no initiative, no passion. I cannot believe you're my daughter sometimes, you know that? You're like him. That's the real trouble. You're just like your father. You do not understand me.*

Jim jerks the car to the side of the road and puts it in park. *Stop it! Stop it right now, Naomi, so help me God.* He grabs her face and they are nose to nose. *If you EVER talk to her like that again, so help me God!* He lets go of her and Mother stares, stunned.

She watches him long after he puts his hands back on the wheel and begins to drive home, just sitting there studying the side of his face. I put my Heathkit and my book on my lap, hold them and start to cry so hard my whole body shakes. Jim reaches his arm back to touch me but I strike it away. I curl up on the seat and don't even try to stop it.

Jim stops the car in front of the hotel and turns around. *Sophia, my girl. It's okay.*

Mother reaches for me, too.

You get out, says Jim. *Leave us.*

But—

Leave us.

I hide my face in my arm and hear her get out of the car.

Jim rests his hand on my head and sighs. *I wish I could fix all this.*

I don't want to move. I try to breathe so I can talk. *I don't know how to swim! I don't know how to ride a bike!* I sit up. *I don't want to go there!*

Hey. I don't think it's going to happen. I really don't.

You don't know. I could live with you. I could help you in the bathroom.

It's a darkroom, he says.

Yes, but it's also a bathroom.

I'm going to take you up now so you can go to bed. Things will look different in the morning.

Mother is waiting for us on the sidewalk. We all three walk into the hotel slowly, carefully moving, walking like our bodies and the street and the sidewalk and the building are all suddenly breakable.

When we get inside the apartment Mother gets on her knees and hugs me. *I am so sorry, kitten. I am so, so sorry.*

It's okay, I tell her. I touch her hair. It's messed up and soft.

Come on, says Jim, *let's get you to bed.*

Don't make me. I don't want to be alone. Please let me stay out here.

Anything, says Mother. She grabs a blanket from the back of the davenport, spreads it out, and waves me over. I get under the blanket and suddenly feel so tired.

Good night, then, says Jim.

No, says Mother, grabbing his arm. *Please stay. We need to talk.*

He shakes his head and says, gently, *I've really had enough of you tonight. I really have.*

Ten minutes, she says. *Please, Jimmy. Sit with me.* She walks over to the settee. He follows.

I'm sorry about how I talked to her, she says.

You'll have to take that up with Sophia.

You know what my first thought was tonight, when I opened that box? My first thought was you. My thought was, I cannot live without my Jim. I will not.

I open my eyes then. Jim's looking at the floor. Mother leans forward so she can rest her hands on his legs.

She takes a deep breath. *I have taken you for granted. All these years. I haven't seen you clearly. But I do now. I do.*

He shakes his head. *I don't know.*

Give me another chance. I can be better.

He puts his hands on her hands. *You live in fantasies. Can you see that? It's good to have aspirations. It's swell. Hell, I got them, too, but this is what's real. Her, me, us.*

The phone rings.

Don't, says Jim.

She shakes her head and answers it. Listens. *Yes, we are,* she says. *We are done. No. I will call you.* She hangs up carefully.

I close my eyes and turn around so I'm facing the back of the davenport. *Please, God and the angels and saints, please let us all be normal again. Please don't make me move to the suburbs. Please don't let anybody drop a bomb on us. I will be good. I will be good. I will be good.*

When I wake up in the middle of the night, I go to the kitchen to get a drink of water and I hear Mother crying softly in her room. Light little sobs. The way you cry when nobody is there to hear you.

I open her bedroom door quietly in case she's crying in her sleep. She and Jim are sitting on the bed, naked, sweaty; her legs are wrapped around him and she is crying. He is holding her hair in his fist and kissing her neck. I close the door and go back to my room.

Lying awake, I look at the ceiling and think: If only my brain were bigger. If I had a big brain like Sister Eye or Mr. LaFontaine, I would know what to think, how I'm supposed to feel. I squeeze my eyes and try to make my brain bigger. Nothing happens. I don't know what is going to happen next. There is no way of knowing that.

Naomi

CHAPTER 34

KANSAS CITY TO CHICAGO, 1955

IN THAT LITTLE apartment above the club, I fell for David, despite all my good reasons to steer clear of him, that I still loved Laura, that Caroline was his girl, that he was my boss. But all that closeness—in the club, the apartment, all the time brushing past each other, sharing a sandwich, catching each other's eyes, smells—it was more than I could withstand. Day after day I put all my steam into my job, cleaned the Sam Hill out of the club with the radio turned up.

One hot afternoon Nat King Cole was on the radio, his voice butter melting on a hotcake. I cleaned and I sang along. *"The world is mine. It can be yours, my friend. So why don't you pretend?"* Suddenly I realized that Elaine was behind the bar, turning off the radio, and David was standing in the door with his arms folded.

Was that too loud? I asked, embarrassed.

Do that again, said Elaine.

What?

Sing a phrase of that song, she said.

I looked at David.

Forget him. Look at me and sing for me. Stand up.

I didn't want to say no to Elaine, so I stood up and sang a sentence.

More. The whole refrain.

I sang the whole refrain.

Now like this room is full and your life depends on it, she said.

I dropped my scrub brush by my feet and felt damp all over, sweat even in my eyes. So I opened my mouth and filled the whole goddamned room with my voice.

Elaine sighed. *Well, I'll be.*

How'd you learn to sing like that? asked David.

Sister Idalia. Records. Elaine, I added, though quietly.

Let's go buy that dress, said David.

Elaine looked confused, *What dress? The two of you?* she said, her arm dropping to her side like it had been shot. *I'd like to see what sort of frock the two of YOU pick out.*

David drove to Giddy Mary's Boutique. It was cool and quiet inside.

Mary looked from him to me and said, *What can I do you for?*

A dress, I said. *Grown-up. Pretty.*

She took my measurements and brought me several to choose from. In the little room with three mirrors, I noticed how different dresses produced different effects. I looked back and forth at the three versions of me and it occurred to me that I could watch my life from an angle, like it wasn't mine, just watch and see what happens. I put the blue dress back on.

You already tried that one, said Mary.

I know that.

It's a bit . . . provocative, she said.

Is that a problem?

Well, no, not exactly, said Mary. *It's a matter of appropriateness.*

But it's your dress. Do you carry inappropriate dresses?

Of course not, said Mary. *It's just . . .*

I settled on the blue one.

Don't you want to ask Mr. Miller's opinion?

No, I do not, I told her.

David stepped up to the counter to pay and I stopped him. He looked at my envelope of money. *Hey, where'd all that come from?*

Don't worry. It's not yours. I don't steal. I saw in his face that he didn't believe me. I saw what he thought I was.

Well, where'd it come from?

It's your father's, actually. Your father paid me to leave Laura alone, to leave Soldier altogether and never come back. "You little cunt." To quote him.

David took a sudden breath and Giddy Mary gasped behind the counter.

Well, I asked Giddy Mary, *do you want the nine dollars or don't you?*

After that, David bought us lunch at a diner. I had a hamburger and a Coke float.

You feeling better? he asked.

Yes. I'm perfectly fine.

I didn't think you stole from me.

I know what you thought.

Honestly, all I can think about right now is you singing. For me. At my club. You clean up good, you got chops.

I shrugged and told him, *I'm going to be famous someday. I'm going to be on the cover of an album. Maybe lots of them.*

He tilted his head.

I wiped my mouth with my napkin and continued, *So it doesn't really matter what happens next. It's all going to the same place. This creek or that creek. Same place in the end.*

I see, he said. *If you're going to be famous someday, you might need to work on your social skills.*

Caroline was at the club when we returned. Her face stubborn, she eyed me up and down and asked to speak to David alone.

For the next week we were all extra polite to one another because she and David had worked it out, whatever it was. They got back on their relationship like you get on a new horse—slow, hand on the pommel like it'll save your life, hoping he's going to be fine and he is until a leaf falls in front of him or a turkey bellows and he throws you off into a fence. That was their love. Always about to throw them into a fence. I watched Caroline. How she moved, lit her cigarette. I watched David watch Caroline, took note of what caused him to stare at her—Caroline walking across the room, Caroline drinking straight from the faucet on the kitchen sink.

I told Sister. *David and his girl are back together again, so that helps. I love singing more and more. It makes me feel like a better person than I am. You gave me this,* I told her. *Thank you. Also, please write me sometime. It doesn't have to be long, just a word. Maybe when the boss lets you out of that cell, you can come get me?*

Most days I tried to help Caroline in the bar but the looks she gave kept me at arm's length.

Once Elaine started singing, everything else fell away. I sank into her voice every night. Sometimes I would catch David watching me and Caroline watching him. Then there would be a big display on David's part—a squeeze for Caroline or a pat on the bottom. *My girl,* he'd say to his friends. I watched it like I was a spider on the high shelf where the expensive stuff was stowed.

It was very late one night, Elaine was done singing, the jukebox was playing, and chairs and tables had been shoved aside for dancing, when Caroline's other man came in, drunk and hollering. The crowd divided almost evenly between those who wanted to scatter out the door and those who were just waiting to hop on the coattails of someone else's rage, to get a few swings in. One fella hit another and set the whole thing off. Sloppy swings because of the booze, stumbling, scary at times, and funny, too. Until I saw David getting the business. Caroline's man pounding him with his fists like it was nothing.

After he was done, Caroline left with the man, looking back at David as he climbed to his feet. *Until we meet again*, he called to their backs.

Elaine was ushered out of the club by two friends of hers.

I went to David, grabbed his arms, and looked in his eyes. He was bloody and inflamed. I felt like throwing myself on this fire of his like a blanket—to put it out or be consumed by it myself, I didn't care which.

Come on, I said, and led him up to the apartment by the hand. He stared at me in total silence while I cleaned up the cut on his eyebrow.

He walked toward the bedroom. I watched. He stopped before the door and looked back at me, still saying nothing. I followed.

He sat on the edge of the bed and reached into his pocket for a cigarette. I stopped him, took the pack of cigarettes, and set them on the end table.

You'll want to pay attention, I told him, and proceeded to take off all my clothes and stand before him.

He studied me silently and reached for me but I stopped him, caught him by the wrist. He put his hands on his thighs and looked. At my body, at my eyes, at my body, and then only my eyes, and I didn't let him touch me until I was sure he was as terrified as I, as uncertain. I would not try to be Caroline for him, or any other woman he'd known—I didn't know how. He put his forehead against my stomach and I held his head. He moved his hands slowly over my body, recording my skin with his rough fingers. All my skin, my hands and mouth and bones and breath, ached for him. So much so that I had to slow it down, control where he touched me and when, keep us just apart, so we couldn't lean all the way in, hide in each other, eyes closed. There was no other way but eyes open. I made him ask me what I wanted and I made him tell me what he wanted, so that what was happening would be marked by us, with words. To make it real, witnessed, spoken aloud.

Over and over, I made him speak. *What do you want now? Now what? Tell me.* I made him ask.

The next morning, I slipped out of bed before he woke up, wiped the makeup from under my eyes with a washcloth, put on my old dress, and went for a walk. As I walked a low, mean voice in my head said, *You're terrible. Possessed.* Hearing it made me stand up straighter, to say to the voice, *Go on. Just go on talking like that. Try me.* I had been changed. I was ready to go to blows with myself.

When I got back David said, *Can I steal a few hours from you this afternoon? I want you to meet someone.*

Yes, I said. *You can steal me.*

CHAPTER 35

ON THE OTHER side of town there was a quiet neighborhood with trees, little brick houses, and respectable cars parked in front of tidy lawns. I'd never seen anything like it. Neat rows of houses for the comings and goings of untroubled lives. It seemed like a neighborhood the devil let alone.

A man in a bow tie, sweater vest, and horn-rimmed glasses opened the door and held it with perfect posture while gesturing us inside.

Ah, Davie, he said, shaking David's hand by holding it with both of his.

This here's Naomi Hutnik. The kid I told you about.

Harvey Gilbert, he said to me. *But everyone calls me Gill.*

Everyone calls me Naomi.

I see, said Gill, smiling at me with perfectly straight teeth. And to David, *Interesting.*

Well, I'm just curious as hell and don't want to waste another minute. He turned to David. *Surely you're anxious to get on with whatever it is you do, hmm?*

David nodded at us and left.

Don't slouch, darling, Gill said, pointing in the direction of my chest. *I hate to be crude but with a pair like this you cannot slouch. Not ever. Understood?*

Yes, sir.

I followed him to the piano. *We'll start with scales on a nice, open "ah."* He sat down and sang a scale; I mimicked.

Again, please. And this time as though your jaw is NOT wired shut.

I went again, my jaw hanging open. I yawned. *Excuse me.*

It's a good sign, said Gill. *You're opening up.*

He turned on his stool and pushed his fingers between my ribs, below my breasts. I was startled. *Try to push my hand away.*

I swiped away his hand with mine. He laughed. *From here,* he said, poking the two-inch space between my upper ribs. *Push with this. Use your ribs.*

I tried to control the space, and once I figured out what he meant, I was able to move his fingers in and out.

Most of the work of singing will happen right here.

Then he had me lie on my back and place my hands on my diaphragm, abdomen, chest, neck, to put the breath here then there. I stood up straight and trilled my lips and made siren noises up and down the range of my voice—one embarrassing sound after another. Soon I felt tired, light-headed.

Can't we just sing songs? I asked.

Gill looked at me over the top of his glasses, stared. My back itched but I didn't dare move under that stare.

He stood up and reached to a shelf behind him, taking down a trumpet, and handed it to me.

Play, he said.

I don't know how.

Try, he said.

I blew on the mouthpiece. It sounded like air on metal.

Why can't you play? he asked.

Because I've never learned. I told you. I don't know how.

Mm-hmm, he said, carefully removing the trumpet from my hands and placing it back on the shelf. He raised his hand above the piano and glared at me.

I have no interest in trumpets, I said.

He sighed. *You will play your instrument after you LEARN to play your instrument. You will "sing songs,"* he said, mimicking a girl's voice, *when you learn HOW to sing songs.*

I scratched my back.

Let's just take a little break here, said Gill. He shut his eyes and took deep, slow breaths.

I looked at the ceiling and could feel David all over my skin, everywhere, like he was still holding my legs open. I didn't want to take a break, to remember.

What's next? I asked.

He opened his eyes. *Consonants,* he said. *Starting on a nice G. Bright. Lee-lee-lee-lee-lee,* he sang. *The lips relaxed, the tongue tapping the roof of the mouth like the wing of a hummingbird. Now you.*

My jaw sprang open and shut like a marionette until it ached.

Can you teach me to sing like Elaine? I asked.

No, I cannot, said Gill, turning the page of the Marchesi book. *Elaine is being done, darling. By Elaine. I can teach you to sing like Naomi. Does this interest you? If not, we can stop now.*

Fine, I said.

He sat back down. *Believe me, you won't be disappointed.*

Back in the car with David, I was exhausted and hungry. He drove a little ways before pulling over.

I think we should talk about last night.

About what specifically? I asked.

He looked out the window. *Well, things are a little complicated right now, with Caroline and all*—

As soon as he opened his mouth, something inside me slammed shut.

Stop, I said, with force. Consonant-vowel-consonant. Punch the diaphragm. Engage the whole mouth. *Don't.* Another good one. I had learned something.

I just don't want you to think— he began.

Have I asked for anything? I said. *Did I last night? Am I now?*

Most gals, he began. And I didn't even have to say a word to stop him. He stopped himself, looked at me for a long time, then began to drive away. A game of kickball was bursting along up the street. The kids cleared slowly to make way for us. We rolled through.

It was nice, he finally said.

Was it? I said, trying to keep the door shut.

We drove the rest of the way home in silence, with just the threads between us—tangled, hot-wired, live.

The next day I had the apartment all to myself and ate everything I could find—a tin of stale crackers, some hard, greasy salami, toast with cinnamon and sugar. I wrote to Sister, told her about David and Gill, told her everything, however bad, because I hadn't heard a word from her. It was like writing to the wind, delivering the story of my life to the Kansas wind, where it would be whipped, shredded, and dissipated. *I wish you would write me. Are you there? I'm not a virgin any longer. I love David or perhaps I just found a way to matter to him, to be noticed. He has made me feel small and I hate him for that but I also long for him. I'm embarrassed. I'll be all right. I will find a way. Maybe I'll turn myself into something he cannot have. I could sure use your help. I don't know what's become of you or why I don't hear word. I'm going to sing soon. Very soon. Here at the club. In public. I miss you.*

The letter made me start to cry, so I took a very long bath and practiced my drills. They sounded better in there. I didn't cover myself when David walked in and pulled me out of the bath and dried my body with a towel and made love to me against the sink. Or afterward when I sat down on the couch and found a cigarette to smoke. I didn't cover myself until Caroline walked in. When I reached for the afghan on the back of the couch, she stopped me.

No, don't, she said calmly. *Not on my account.*

I crossed my arms in front of myself. David approached her, pants on, shirtless. *Baby*, he began.

You, too. Don't you move either. I want to take this in.

As she lowered her turquoise suitcase to the floor, she stared back and forth at us, thinking. *Just want to be absolutely sure I'm seeing what I'm seeing.* She kept rubbing her fingers together like something was stuck on them. *I am, right?*

David looked at her. *What?*

Seeing what I'm seeing?

Yes, you are, he said.

I lit my cigarette and stared at the wall.

Caroline sat next to me and crossed her legs. She looked over my body like it was a bolt of fabric she was considering. *I came to tell David that I left Charlie. That it's over, that I'm all his now. And here we are. I come home to this little surprise.*

Caroline, said David.

YOU don't say a word, she shouted as she stood and tugged on the laundry line that she had used to dry the money.

I know a lot about you, don't I, Davie, she said, pinching the line. *So many memories. You'd probably hate to kick me out what with everything we've shared.*

She walked to the window, looked out. *I'm not going to let you off the hook, just like that. Or you*, she said, pointing at me. *I'm also not going to let you out of my sight. Either of you. ESPECIALLY you*, she said, bending over me. *Look at this. All naked and delicious. You little snake. You're not a woman. You're a child. You cannot compete with me.*

I watched David carefully, stared at his love for her, his respect for the speech she gave, for the way she commanded our attention. She knew how to unsettle him, surprise him, and she was right. I could not compete.

He was the only one who believed your little story, doll. Cast out from the country, penniless, not a friend in the world. I never believed you, not for a second.

Leave her be, said David.

Caroline glared at him. *Not a chance,* she said, putting her hand in my hair.

I tried to catch my breath, to breathe from my diaphragm.

The phone started ringing and we all looked at one another. Caroline said, *Let's let that go,* but I stood and answered it.

May I please speak to David, said the voice. Laura's voice. I turned my back to them and held the receiver tight in my hands, close, like it could be snatched right out the window.

Laura, I said.

Who's this? she said with her singsongy bank voice.

It's me.

I listened to her breathe. I'd memorized her breath without knowing it, a pause at the top of the inhale and then a little push to let the breath out.

She hung up.

Laura, I said. *Laura.*

CHAPTER 36

THAT NIGHT CAROLINE paced the apartment waiting for David to come home from the game at the Continental. She wore a red nightie with a lace bodice and a matching robe that she left hanging open. I sat at the little table and made notes in my notebook, adding up how many hours I would need to work in order to make enough money for a security deposit on my own place or a train ticket to someplace else.

Finally David walked in, his jacket over his shoulder and his sleeves rolled up. Elaine followed behind him.

Well? said Caroline.

David shook his head, making us believe he lost, but Elaine gave him away by doing a little dance and singing, *"We're in the money! We're in the money! We got a lot of what it takes to get along!"*

Elaine and Caroline hugged. *Davie could get an Academy Award for what he does at these tables, I swear to heaven.*

He can bullshit with the best, that we know, said Caroline, glancing back at me. *What do you say we go downstairs for a nightcap?*

Good idea, said David.

You coming? Elaine said to me.

She's all tired out, Caroline said. *She needs her rest.*

An hour later Caroline and David came back up, passed me on the davenport, and went into the bedroom. Caroline hummed. I heard her humming get closer and I pretended to be asleep.

I know you're awake, she whispered as I lay there still pretending. *Come in here.*

Naomi, she said. I opened my eyes. She stood there with her head tilted, her robe hanging open. *Come on.*

I don't remember making a choice, only standing and going with her, David sitting on the edge of the bed.

Caroline, what are you doing? he said.

I wrapped the afghan around myself and watched them kiss.

She pushed him onto the bed, put her hand on his crotch, and looked back at me.

At the very least you might learn something, she said.

Then she kissed him, put her full weight on him, slid her hand back to his crotch. She pulled his pants off, felt him, cocked her head. *Oh, no*, she said, *are we spent?* David looked at the ceiling.

But you're not, she said to me. *Are you? You never are. You are hungry all the time, aren't you? I see how you look at Elaine.*

I hated Caroline then. And I wanted to be in charge of her, to watch all the power run out of her. I knelt on the bed, turned her over on her back, and held her head down so that I could kiss her neck, grab her breast, and she looked at me with a challenge on her face. I pulled at her with my teeth and ran my hair against her skin. She shut her eyes and arched underneath me. I rested my hand inside her thigh and she closed her legs around my arm, squeezed, moved her hips this way, that, but I didn't move my hand. I didn't move my hand up to her until she asked. *Say please*, I ordered, watching her face all the while. Every time she caught my eyes, there was an expression on her face that said, *I dare you.* I didn't let her body release itself—the flood, the shudder—until that look was gone, until she was completely powerless. Until she didn't even know I was there, or David, or anything.

When we were done I stood up and looked at David, sitting on the edge of the bed.

He pulled me to him but I turned in his arms as we fell on the bed so that my back was to him and I faced Caroline. When she reached up and touched my face, it was like she'd never seen it before. She put her hand in my hair and said, *You're a monster.* And then we made love like this with me between them. I loved his whiskers against my bare back.

It was almost noon the next day when I heard someone come up the stairs. I opened my eye to see Elaine standing there, her hand on the doorknob.

What in the name of God, she said.

Aw, come on, Elaine, said Caroline.

Just when I think I've seen it all. She threw a large envelope at me. *You bring trouble wherever you go. I knew that from the start.*

Shit, said David. *God damn.* He got up and yanked his clothes back on so he could go after Elaine.

Caroline took her time getting dressed. *There's no telling what a day may bring, is there? Around here.*

I turned over on the bed and held the package. Old, shaky handwriting—*Naomi Hutnik, c/o David Miller.* "Care of" indeed, I said out loud as I tore it open. There were a dozen letters from Sister Idalia. I pulled them out and arranged them by date and read them all. The last one made me shudder.

I subjected myself to the utmost humiliation yesterday. Mother visited me. I was so certain she intended to let me back into the community but she wouldn't. She was praying about it still. I begged her to let me out, begged her forgiveness and her mercy. I fell to my knees and grabbed her, clutched at her habit, wept and then screamed, and suffered her silent stare and the swiftness with which she removed herself from me. I do not know what to do. I can't bear another day. God have mercy on me and the terrible thoughts I now entertain.

I turned the envelope upside down and shook it. A little note fluttered out. Sister Windy's writing. *No more letters, dear. Sister Idalia is gone.*

I rose to my knees on the bed and read the tiny note over and over. *Oh, Jesus, please God. Oh, Jesus.* I ran to the phone and called the Mount. A student was working the switchboard and wouldn't put me through to anyone or answer my questions. *The community is not to be disturbed today* was all she said, over and over.

As I was dressing, David returned and asked what was wrong. I tried to explain and asked him to take me there but he shook his head. *I'm sure she just ran away, I'm sure she's fine,* he said. *There's no use going there.*

I fell to my knees and cried. He lowered himself and held me. *Listen here, doll. She's gonna contact you, I promise. You just sit tight. I know she will.*

She's my family, I cried to him. *She's all I have.*

You got me, he said.

No, I don't. You know I don't.

Look. Tomorrow is Sunday. Let's just concentrate on our work tonight and tomorrow we'll drive down there. Get some questions answered. It's a bunch of women. How hard can it be?

I hugged him and thanked him.

It took all the concentration I had to work at the club that night. Caroline flirting with me all the while like I was some man. I finally couldn't stand it any longer. *I'm trying to work,* I snapped, which hurt her and caused her to drink way too much.

By the time it was her turn to sing, she was three sheets to the wind—and Elaine still nowhere in sight.

It was Saturday night and the place was packed. I was sweating from covering all the tables. David was in his shirtsleeves running drinks, trying to keep an eye on Caroline, maybe wondering just what kind of mess he'd made.

He approached me. *Listen, I need you to sing. I need you to get up there.*

Absolutely not, I told him.

I beg you, doll. Just go up there and talk to the guys and do what you do. They can play any old song you sing to yourself, anything.

He walked me to the stage and got me up on it; the guys smiled and the crowd cheered. I stood there sweating, my dress sticking to me. Caroline cocked her head. *What you got for us, kid?* said the Negro man sitting at the table right down in front of me.

I swallowed and pointed to the drink in front of him. *May I?* He handed it to me. I took a big drink and handed it back. *Owe you one,* I said, and to the band, *"Ain't Nobody's Business."*

What the kid wants, said the guy on the bass, who then popped out a line that hopped and danced. I held the mike by the neck, closed my eyes, and pretended I was Elaine, saying, *You in a hurry, friend? Let's take this nice and slow.* The crowd clapped slowly and the people said, *Mm-hmm* or *Okay.*

"If I should take a notion." I sang real slow and gentle. *"To jump into the ocean."* Pause. *"Ain't nobody's business if I do."*

There was a burst of sound from the crowd—vocal, surprised, intimate—and I felt their reaction in my lungs, between my legs, behind my eyes. It was so deep I could hardly remember what came next. The band watched me, followed me close, moved under me like firefighters with a safety net with me teetering on a ledge.

"If I go to church on Sunday, then cabaret all day Monday," I sang. *"Ain't nobody's business if I do."*

I was someone else on that small platform, something else entirely.

And I knew that I would not be happy until the whole world saw what I could do.

Late that night, I lay there on the davenport playing the show over and over in my mind and worrying about Idalia. David lay down behind me and held me tight as he fell asleep. It was sweeter than I'd imagined.

CHAPTER 37

THE NEXT MORNING I called the Mount again, asked for Sister Idalia, and the young nun on the switchboard blurted, *Oh, she's run off!* Then she quickly tried to cover herself but I hung up before she could finish.

I sat at the little table with my head in my hands, shaking with relief. David woke and stood behind me. *She's fine,* I said to him. He pulled me up by the arm and into the bedroom, where Caroline had just woken up. We fell silently into a confusion of limbs, hair, skin, breath. Right there in the light of day. No booze or anger or darkness to hide us.

We carried on like this for the next two days. My mind was always on one of two things: the bed and the stage. These things left me intoxicated all the time. Until I saw this look on Caroline's face—the faintest trace of jealousy, hurt—and I knew it was over. The thin membrane that was keeping us even had broken. I didn't know when or how, so I returned to the davenport.

Tuesday night the crowd was sparse and without magic. David was at a poker game, and Caroline and I snuck drinks from the bar while a lonely man played songs from the jukebox. We should have closed down but among the dozen people left there was a feeling that this dragged-out, tired night was still a shade better than the life that waited outside.

Caroline and I danced. I closed my eyes and thought of Laura and me, back in the schoolhouse. A man walked in and I left Caroline so I could tend to him. He was a slight man with his collar turned up and a too-big hat. When I got close he turned to face me and I saw that it was a woman, and then I saw that it was Sister Idalia. We hugged each other so hard, cried and held each other's face. *Look at you*, she kept saying. *Heavens, look at you.* Her hands trembled against my cheeks.

What are you doing here?

I'm just passing through. I won't keep you. I'm visiting a sister, a friend in town. She teaches at Donnelly College.

I studied her face. So strange and so familiar all at once.

I'm going to see her in the morning, say good-bye before I leave. Her mouth trembled a little.

Will you stay here tonight? I asked her.

Caroline let us have the bedroom. Sister and I lay face-to-face in bed. *How did you get out?* I asked.

Sister Windy, she said. *We planned it for weeks. And then it just went off without a hitch and I was free, but— it never occurred to me I would have to say good-bye to her. I will never see her again. Or any of my sisters. I didn't realize how final it would be. All I could think about was getting out.* She cried and tried not to cry. I rested my hand on her head and said, *I know, I know.* Because I did.

Will you stay with your friend at the school? I asked.

No, that won't be possible. The whole community knows by now.

But where will you go?

Chicago, she said, a smile appearing. *My brother is expecting me. He tells me he will help me start a new life. He has always wanted me to be free. Freedom is more exciting to him than to me*, she said.

I think I would like your brother, I said. *I don't believe a woman should be trapped.*

Sister smiled. *I have missed you.*

I'm going with you, I said.

What?

I sat up in bed and looked down at her. *I'm going with you*, I repeated. *To Chicago. Would your brother mind?*

Heavens no.

I need to leave here, I whispered.

Chicago, then, said Idalia.

I lay there steering my thoughts from David to Chicago over and over again. Every time my mind leaned toward David—his heat, his desire—I steered it back to Chicago.

As my head got heavier, it became clear that my problems would all be solved by going to a new place. I would start anew. No one would know me and I would not hold myself back.

The next morning I stalled, hoping David would turn up before we left. I felt I couldn't leave without saying good-bye, or maybe without finding out if he would fight for me.

Sister went to Donnelly College to visit her friend and we made plans to meet at the bus station at noon.

I packed the few things I had in my bag as Caroline watched.

You can't carry that awful old satchel, she said. *Let me help you.*

She gave me her turquoise suitcase with silver metal trim, put it on the bed, and popped it open. Then she pulled some dresses and skirts out of her closet and took out the hangers.

What are you doing? I asked.

Just a few things to tide you over. I'm tired of them anyway, she said, folding them gently into the suitcase.

David came in and stood in the doorway. *What's this?* he said to Caroline. *You going back to Charlie?*

Caroline took a garter belt, a pair of stockings, and a half-slip from the bureau and tucked them into the elasticized pocket in the lid.

What's going on here? David insisted.

Our girl's moving on, said Caroline.

I slid past him and sat to put my shoes on.

He followed me, standing close. *What is this?*

I was shaking so bad I couldn't fasten my shoes.

He bent over. *Doll*, he said.

I didn't look.

He got down on his knees in front of me, slid his arms along my body until he held me by the hips. *Stop*, he said. *Just stop.*

I'm leaving, I said.

He shook his head. *Don't be silly. What are you talking about? What's she talking about?* he said to Caroline.

I fastened my shoe and thought, If I don't stand up right this minute, I'll never leave here.

I understand, doll. It's all too much. We can, we can slow it way down, right, Caroline? We can all just take her easy.

No, I said.

He put his forehead on my lap. I touched his hair, slid my palm along his whiskers one last time.

I would have learned to love you better, he said, looking up at me. His longing washed over me, made me sweat. It's what I wanted, to be looked at like that.

Come on, doll. I've got no aces here.

I have to go. I left then, telling myself all the while, This step. Now this. Now this. Now this.

CHAPTER 38

IDALIA'S FRIEND DROPPED her off at the bus station and they lingered by the car a long time. They hugged and her friend pulled away first, taking Idalia by the shoulders, before getting back in the car with a quick snap of her habit.

Idalia watched her drive away, watching long after the friend was out of sight, then she walked slowly into the station.

She nodded at me like she'd lost her voice.

We bought our tickets and waited in silence.

You can talk to me if you want, I told her.

I know. She looked at her hands and closed her eyes. She was so sad she breathed slowly.

Are you talking to God right now?

She nodded.

Tell Him I said hello.

She smiled. *Tell Him yourself.*

Oh, I can't. I'm in the devil's hands, I said with a grin.

Are you, now? she said.

I nodded.

Her name is Sophia, said Sister.

The nun? Your friend?

Sister looked out the window. *I met her when we were both novices, sat next to her in Latin. She was just terrible, had no knack for it. I don't recall her ever conjugating a verb correctly. And oh, Sister Helen would get so angry, red in the face, but Sophia remained calm, unaffected. I fell in love with her,* she whispered. *I thought, Here is a person who can wear the world so lightly. Who wouldn't love her? Who wouldn't want to be by her side forever?*

You got in trouble for loving her?

Of course. But there's no real effective punishment for love. Is there?

We boarded the big chrome bus, and in a matter of minutes, it felt like our whole lives were behind us, everything we'd known and done.

I thought about my family, the kitchen table, Laura, school, Soldier Creek and David, Gill's lesson and Caroline's arching back, the small, hot stage at the club, and it felt like too much to have to let go of all at once. I cried. Then this voice in my head said, *I'll give you five minutes for this sadness and no more. Do you hear me?* Out the window, the fields passed in a blur of gold and light.

For the first few hours of the trip, I felt nauseous, a thin layer of sweat covered my body. Sister gave me a sandwich but I couldn't eat, so I just let it sit on my lap.

I watched Sister think about her love, pain radiating off her like a fever. I had long thought of love as a thing I'd like to hurt, and with Sister suffering from it, I wanted to beat it, rip its hair out. It was surely the thing to avoid at all costs.

A woman across the aisle stared at me and at the sandwich in my lap.

Would you like this? I asked her.

She waved her head and hand no.

Please, I said. *I can't eat it.*

She took it from me slowly. Dziękuję, she said. ("Thank you.")

Nie ma za co, I told her. ("It's nothing.")

Her eyes grew large when she heard her native tongue.

Moja matka jest Polką, I said. ("My mother is Polish.") I thought about my mother and then I tried to stop.

She continued to talk happily, though I understood little. Eventually she was content to just nod and smile occasionally.

After a few hours, we crossed the border into Illinois.

Have you been to Chicago? I asked Sister.

Yes, she said. *To see Ricky. Naomi, Ricky is not like other men.*

Well, that can only be good news, I said.

Sister laughed. *Aren't you worldly now?*

Am I going to fall in love with him? I asked.

Sister smiled. *Probably*, she said. *But maybe in a way that won't hurt as much.*

Oh, terrific, I thought.

CHAPTER 39

Chicago at night was a rushing, sparkling, raging city that surged and sang with life. When we unloaded ourselves at the station and stepped out into the wind and the speed of the town, I was slammed with the certainty that this was my home.

But first I had to go back into the bus station and be sick. As I steadied myself against the stall for a moment, I heard a woman crying in the one next to mine. I looked down and saw the brown carpetbag of the Polish woman from the bus. I left my stall and knocked on hers, asking if she was sick. Jesteś chory?

She came out, her face wet, speaking way too fast. I gleaned that she was alone and lost but that somewhere in this big city there was an enclave of other Poles.

Sister knew of the Polish Triangle and we took the woman there. *It's not out of our way,* Sister told her loudly.

There was a small grocery in the Polish Quarter with a sign in the window that read *MÓWIMY PO POSKU* ("We speak Polish"). I asked the man behind the counter to help us. *You look like a proud man*, I said, touching his arm. His back straightened and he introduced himself to the Polish woman, who flooded in her native tongue. They laughed as he led her to a chair, and they were already talking about the war when we began to leave.

The woman rushed toward me then, digging in her bag for a piece of paper and a pencil nub. She asked me to write down my name and address. I wrote my name and Sister wrote Ricky's address. The woman told me she'd send me a letter of thanks. W języku angielskim. In English.

Sister nearly dragged me to Ricky's apartment. There was so much to look at, so many different kinds of people, such a concentration of life. I felt nearly invisible in that rush of humanity—irrelevant—and it was refreshing. I got the idea that what I did, who I was, wouldn't matter a lick in that big city.

I stopped Sister and held her arms. *This is the perfect place to make a new beginning*, I said.

She said nothing and smiled weakly like she had never wanted to make a new beginning.

We turned on to a noisy, dirty street that was bustling, even at the late hour. Sister opened the front door of a tall old apartment building and we climbed three flights of stairs. She knocked and the door opened almost immediately.

Her brother threw his arms around her and I was startled because he was wearing a long woman's robe—blue with large orange flowers and white cranes—which I was sure belonged to a woman he had there.

Are we intruding? I said, before I could even shake his hand.

Heavens, no, he said, *I've been waiting on this one for months. Months!*

Ricky took Sister's face in his hands and said, *Jesus, what did they do to you? You look perfectly terrible. Let me take your coat*, he said, helping her out of it. When he snatched Sister's hat, she immediately put her hand to her head like she could hide it somehow. Ricky gasped, *My God, your beautiful hair.* He slowly reached out for her head, pulled it close, and kissed it.

It's just hair, said Sister.

Ricky touched his own shaved head. *We look like we just got back from the war, you and me. Happy homecoming, huh?*

And you, he said to me, *the troubled girl?*

Sister shot him a scowl.

What? I feel like I know her. It's all so scandalous.

We tell each other things, Sister said to me. *I'm sorry.*

You don't know the half of it, I said, dropping my coat on the hall tree. *Neither of you.*

Ricky gasped. *She's terrible,* he said as he walked a circle around me. *Not to mention brimming with potential.*

I smiled at him and tried to figure out what was different about his face. It was his eyebrows. He didn't have any. I looked around his apartment. There were scarves over the lamps, tapestries hung on the walls, piles of books and records on the floor, and it smelled like a mixture of hairspray and cigarettes. Surely a woman was around there somewhere.

I studied a black-and-white photograph on the mantel.

Veronica Lake? I asked. *I love her.*

Ricky laughed and so did Sister.

I knew we were going to get along, he said, and Sister shook her head.

It's me, kitten, he said. *The lady is me.*

CHAPTER 40

SISTER AND I slept on a pallet of blankets and pillows on the floor. I woke to Ricky tiptoeing around the apartment in pedal pushers and a red checked shirt with a bright blue scarf wrapped around his head.

Oh, did I wake you?

I shook my head no and climbed up on a stool at the little kitchen island. Ricky made coffee and filled the sink with water. He took a bottle of shampoo from the cupboard and poured a capful into the sink. The way he moved made me jealous.

He lifted a long blond wig from the counter and slowly lowered it into the sink, moving it back and forth.

Thanks for letting me stay the night. I'll look for a place today, I told him.

You will not, he said. *I'm going to take care of you two, for a little while, at least. My refugees from the High Plains.*

Maybe you can teach me a few things, I said.

He lifted the wig out of the sink, turned on the faucet, and let the water run over it. *A few things?* he said. *I will need to teach you everything. Sitting there like a boy on a stump. Heavens.*

He dried his hands on a dish towel and threw it over his shoulder. *And, kitten, I'm called Rita. "Ricky" is back in Kansas somewhere.*

Okay, Rita, I said. *So, do I call you "he" or "she?"*

"She" would do nicely, said Rita, as she laid the wig on a towel and blotted it.

Suddenly I felt the urge to be sick, and ran to the small bathroom. I sat on the floor, resting my head against the pink and black tile, and hoped this bug would pass soon. It was getting in the way of my new start.

Once my stomach was steady again, I returned to the kitchen. Rita pulled two pieces of toast out of the toaster oven and set them on a plate. She put this and a cup of strong black coffee in front of me.

Did I upset you? she asked.

I'm feeling off. I wasn't even able to eat yesterday, which is odd for me because I eat all the time. I'd say I eat every chance I get.

I buttered the toast and tried to keep from devouring it while Rita watched, smoking a cigarette.

So what brings you to Chicago, Naomi of Kansas? she asked. *Or is this just the only town you've not yet been run out of?*

I stared at her until she laughed, a deep, bottomless laugh that made me feel a bolt of joy inside.

We laughed while I ate my toast.

Rita put more bread in the toaster oven. *Do you have aspirations?* she asked, studying me like she was sorting out something complicated.

Well, I want to sing.

She nodded, pulled a drag off her cigarette. *So I heard.*

I looked at the coils growing red in the toaster oven, listened to its ticking sounds.

It's not enough, you know, she said.

Beg your pardon?

She retrieved the toast with a pair of tongs and dropped it on my plate.

To want to sing. Or frankly, to be able to sing. Singers, pretty singers, are a dime a dozen around here. She nodded toward the window.

I buttered my toast slowly as she perched on the stool next to mine, facing me.

Look at you, slumped over your fourth piece of toast, your legs all twisted around each other. What are we, four? Five?

I untangled my legs and sat up straight.

Your body is a work of art, an enticement, and it must appear so at all times.

I looked at her sitting on the stool, her body a beautiful zigzag perched on her hip, her cigarette raised. She took a drag, blew the smoke, raised her chin.

You cannot afford a moment's sloppiness, lest you forget yourself at the wrong time, she said, raising an eyebrow. Eyebrows. They were penciled in now.

I understand, I said.

She got up and retrieved a bag with strawberries on it from a drawer. She unbuttoned the bag and pulled out a handful of curlers, some green, some pink, then she fished around for the little plastic pins. One of these pins she held like a tiny paintbrush, making little strokes in the air while she talked.

It's like this. You are a fantasy and you must always appear as such.

She leaned on the counter and pointed at me with the pin. *So your public must never see that you are just like them.*

We stared at each other for a long time.

I know, I know. It sounds like an impossible amount of work, to be so aware all of the time, but really, kitten, there's just an initial hump, a period of adjustment, and soon you will forget that you were ever any other way.

I heard the word *forget*. *Teach me*, I said.

I will, kitten. She turned back to her wig and gracefully, artfully, wrapped sections in the curlers.

Sister was up and moving around now. *Teach her what?*

How to impersonate a woman, said Rita.

CHAPTER 41

WE WENT TO Rita's club on Wells Street. With one of Rita's scarves tied around her head, Sister looked like a bohemian. Some of the patrons recognized her and approached after we sat down. There were men dressed as women, women dressed as men. The rules of men and women seemed flexible here, something to play with. A few women approached our table and teasingly asked Sister who her new friend was. It took me a minute to realize we were being mistaken for an honest-to-goodness couple. It made me feel a part of something, this awareness, and it scared me to death.

Close your mouth, said Sister.

I can't help it. I've never been anyplace like this.

In all your world travels? she said.

I grabbed her arm and wiggled her. She gently pulled away and looked around. *No touching*, she said. I threw my arm around her just to disobey. She pulled it off me fast. *I'm not kidding. We could be arrested for that.*

What? I said.

Just then a round bald man with the deep voice of a movie star hopped up onstage and raised his arms. The crowd applauded, whistled, and catcalled. He introduced the revue, which started with a large dance number involving feathers, large headpieces, and scandalous costumes. I saw Rita and soon realized every performer up there was also a man. The rest of the revue consisted of number after number of songs, dances, skits. My whole body longed to move like that, to hold a crowd like that, make them laugh, make them sigh.

Do you like it? said Sister.

I feel I could burst, I said, breathless.

When it was done, Sister took me backstage, and Rita made a big show of introducing us to the girls.

A new singer up from Kansas City, Rita said of me.

Oh, the girls said, looking me over.

A skinny gal in a fringe dress sang a little gibberish tune and did some country steps. *Like that?* she asked. I didn't realize right away that she was making fun of me.

Yes, just like that, I said.

Maybe if she's any good she could join us, said Rita, smearing cold cream on her cheeks.

The other gals shot big-eyed, angry looks at her.

The skinny one tilted her head. *Might do us good to have a jam on-stage.*

The others considered what she said.

We'll see, said Rita.

I whispered to Sister, *What's a jam?*

She sort of tilted her head. *A heterosexual.*

I started by hanging out backstage, helping the girls with their costumes, wigs, and makeup, learning their tricks—creating a waist where there wasn't one, sculpting a jaw with shades of foundation, playing up the eyes with false eyelashes, shadow, and kohl. I'd never seen that sort of artistry in my life, a whirlwind of brushing, lining, pulling, teasing, squeezing, curling, turning a roomful of nondescript young men into a clique of bombshells.

Over time, I got to know the numbers by heart. The strengths and weaknesses of each performer, what worked, and what didn't. I learned that it's not invisible, what goes on inside a singer's head; it's all over her face and body if you look carefully enough.

Rita's training went something like this: her studying and critiquing how I sat, stood, read, what I did with my eyebrows, how I moved my hands when I talked, how I wore my dress, the color of my stockings, the condition of my shoes. We listened to songs over and over, her picking up the needle and moving it back. *Do you hear that? The way she moves, glides really, over the break in her voice, how seamless it is? Listen again.*

I worked the phrases over and over, learned every tune she had in bits and parts at first. Soon I was singing everything, and I was tired.

Hang in there, kitten. We're not just making you into a lady. That part is easy. We're making you into an icon, Rita would whisper, and the hair on my arms would just lift right up. It would solve everything, fame. To be loved. Seen. To never be at the mercy of anyone else, ever again.

Rita called herself the club's artistic director. She managed everything—performing, choreography, costumes, wigs. When she first asked me to come with her to rehearsal, I went begrudgingly. When I got there the girls surprised me with a small wardrobe they'd put together from extra parts and spares. They even filled a small tackle box with makeup and brushes and sponges and puffs. I moved the little tray in the tackle box back and forth and touched the three tubes of Revlon lipstick. It all blurred through my tears.

Oh, God, stop it, said Skinny Edie, *your lashes won't curl if they're wet.*

They dressed me, fixed me up, and I rehearsed with them. They decided to let me in on three of the big dance numbers, and though I already knew them by heart, it was much harder to move than I imagined with the weight of the costumes and the constriction. The costumes left bruises on my hipbones. I performed with them that very night.

During one of the numbers, there was some skirmish in the bar and I forced myself not to look, though I could tell from the faces of the other girls there was cause for concern.

When we got offstage the girls gathered and watched the crowd. Two men were handcuffed and being taken out of the bar by a man who I thought was a patron. Back in the dressing room, everyone was quiet.

I whispered to Skinny Edie, *What did they do?*

Edie looked up at the ceiling for a moment. *There are city ordinances against two men touching, dancing.* She peeled off her wig cap and rubbed her hand over her head.

What will happen to them? I asked.

They'll be booked, charged, said Edie.

Charged with what?

Inmates of disorderly houses.

Is this a disorderly house? I asked.

Have a look around, someone behind her said.

What will happen to them? I asked.

Their names will be published in the papers, said Rita. *And their addresses.*

Where they live happily with the wife and kids, said Edie.

Edie, said Rita.

And everyone was silent as they transformed themselves into everyday men again.

CHAPTER 42

I WENT TO THE club earlier than everyone else because I didn't use wigs and it took me a long time to set my hair. Edie sat down next to me and handed me curler pins, watching me in the mirror as I rolled the last few curlers.

Let's go get a drink, she said.

Like this? I asked, touching my hair.

She snagged a scarf from the station next to her and wrapped it around my hair. *There,* she said. *And besides, there's nobody out there at this time. No one that matters anyhow.*

We sat down at the bar. Edie ordered us two gin and tonics. *Heavy on the tonic for this one here,* she said, pointing at me.

The bartender made us our drinks, and Edie raised hers. *To the end of your career,* she said.

I was about to drink but stopped. *Come again?*

Edie smiled. *You're no chorus girl*, she said, drinking.

I considered this. Of course she was right.

You think these queens are going to let you show them up ad infinitum? she said.

I don't show you up, I said.

Edie eyed the other customers like she was looking for something, then leaned in to me and whispered, *Hate to change the subject but you see the bloke at the end of the bar?*

I turned around in my seat to get a look at him.

Edie pulled me back by the arm. *God, child, you are about as subtle as a car wreck.*

I looked down at my drink.

Here's what you'll do, she said. *Touch the back of your neck and make like you're doing a little stretch. Glance at him. Okay, try it now.*

I did what she said. A man perched on a stool in a brown coat. A full glass of beer in front of him.

What about him? I asked.

He's a cop, said Edie.

How do you know that? I asked.

I know, she said.

I looked at him again, trying to see what gave him away.

So I have this crazy idea, she said, her eyes shining. *You have a good, what, twenty minutes between your first number and the second, right?*

Yes. About.

What if you were to come out into the house in between, say to fetch some more water for the gang, and you sidle up to our cop friend, she said, looking at me expectantly, as if to wonder whether or not I understood.

And? I said.

And, I don't know. She tapped her finger to her lip like she hadn't thought it all through yet. *And you flirt with him*, she said, as though it's just occurred to her. *You work your wiles on him.*

I considered this. *Why would I do that?*

Edie leaned forward on the bar. *It's like this. All the cops have quotas.*

He can either arrest a bunch of nellies here at our place of employment OR some goon with a Beretta in his pants. Which would you choose if you were him?

I scratched the place under my scarf where a curler pin was poking me and looked at the cop. *So what is your idea exactly?*

She shrugged. *Maybe if he had a friend in here, he'd ease up a little.*

Why me?

Edie stood up, pushed her glass to the back of the bar, and sighed. *Your looks betray how very young and dim you are, don't they, kid?*

She put her hand on my shoulder. *Think about it. A little friendly chatter is all. To soften him up a little. Honey, all we need is one of these ass-holes on our side. Just one. If folks keep getting arrested here, nobody comes; if nobody comes, this whole flock a chickens is out of work, including you.*

Later that night after we finished the first number, I went to the dressing room hot and excited, all my cells humming. I lifted my headdress off and tried to fluff out my hair where it had been crushed. Edie looked at me from her station, raised her eyebrows. I smiled at her, shrugged, and pranced out into the house.

I couldn't see him at first as I approached the bar. The bartender was busy with a cluster of boys talking all at once and the man had moved to a table. I wondered what to do. The bartender asked me if I needed something, so I asked for some soda water, started to walk away, glanced at the man, then smiled and waved, rushing over to him.

I set my glass on the table and clasped his hand with both of mine. *Oh, you MUST be Patrick,* I said, shaking his hand vigorously until he struggled to take it back.

You've got me mistaken for someone, he said, looking away.

Oh, no! You're not Patrick? Gosh, I'm terribly embarrassed. My friend Rita, she said her friend Patrick was coming tonight. Tall, handsome fella. Glasses. Shy, too, she said. And I saw you and thought, Well, that's surely Patrick.

The man put his hands in his pockets and looked around.

Nope, he said.

I perched on the chair. *Mind if I sit a minute? These shoes are a bear.*

I'd rather you didn't, he said, crossing his arms and looking at the door.

Oh, you're so right, I told him. *I shouldn't be out in the crowd dressed like this. Hardly dressed, you might say.* I stood then, bent over in front of him, and smiled. *My name's Naomi.*

Is that so, he said, looking away from my breasts and back at them again.

Baptized, I said, picking up my glass as he looked at my hands.

He stared at me and breathed with his mouth open for a minute. *James*, he said finally. *Baptized James.* His mustache twitched.

James, I said. *The fisherman.*

That in the Bible or something?

It most certainly is, I said. *Are you a fisherman, James?*

Something like that.

Well. Enjoy the show, I told him.

As I made my way back to the dressing room, I saw Edie duck back in. She'd been watching me.

Where'd you go? said Rita.

Just to get a little soda water, I said. *My stomach's acting up again.*

Don't go out there again, said Rita. *You don't understand how things work around here.*

I'm sorry, Rita, I said, as I walked to the dress rack to fetch my next costume. Edie stepped up next to me, smiling. *Brilliant*, she whispered.

I know, I said.

The next night I watched for James but he never showed up. I didn't notice the tall blond who, like James, never touched his beer. The club was raided again and six patrons were arrested, including the guy that Edie loved.

Why don't they ever arrest the women? I asked them.

They all looked at one another.

Kitten, said Rita, *no one cares what women do.*

Some of the other girls laughed quietly to themselves and I suddenly remembered that I was still, despite the feathers and glitter and heels, in a room full of men.

CHAPTER 43

THE BAR WAS half full for the next week. Back in the dressing room, the owner explained that he was going to have to dock our pay. The gang looked at him in silence.

The way I see it is, either they'll get the best of us and we close down, or they get bored and leave us be. Either way, we keep our chins up, right, ladies? he said, raising his arms.

I walked out to the bar to get a drink. James was back in his usual spot, full beer in front of him. My robe was coming a little loose in the front and I let it. I saw James look and look away, so I tightened the robe, pretending to be embarrassed.

Haven't seen you around in a while. Did we bore you? I said, standing too close to him. The slightest lean forward and my breast would press into his arm. He adjusted himself like he wanted to move back but he didn't actually move back.

I've been busy, he said.

With the fishing? I asked.

With the fishing.

I stood, fixed his collar, and told him, *Well, I, for one, am glad to have you back on dry land.*

He flushed and stared and turned his beer glass. *Yup.*

Maybe if you're still around after the show, we could have a drink, I said.

Maybe.

After the last big dance number, I was quick to change out of my clothes and head to the bar. James wasn't there. I was silly to think he would be.

I grabbed my bag and coat and walked down the long hallway that led to the back door. I opened it, ducked my head into my collar against the wind, which was flaring down the alleyway, and there was James, leaning against the building, protecting his cigarette with his hand.

What are you doing here? I asked.

Holding up the building.

How'd you know about this entrance?

Well, you don't use the front door, now, do you? he said.

I began to walk.

Can I buy you a cup of coffee? he asked, following me.

No, I said, my chin high. *I'll need more than a cup of coffee. Were you not watching me tonight? I could eat a horse.*

Let's go find you a horse, then, he said.

At Mitchell's Diner on Division I told James all about Soldier, Kansas, and asked him about his family. His parents were immigrants, too. Italians. They had wanted many children but only had James.

Moved halfway across the country to escape my mother's disappointment, he said, pushing up his glasses and laughing at himself.

Me, too, I said. *What a coincidence. Surely she's proud you're an officer of the law.*

James stared at me.

Did you honestly think I didn't know?

I'm no actor, that's the truth. He poked his pie with his fork. *Not much of a cop, for that matter.*

What are you, then?

What do you mean? he said.

What would you do if you could do something else?

He looked out the window and his mustache twitched. I began to understand this twitch as a replacement for smiling.

I'll tell you what. I got in a little trouble while back. Nothing serious. But for my punishment, the captain thought it would be clever to make me take pictures—mug shots, crime scenes—and develop them in the lab. He leaned in and said in a low voice, *Best three months of my life.* His eyelashes were so long they ran into his lenses, his eyes like a boy's. His black hair colicky, beyond hope. *I saved up and bought my own camera after that. I hate to admit it but it's the one thing I get a kick out of, taking pictures.*

I'd like to see your pictures sometime, I said.

When a person knows they're being photographed. Well, it's interesting, but it's not them. I like to catch people unguarded. That's the story. That's the real deal, he said with a little twitch. He studied me when he talked, stared at my mouth, my ear, my fingers. I couldn't tell if I had feelings for him but I knew that I loved his eyes on me. How boldly he looked at me.

So become a photographer, I said.

Too unsteady.

He looked at my hair. I watched his face.

James took a sudden deep breath. *Hey,* he said.

Mm-hmm?

You think the guys . . . the performers at the club would let me photograph them? You know, just for my own purposes. Not to bring any trouble. Heck, they could even use the photographs if they wanted. For promotion or something. What do you say?

Don't you want to photograph me? I said, striking a little pose.

Nah. If I started photographing you, I'd never stop, he said, and I could feel the tension between us tighten.

I see, I said. *I better get home. My roommates worry.*

I'll walk you to the El, he said.

We walked in silence.

I'll talk to the girls at the club, I told him. *It's possible they might be willing to make some sort of arrangement with you.*

He smiled.

We stood on the platform and looked for the train. James tapped both feet.

Can I offer an opinion? I asked.

Sure, he said.

If you follow this little idea of yours, heaven knows where it will lead you. I folded my arms across my chest. *You should believe me about this.*

Are we talking about taking pictures or are we talking about you?

Either, I said.

I could hear the train but I couldn't see it yet.

By the way, he said.

Yes?

Nobody calls me James. Name's Jim. Please call me Jim.

The train appeared in the distance.

Jim, I said, just to hear it, and my heart pounded a little.

Know what I think? he said.

What?

I think you're going to let that train go on by and come home with me.

We stared at each other and kept staring as the train stopped. Then we stood there while the doors opened and the doors closed. We climbed back down the iron stairs and walked to his apartment.

It was a small, cluttered place, and I was so nervous I asked to use his restroom. I closed the door behind me. It smelled strongly of vinegar. A board had been placed along the length of the tub. At one end was a large machine like a giant telescope and next to that were three trays filled with the liquid that was giving off the smell. A big square black timer hung on the wall. Black-and-white photographs were strung up on a laundry line, pictures of buildings, windows, a dandelion coming up through the pavement, and one of a woman in a window.

I looked at myself in the mirror.

Go on, I told myself. *Let him see you.*

CHAPTER 44

OVER THE NEXT few weeks my costumes, which had always been plenty roomy in the waist on account of the fact they were made for men, became snug. I tried not to eat so much, but still. Several times I tried to let them out, but wound up making a mess and pinning them back together.

One afternoon someone rang the apartment, a round woman on the stoop in the cold, holding a covered plate in her hands. *I am the woman you helped. From the bus station. I am Polish. Your mother, too?*

I invited her in and brought her upstairs.

I was going to write you letter to say thank you. I try. English is hard. I bring kolaches.

What's your name?

Hilda, she said.

We sat in the small kitchen and ate the *kolaches. Have you found work?*

I work in factory. All day long I sit and make little hem on the side of flag. Same hem, new flag, all day long. In Poland when I am your age I make beautiful gowns for rich lady.

At that, I ran for my costume and showed it to her. *Can you help me? It's too small.* I put my hands around my waist.

Hilda can fix anything, she said, removing the safety pins. *I can get maybe two inches but you cannot get more fat.* She whipped a measuring tape around my waist and bent over to read the number, touching her palm to my abdomen and cocking her head.

Not fat. You will have baby, she said, smiling broadly, patting me again. *Your husband will be very happy.*

She sewed the costume while I stared at her, counting weeks and months in my head. My legs suddenly seemed to be made of ribbon, and as I sat there I began to cry—big, choking, gulping sobs. Hilda knelt beside me and put her arm around me, mumbling in Polish.

Z przyjemnością, she said, touching my cheek. *Be happy.*

It took me forever to set my hair that night. I became tired holding my arms above my head for so long and the bulbs made me sweat. I turned the lights out and stood in the dark while the bulbs cooled, my eyes adjusting until I could see faint bits of light coming off sequins here and there, and the cooling filaments in the vanity bulbs. It seemed I stood in the middle of a constellation, suspended in it.

I unscrewed every other bulb at my station and turned the lights back on; there was less heat that way.

Rita showed up and went to work on herself, humming as she did. She bounced when she walked and admired herself in the mirror.

Finally she set down a powder puff and turned to me. *Don't you just feel so excited sometimes?*

About what? I asked.

Oh, I don't know. The future, she said.

I thought of the future then I tried to not think of it.

I have news but there are still a few bits to be ironed out. I cannot wait to tell you.

I would settle for potentially good news, I said.

She faced me. *Oh, all right. You know Carl? Edie's lover? Well, ex-lover*, she said sorrowfully. *He has an annual Christmas party. Anyone who is anyone goes. And I have procured you an invitation.*

How'd you do that? They don't know me.

I threatened to tell Carl's wife about Edie, said Rita in a low, slightly ashamed voice.

That's awful. Why would you do that?

You'll sing, of course. In front of a real crowd. You can't understand now but trust me, it's just the ticket.

I left her to her makeup and her ridiculous plan, and went out to the bar. Jim stood when he saw me and kissed my cheek. He stirred me, that attention, and his eyes made me feel more substantial than I'd ever felt.

I sat down with him. *I cannot be your girl*, I told him. *Last week. Well, it was lovely. It truly was. But suddenly my life is more difficult than it was then and I don't want you to see this. Or expect you to stick around.*

I don't got a say in this?

You just. You don't know me. At that, I stood to leave.

Maybe you need a friend, he said, standing with me. *I don't have any ideas about what this is. What we are.*

We'll see, I said, then left him quickly so he wouldn't see how this bit of kindness brought tears to my eyes.

CHAPTER 45

THE NEXT DAY I gathered all my dresses and costumes to take them to Hilda's apartment so she could let them out.

There was someone at the bottom of the stairs but I didn't really try to see who it was as I went down because my arms were full and my body ached.

You running away again? the man said.

I peered around the pile of dresses and saw that it was David. He touched his hat as he nodded at me. Some of the dresses started to slip. He helped.

What are you doing here? I said.

What, you act like I'm some kind of criminal. You left me, remember?

I looked up at him, let my eyes settle on his features for a moment . . .

He tried to hug me, to kiss me on the cheek, but it was all made awkward by the load in my arms. I stared at his face. It had only been months. How easy it would be to fall into him, his sad eyes, his reach, I had missed the way he wrapped himself around me.

He took the clothes from my arms and looked me up and down, shaking his head. *My*, he said. *You look . . . you look like a woman.*

What else would I look like? I asked.

I want you back, Naomi. I'm here to bring you home, where you belong. We let things get complicated, he said.

I have that effect, it seems, I said, and began walking toward the train.

Listen, he said, following me. *I'll let you feature at the club and I'll pay you right. I'll even let you work other places, see what happens.*

This is my home now. I have work, I told him.

Singing in some underground joint with a bunch of queers? he said, laughing.

I stopped and looked at him. The blue striped suit, the shadow of whiskers, the dark eyes, a pile of glitter and sequins, tulle, and lace so easily held by his long arms.

None of whom have tried to have sex with me once, I said.

This city will turn you hard, he said. *You don't know.*

The threads between us were tight as ever, and I started to feel myself slipping into him, toward him. As he talked I nearly told him I was pregnant, but something stopped me.

We climbed the platform to board the El and I took my dresses back.

Come on, doll, give us a chance. Come back with me.

No, David. All of me was shaking. I just wanted him to wrap himself around me and hold me together. *No.*

The train came then. He took my arm. *We're not going to get this again*, he said. *What we have. There's no man going to love you like I do.*

Let me go.

He let go of me.

I don't love you. I never did. Believe me. I rushed on to the train and found a seat, watched him through the window, smiled and waved like I was fine. I waited to cry until we were moving. I cried long enough to miss my stop, the other passengers moving away from me, nobody sitting anywhere near me, my crying, my dresses hanging from my arms like lifeless bodies.

I cried to Hilda, let myself be overcome with feeling, and in the midst of it all I lied. I said I told David about the baby and that he left me. It seemed the only way, this lie. How could I tell her the truth? That if he had to, David could do the right thing. Marry me. Take care of us. How could I tell Hilda, or anyone, how much I feared such a life, a *normal* life? How much I feared becoming invisible again, powerless, dependent. I wanted to do the right thing but I wanted something else more. To be known. To be loved. How much easier to say, *A terrible, no good fella*, tears and all, and be done with it.

She stroked my hair and shook her head, saying, *Men like him*, and I felt lighter on the way home, without the dresses.

When I got back Rita and Sister were home and they threw their arms around me before I was all the way in. Rita touched her hand to her chest and looked at the floor, saying, *Oh, thank God you're all right.*

We thought you'd run away, said Sister. *Where did all your clothes go?*

Some man came by the club today asking if you were there. He was very aggressive. I refused to tell him where you were but one of the girls caved and spilled the beans. Stupid queen. Who was he? Rita said, overwhelmed. *And then I come home to find you gone?*

Where have you been all day? said Sister.

I'm having the dresses let out.

Rita glanced at Sister. *She's still filling out. Completely normal.*

I'm pregnant, I said.

They looked at me.

Rita sat. Sister covered her mouth.

David found me. I don't know how but he did. I told him about my condition and he doesn't want anything to do with it. I was still startled by how easy it was to say this lie, this big lie.

That bastard, said Rita.

It's okay. All he does is confuse me. I stood up and looked down on them, sitting side by side on the davenport. *I have plans for myself, clear plans. I'm a singer. Who needs him? I have you. You love me.*

We do, said Rita.

Idalia nodded and patted the cushion beside her and I sat. *We're going to be fine.*

Rita rested her hand on my thigh. *I know someone,* she said.

Someone what?

Who can take care of this. Make it go away, she said gently.

Is that safe? I asked.

Let's all just slow down, said Sister.

I don't know, said Rita. *I think so.*

We're going to be all right, said Sister, stressing the word *we,* like she wanted me to erase the word *I* from my head. I scowled at her, got up, and walked around the apartment. It felt terribly small.

Rita said, *We have bigger concerns right now.*

What on earth could be bigger than this? asked Sister.

We just need to get you through the party, said Rita.

I could not talk about the party. I couldn't talk or think or even stand for another minute. *Thank you both,* I said, and went to bed without eating or taking off my clothes.

CHAPTER 46

THE DAY BEFORE Carl's party Rita took a dress bag from the back of her closet and pulled out a black satin gown, full length, sleeveless, with a matching stole.

I touched it.

I bought it with the intention of modifying it, she said, *some sort of strap or sleeve, but I never got around to it.* She held it up in front of me. *God, I hope it fits you.*

It did. We practiced walking in the gown. She frowned and thought with her finger on her mouth. *In this dress you have to walk as though your legs are separate from the rest of you, and take close, gentle steps. Quick.* She put an empty cup on her head and walked around the room. *You don't walk, darling. You glide.* I walked with the cup until I got it.

Then we practiced sitting.

I don't know if I can do this, I said.

And another thing, she said. *I've been thinking about your name.*

What about it?

It's horrible, kitten. Hutnik, she spat.

It's Polish.

I realize, she growled. *We're going to call you Hill from now on. I've given it much thought. Naomi Hill. Easy, memorable.*

I sat there with the big gown billowed around me like a cushion between the world and me and felt tired. Sister watched from her desk as Rita lowered herself behind me and put her dry hand on my bare back. *Darling*, she said gently, *we don't get to live two lives at once. We must choose between who we were and who we would like to be. I know this better than anyone. You can believe me.*

The next day Rita transformed me. She put me on a stool by the kitchen sink and saturated my hair with a dark brown solution and let it sit there for a long time. When she finally washed it out, my light red hair had turned to a deep, dark crimson, like cherrywood. After it dried, she mixed another terrible-smelling solution in a bowl and combed it through my hair. I asked her what it was.

Nothing you'll find in a white neighborhood, I'll tell you that, she said. *A queen worth her salt will go to any lengths for beauty, mark my words.*

When she rinsed it out, my frizzy curls were nearly gone. My hair was straight, like Laura, like pretty girls. She wound it up tightly in several big rollers. Then she took a damp sponge covered in foundation and patted it over my skin until my freckles were invisible. I kept staring at myself, not believing it was I. But there was another me underneath, safe, hidden. This made me happy. Rita teased, sprayed, and pinned my hair. It was elegant. I was elegant. Naomi Hutnik was gone.

Idalia cried when she saw me.

I'm sorry, she said, *but you somehow look entirely yourself and not yourself at all. I don't know what to make of it.*

When she was done with me, Rita went back into her room and

closed the door. She was in there for a long time. Idalia and I stood in the living room. I was afraid to sit.

I'm nervous for you.

It's just a party, I told her.

Not just the party.

Then I was mad at her for making me remember. I thought of what Rita said. *I know someone.*

I didn't want to go. I didn't want to walk in there alone.

Rita cracked the bedroom door an inch and said, in the rapid-fire voice of a freak-show announcer, *Ladies and ladies! What you are about to behold is a never-before-seen sight for the senses, never to be repeated, so feast your eyes for this ONCE-in-a-lifetime experience.*

She pushed the door open with a black cane and Rita was, for the moment, erased. This was Richard. Black tuxedo with tails, the slightest bit of sheen from use on it, top hat, beautiful shoes. He stood with his legs slightly apart and his hands resting on the top of his cane, and said, in a deep voice, *Where's my gal?*

On the taxi ride to the party, Rita gave me more instructions. She took a deep breath when she was done. *Above all else, never lose sight of the vision of your self. Not who you are, but who you are becoming.* She smoothed down a stray hair with a light hand and I felt myself blush. Rita, the man, made me dizzy.

It was a beautiful party full of beautiful people. Rita whispered to me, *They need to be taken away. Take them away, Naomi.*

When the pianist asked me to sing, I acted shy at first, but then I pushed my whole body and heart into the notes. I sang like it was my home, all that beauty, and they were my people. *Take them away, Naomi.* On their faces was love and longing and want. Something started to burn in me right then, a very particular hunger. For this, to be here at the hot center of all these people, holding them with my voice. I'd never sung better in my life. I felt like I'd been standing at the edge of my old life all this time and all I had to do to find myself—my voice, the power in me—was to jump. So I jumped. Even Rita was taken aback. *It has begun*, she said when we left.

We walked all the way home, faster and faster as Rita outlined her plans for me. She never once mentioned my condition, like it was a problem that had left on its own. We walked as fast as my shoes would allow, and as the cold wind numbed our faces, I felt myself divide into two. One of me was going to become a singer, to be famous, known, loved, at all costs. The other me was not going to get rid of you, planned to have you, love you, be loved by you, and it was as though these two sides stood back to back, not knowing the other existed at all.

Could you feel how much they loved you? said Rita. *Do you see how loved you will be?* I nodded and smiled.

I see, I told her.

The next day a man called Rita, wanting me to sing that Thursday at his little bar, a restaurant lounge in downtown Chicago. I opened for an opening act, which amounted to four songs.

Under the lights, in the gaze of the little crowd, I felt I was exactly where I was meant to be and everything that led to that point suddenly became right, each moment the correct variable in a long equation. I felt large on the stage, by myself, too large to be hurt, and I suspected that if I were ever going to have any certainty in my life, it would be located there, on the stage.

Rita and Sister were there. Jim was there. The manager paid me by letting us eat for free. Jim reached over the table, took my pickle, and ate it. I said to him, *I'm going to have a baby*.

The women looked at me.

What do you know? said Jim, looking at his plate.

I'm going to need help, I said.

All right, said Jim.

What do you hope to gain by this? asked Rita.

The others looked at her like this was an ugly question. But I thought about it honestly.

I believe it will make me a better person.

As we left the club, the women walked ahead and Jim walked beside me. He looked puzzled.

What is it, Jim?

I have to ask. Is it mine? Is the baby mine?

We stopped walking and looked at each other. *I wish it was*, I said.

He breathed and nodded. *Come on, then*, he said, walking. *You've had a long night.*

In the *Chicago Sun-Times* the next day was a little sentence about me. They said I was someone to watch, they said I was *a real pearl.*

You made me glow. You made me big, full. You pushed my voice, you gave me a woman's voice. *A real pearl.* Before I even knew your name, you lit me up. *I think I'll keep you*, I said, holding the paper and looking down, *whoever you are.*

I keep you.

PART SIX

Do Nothin' Till You Hear from Me

Sophia

CHAPTER 47

CHICAGO, 1965

IT IS MORNING and now I am eleven. I kick off my blanket, get out of bed, and look at myself in the mirror, wondering if I look different because of what I've seen, the grown-ups at the party. How everything goes wrong. Mother and Jim wrapped around each other in her room last night. I don't, though. Somehow I look the same. I rearrange the little ceramic raccoon family on my dresser so that the baby raccoons are all lined up on the edge about to jump. Then I lay the mother raccoon on her side. She is asleep and doesn't know about the babies. I look in the mirror again. Nothing has changed so far as I can tell.

My dress hangs over the chair. The hole in my skirt is larger than I thought and it still smells like something burned. I sit on the floor, take the lid off my record player, and put on Skeeter Davis, keeping the volume low so they don't know I'm up.

My notebook is on the floor next to my record player. I stare at it.

Finally I turn to the list in the back. Under *David*, I write *Jim*. And in the characteristics column I write: *my friend. my dad (kind of)*. I look at all the names on the list. All the people who loved her are gone now, except for Jim. All you have to do is look at my list to see what's going to happen.

I hide my notebook way under my bed, not wanting to look at that list of names ever again.

My stomach growls. I go into the kitchen.

Morning, kitten, says Mother. I wave.

Jim pulls out a chair for me.

Whatcha doin'? Jim asks.

Getting something to eat.

You still sore at me about last night? says Mother.

I stare at the toaster, the coils brightening.

It's okay if you are, she says.

I ignore them both.

How about we make some pancakes? says Jim.

Don't have the ingredients.

I'll go get the makings, he says. *Okay?*

I shrug.

I'm off, then.

I look at Mother and then run after Jim. *Wait. I'm coming with you.*

At Clanton's, Jim opens a container of eggs to make sure none is broken.

How are they? I say.

All good.

I open the lid for myself while he's still holding it. *Yup.* Then I pick up one of the eggs, study it, hold it out in front of me, and let it drop on the floor.

Jim looks at me, then at the egg mess. *What the hell?*

What? I ask. *You could photograph it.*

Jim stares at me for a long time. *Fine. Sit right there.*

I sit on the edge of the cooler. He photographs me there, my shoes very close to the egg, which looks like a planet exploded.

Do we need flour? he asks.

Probably.

We get flour and syrup and put them on the counter next to the register.

There's an egg on the floor back there, Jim says to Mr. Clanton.

As we head home, I take a deep breath and tell him, *I saw you last night.*

What do you mean?

With Mother. In her bed.

He stops, frowns, moves the bag of groceries to his other arm. *Oh, doll.* He shakes his head. *You gotta stop sneaking around. There are things kids just aren't meant to see.*

Too late.

You want to talk about it? he says.

What am I supposed to say?

I don't know. How you feel?

Mad.

Okay, he says. *Because—*

You're stupid.

Why am I stupid?

I stop walking and face him. *You ruined it! We were fine! The way it was! Now you're on the list!*

Sophia, everything is fine. This isn't going to change anything.

Everything's always changing, I tell him. *Nothing sticks. Ever.*

Let's hold on a second. We sit down on a curb. I put my head on my knees and cry a little into my jeans. Jim rests his hand on my back.

What's different about me, what I don't think you understand, is that I'm not going anywhere, whether your mother loves me or not.

He lifts my face up, holds it in his hands, and peers down at me over the top of his glasses. *You want me to be your dad?*

I nod.

Then it's settled. My love for you is separate from her. You under-stand? You taught me that. End of story. Anyway, we gotta stick together, you and me.

He puts his arms around me and holds me really tight. It feels like he's going to hold me forever. Some people can hold you forever and some people can't. That's all of it, I think.

Let's go up and make pancakes and have a good day, okay? he says.

I take his hand and we walk toward home. We pass a fire hydrant and I stop to look at it. How did I forget to put fire hydrants on the list? Where does the water even come from?

CHAPTER 48

The rest of the day feels like maybe the most normal day I've ever had. We make pancakes and eat them. Mother and Jim read the paper while I study my new nuclear-fallout book. They teach me gin rummy and it turns out I'm pretty good at it. They smoke cigarettes and sip drinks while I have a bottle of Coke. We change the sheets on our beds, sweep, and do the dishes. We have cheese sandwiches in the afternoon. Then Jim helps me get ready for my spelling quiz. Meanwhile, the phone rings all day, so often that Mother and Jim don't even look at each other when it does.

I call Elizabeth and her mother answers. I almost hang up.

Thank you for bringing Elizabeth to the party last night, I tell her.

That is very polite of you, Sophia. I hope you had an enjoyable evening.

I don't say anything about that.

Anything else? she says.

May I please speak to Elizabeth?

For a moment.

Then there is Elizabeth's voice. *Have you seen your new house yet?*

I don't think we're going to move now.

What?

I think everything has changed, I tell her.

Elizabeth sighs. *Nothing ever changes in my life.* Then she calls out, *Coming! I have to go. I'm going to the library with Dad. I wish you could come.*

See you at school tomorrow, I say.

When I come back Jim is sitting on the floor in the living room, bent over the coffee table. He's moved a lamp so that it's next to him, lighting a photograph of Mother and me. I sit on the floor opposite him. In the photo, Mother is squatting in front of me holding my hands in hers, and we're smiling at each other. There are other people in the picture but it's like they're not really there. The picture seems to be about how much she loves me. You'd never know by looking at her that she ever loved anyone else.

Jim is dipping a little paintbrush into a tiny vial of black liquid and touching the brush lightly on some white spots and squiggles on the picture.

What are those?

It's from dust on the negative.

What are you going to do with that picture? I ask.

Mother comes in for a drink.

I'm going to send it to Look *magazine. The editor says he wants more pictures of your mother, surprise, surprise. I reminded him that this was ORIGINALLY going to be a story about Chicago, its beautiful architecture, and how it's getting destroyed before our eyes.*

Progress, I said.

Yeah, progress. And he says he wants the buildings, sure, but he also wants the singer, says he wants to create a whole picture: the rising star in a city that's falling down, or something to that effect.

It sounds terrific to me, Mother says.

Well, it would, Jim says, shaking his head and grinning at her.

I would like to have that picture, too, I say.

While it dries, he looks through his stack of photos. Church, theater, tall building, Mother, Mother and me, Mother and our friends, grand entrance, archway, column, staircase, Mother onstage, Mother backstage.

Jim thinks, takes a deep breath, then he sets them in an old photo-paper box and puts the lid on. A small piece of paper with *Look* magazine and an address is taped to the lid. He taps it with his finger.

I think they look pretty good, I tell him.

I don't know. There's something missing. He faces me. *I don't think these give you a true sense of the destruction. It's altogether too romantic, don't you think?*

God forbid, says Mother, laughing and wandering back out of the room.

That night Mother tucks me in. She's changed into a long caftan, something Jim likes. She sits down on my bed. *Let's talk.*

About what?

I'll start. I said some awful things to you last night.

I stare at the dead bugs in the fixture on the ceiling.

I also want to tell you that I think I've made a mistake with you. I always think you're all right. Because you're so smart and self-sufficient. So I guess I leave you alone. I don't worry. But maybe I should.

I'm fine.

Well, I'm going to try to think of you more.

Okay.

I really like Elizabeth. I think she's a very good friend.

I nod.

Is there anything else you want to talk about?

I shrug.

Go ahead, she says, sitting up straight, like I'm going to punch her.

I think you're going to hurt Jim. Like the others. And he's going to leave us and then what will we do?

She looks down at my bedspread and tugs at a piece of thread.

We are adults, she finally says.

I thought you loved David.

She stands up. *I do but . . . You know, darling, David is like a strong current and you can swim as hard as you like, but you will always end up going his way. We've worked so hard.* She looks down at me.

So you're going to be with Jim now?

We've really always been with Jim, haven't we?

You're not going to mess it up?

Her mouth tightens. *I hope not. I really hope not.*

I pull the covers tight around myself, close my eyes, and let myself feel a little bit happy.

CHAPTER 49

JIM STAYS THE night and they're both up early. Mother is smiling a lot. Mother smiling makes Jim smile makes me smile.

Before we leave for school, he takes Mother's face in his hand, almost the same as he did in the car two nights before, but this time he kisses her.

Oh, brother, I say, looking away and pretending to be disgusted.

Sister Eye is waiting for me outside school. *I'll take her from here, Jim,* she says, and he says thank you and gives her a kiss on the cheek. *What in heaven's name,* she says, touching the place where he kissed her as he walks off.

How's my girl? Sister says to me.

Fine.

I've been worrying about you. I tried to call.

We hold hands while we climb the stairs. *What did you want?*

I wanted to tell you that I think your life is too often . . . crazy. Unpredictable. Do you know that word?

I shake my head no.

You never know what's going to happen next, she says.

You can say that again.

That's all, she says. *I see you and I wish it were different.*

Later in the week, Mother offers one of her closets to Jim so he can make a darkroom in it. While he's in there nailing a clock to the wall and Mother is getting her makeup on, Big Doug shows up at the door. He asks to speak to Mother alone but she says, *No, they're my family.* We all sit down in the living room. A family. Mother offers him a drink but he doesn't want one.

You know why I'm here, he says to Mother.

She nods.

It's been swell. I'm your biggest fan, you know that.

I know, says Mother. She puts her hand in Jim's.

Big Doug folds his hands in his lap. *We kept the Angel plugging along for quite a while, you and me.*

You found someone new?

He nods.

How much longer do I have? she asks.

Three more weekends, he says. *Plenty of time for you to find another gig.*

All right, says Mother.

Besides, you don't want to be stuck in some old joint singing the old songs. You got to get out there! Find your fame!

I had hoped it would find me, Mother says, standing and extending her hand. *Thank you, Douglas. For everything.*

Can't wait to say I knew you when, he says cheerfully on his way out the door.

After he leaves, Mother and Jim sit on the couch a long time.

It's going to happen for you, says Jim. *Don't think for one minute that it won't.*

CHAPTER 50

HILDA MAKES MOTHER a new dress for her last performance. When she asks Mother why she would want a new dress for her last show, Mother says, *This is not the end, Hilda. It's the beginning.*

They argue for what seems like an hour over the sexiness of the dress. Mother keeps saying *more*, Hilda keeps saying *too much*. Mother doesn't want me to see it because she wants me to be surprised along with everybody else.

We've got three weeks, Mother says. *Will it be ready?*

Yes, yes, yes, says Hilda, resigned.

When we get back from the fitting there is a note from Jim. He's gone out to take pictures. *Just a few. Back before lunch.*

Let's have a picnic! she says.

It's a beautiful day, a windows-open kind of day. We do our chores around the apartment, go to the grocery store, and prepare lunch.

Do you have a new job yet? I ask her.

No, she says, scrubbing potatoes and glancing at the potato salad recipe in the *Redbook* on the counter.

Are you sad that you only have a few performances left?

Mother raises the potato peeler in the air. *It's funny, kitten, but I'm not. I'm not sad at all. I have a feeling, you see. I can't explain it. I believe it's all going to work out for the best.* She looks down at the recipe in the magazine. *Did we remember to buy an onion?*

I hand her the onion. I like working beside her, cooking, thinking about a picnic with Jim in the park, in the sun and wind, just the three of us. A family.

I love you, Mom, I say.

She stops peeling and looks at me.

You do? she says. Her breathing quickens and all of a sudden she has tears in her eyes.

I nod. *Yup.* She pulls me to her and hugs me with her face against my head.

I love you, too. I swear to God I do, she whispers into my hair, crying just a little.

In the end, the potato salad is a pale yellow dry mush. We stare at it. I taste it. It reminds me a little of the papier-mâché mix we made in art. Mother adds salt and some A-1 sauce, tries it again, and winces.

You think we should ring the kitchen?

I think we better, I say

Well, shucks, she says, staring at the bowl of mush.

I try to stifle my laughter while Mother is on the phone, wrapping the cord around her finger, flirting with the kitchen guys, describing the disaster. *No, you should really see it,* she says, laughing, *it's perfectly terrible.* I imagine her telling Jim the whole story when he gets here. And of course Mother will make the story worse, more dramatic. She'll act it out at the picnic maybe, standing barefoot on the blanket, and we'll laugh because this is how she loves us. We know this because we're the ones who know her, Jim and me. We're the ones who understand.

Just in time! Mother says when a guy from the kitchen brings us potato salad. *You're a lifesaver.* We finish packing the picnic basket and Mother looks at the clock. *Well, mister, where are you?* she says to herself.

She looks out the window. *It's warm out there today.* She goes into her room and puts on a different dress. I look out the window at the street. I'll be able to spot Jim by his tripod.

An hour passes and then two more. *You know Jim*, says Mother. *He always loses track of time when he's taking photographs.* She takes the blanket out of the basket and spreads it on the living room floor. *I understand this. Same thing happens to me when I'm singing. Whole night just goes by like that*, she says, snapping her fingers.

We have our picnic on the floor.

I'm gonna miss the Blue Angel, I tell her.

I know, sweetie. Me, too. Bigger and better things! she says, raising her sandwich in the air like a toast. We tap our sandwiches together and laugh.

We save plenty for Jim.

After pacing and smoking for a little while, Mother says, *Well, I need to be getting ready.* She makes herself some coffee and heads into the bathroom. After she finishes her hair and makeup and changes her clothes, she comes into the living room and puts her hand on my shoulder. *You may as well stay here. He'll be home any minute. Is that all right?*

Yes, I say.

Okay, kitten, she says. *You know what? Even though the day didn't go as planned, I sure did enjoy myself. We had a good day, didn't we? Just the two of us?*

I smile and nod. *You're going to be late. See you later, alligator.*

After she's gone, I wander around the apartment. I eat some ice cream out of the carton, turn on the television. First I watch *Flipper*, then I watch *I Dream of Jeannie*. During the show, I look at the door, cross my arms in front of me, and bob my head like Barbara Eden. *Please bring Jim home now,* I say. But he doesn't appear in a poof of smoke. I didn't really think he would. I'm starting to get mad. *You could at least call.*

Mother calls during intermission. *Any word?* she asks. *No,* I say. Sometime during the NBC Saturday-night movie, I fall asleep. When I wake up the apartment is entirely dark except for the television. No Mother yet, no Jim. The news is on. A reporter says, *A portion of the old Chicago Stock Exchange, which was in the early stages of demolition, has collapsed. No injuries have been reported but citizens are asked to avoid the area until further notice.*

The phone rings and I run for it, already relieved. I know it's Jim. Finally.

Doll, it's David. His voice sounds tight. *Your ma home yet?*

No.

Jim there?

No.

You alone?

Yes.

Why are you alone?

David?

Yes?

The news just said that the Stock Exchange building collapsed.

I saw it, he says.

I swallow. I feel myself breathing. *Jim . . . Jim went out to take pictures today and he said he'd be right back and he never came back and he never called.*

When was this?

This morning.

He'll turn up, doll. He will. You two photograph every building in town practically. I'm sure he's all right. He's a smart guy. You worry a lot. You really do.

That's what Jim says.

Why don't you make sure the door's locked and go to bed.

Okay, David. I hang up the phone and lie back down on the couch.

CHAPTER 51

WHEN I WAKE up, Mother is sitting in the living room, smoking, in the same outfit she was wearing when she left. I can see by her face that she hasn't slept.

She forces herself to smile. *Good morning, love.*

Did you hear from him?

She shakes her head no.

Did you see the news—

I know, she says sharply. *I'm not worried.* She takes a deep breath and touches her eyebrow. *You know, he's just so worked up about this* Look *magazine spread that he's not himself.*

Okay, I say. *What do we do?*

I don't know. She puts out her cigarette and lights another.

We spend the next few hours in silence, walking around the apartment in circles like fish in a tank, avoiding each other. I go from feeling scared to feeling panicked. When the phone rings, we both jump like a gun went off.

Hello, says Mother. *Yes, yes, this is she. Mrs. Piccolo. Nice to meet you, too.* She listens. *I don't know where he is either. Yes, if I hear anything, I'll let you know. Right away. I will, ma'am. Please don't be upset.*

She hangs up and steadies herself against the wall.

Who was that?

She shakes her head.

Who was that? Answer me! You have to answer me!

She looks startled. *Jim's mother. In New York. She said he calls her every Sunday morning at ten* A.M. *No matter what. He didn't call this morning. He's never missed a Sunday. I didn't even know she was alive.* She laughs a little bit. *There's so much I don't even know about him.*

She stands up straight. *Go put your shoes on.*

I can't move.

Go! she shouts.

As we get closer to the Stock Exchange the traffic becomes more and more congested. While we are stopped at a long light, Mother just gets out of the cab and starts walking. I run after her. What is left of the Stock Exchange is hugged in dust. We keep walking until we run into the sawhorses that have been set up around the sidewalk to keep people from getting too close. Cars are parked haphazardly in the street.

Mother tries to get close but a guy in a hard hat stops her. *Sorry, ma'am.*

Excuse me, she says, *please let me pass.*

I can't do that, ma'am.

She straightens. *I believe my . . . There may be a person in that building,* she says, her voice shaking.

The hard-hat man smiles and shakes his head. *Now, ma'am, ain't nobody been in this building for six months.* He pats her arm with his big gloved hand and points to the doors and windows at street level, talking to her like she's a child. *See there? She's all boarded up.*

I move myself in front of Mother. *I've been in it. I was just in it last month.*

He looks at me and tilts his head. *I don't think so.*

I have so! I shout. *You don't know!*

He raises his arms to the side. *Why don't you two girls head on home now.*

I zip around him and run for the building. He tries to follow me, yelling, *Hey! Kid, you come back here this minute!*

I go straight for Jim's secret entrance and slide the small pallet of boards off the opening. Inside there is only dust and darkness, and I try to walk, feeling my way through the mess with my feet, my arms outstretched and reaching. I try to remember what way we went but I'm so scared I can't think or tell where I am at all. Through the commotion, I can hear Mother's voice calling my name. Then my arm runs into a railing and I grab the banister, turn myself around it, and head up the stairs. I get pretty far until somebody snags me like a cat, carrying me down and back outside.

The hard-hat guy sets me down on the pavement and crouches in front of me. *You telling me the truth that you been in there recently?* Mother rushes over to us.

I cry and cough. *He could be in there. Please, pretty please,* I say.

This better not be some kinda prank. He points at me.

How dare you? says Mother.

I'm telling the truth, I say.

He stands and puts his hands on his hips. *Shit.* He walks over to a group of men and talks to them. They look at us and at the building. Then they all go to Jim's secret entrance and file in one at a time.

Mother and I sit on the curb and wait. She holds me, rocks me, and hums a little. Now that I've started crying, I can't stop. A fire truck arrives and some police cars.

It starts to get dark. A policeman walks up to us and asks Mother a lot of questions. What does Jim look like? What was he wearing last time you saw him, on and on. *And what was he taking pictures of exactly?*

Mother looks at me.

The railings, windows, little beautiful things, I say.

He frowns at me and says, *I see.*

He tells us to go home and promises to let us know if they find anything. *I seriously doubt that your boyfriend is in this building, ma'am*, he says as we begin to leave. Mother looks at me and nods, trying to smile. I look away.

At home we sit in the living room with the lights off. We don't want to see or talk or eat or anything. We just wait.

Hours pass and the apartment is almost black. The only light is the light leaking in from the street and the flaring tip of Mother's cigarette.

Then there's a knock on the door.

We don't move.

Mother breathes heavily. Then she bends over, holds her head, and makes a sound.

I walk toward the door, stop to turn on a lamp, and open it. It's the policeman who talked to us. He turns his hat in his hands.

He seems to not know what to say. We just look at each other. He swallows. *Is your ma here?*

I am frozen.

He steps closer. *Sweetie, is your ma home?*

I hear her get up and take a few steps toward us but not all the way.

He looks at her and thinks very hard about every word he chooses. *Ma'am. We have uncovered . . . a man we believe to be your friend. There is a chance it's not. But he fits the description you gave me exactly.*

She moves silently back into the room.

I'm sorry, he says, looking down at me. He shakes his head and walks away.

I stand there staring at the hallway for a long time while Mother makes terrible, painful sounds in the dark. In between, when she's catching her breath, I hear the hallway lights buzz. I can't shut the door. I will wait forever. And watch. I will stand here all night.

CHAPTER 52

ALL THE NEXT day, Mother doesn't leave her room and I stay home from school. In the afternoon, I sit at Mother's desk and write a note to *Look* magazine telling them what happened to Jim. I think it's their fault, though I don't say that. I place the note in his box of photos and take it downstairs. Sal is at the front desk, so I ask him how to get to the post office.

You need to mail that?

Yes.

You got money for postage?

I look at the box, uncertain.

Let me take it for you. He reaches out to take the box.

It's very important, I say, before I let him have it.

Okay, kid.

Thank you, Sal.

I go back up to the dark apartment and sit. Sister shows up around four.

Why weren't you in school? Are you ill? She walks in and turns on a light. *What's going on here? Honey, talk to me.*

I stare at her. Her face gets stern. *Sophia!*

I want to tell her and believe I can somehow divide the pain if I can tell her but I cannot speak.

What on earth, she says to herself as she walks into Mother's room. I stand in the hall and listen to them, to the clock on the shelf, to the horns on the street. I walk to the window and it's the same as always—cars, yelling, honking, wind, the El—like nothing has happened, like everything is fine.

Sophia, says Sister when she eventually comes out. Her eyes are red and her voice shakes. *I would like you to gather up some things. You're going to stay with Rita and me for a few days. Mama needs to rest.* She walks into my room and pulls my blue-and-green-flowered suitcase out of my closet.

Help me, she says.

I hand her my uniform skirt, blouse, and shoes, and my nuclear-fallout book. I start to hand her the Heathkit from Jim but decide I want to hold on to it.

Before we leave, I check on Mother. She's barefaced with all her freckles showing.

Just a few days, she says. *You need to be taken care of right now.*

When we arrive at Sister's apartment, Rita says, *I just heard.*

Can I speak to you alone? says Sister.

After talking awhile, they come out of the bedroom and Rita walks to me with her arms open. She hugs me, sniffling. Sister stands nearby with her eyes closed.

Are you talking to God? I ask her.

She nods and I stare at her. There is no such thing, there is no such thing, there is no such thing. Sister opens her eyes and looks at me like she heard my private thoughts. I look away.

Do you have a bomb shelter here? I ask.

Sister and Rita look at each other. Sister shakes her head no but Rita stops her.

Of course it does, says Rita. *Come with me.* She grabs her keys and we leave.

I follow her down several sets of stairs and through a door. It's dark. She flips on the light and there is a long aisle lined with cages, each cage has a padlock on it. We walk down the aisle, looking in the cages. They are full of stuff, some more than others. Furniture, boxes, lamps, a few lanterns, rolled-up rugs, Christmas decorations, crates of records.

What is all this? I ask.

Stuff we might need, says Rita. *After the bomb.*

I look into the cages. A box of toys. A bassinette. A guitar case.

Do you feel better? says Rita.

I don't know how to tell her that I will never feel better for the rest of my life. She rests her hand on my back. *Let's go back upstairs. Bomb shelters do nothing for the spirit, do they?*

Sister makes noodles and butter and I eat three helpings. She asks, *When did you last eat?* I shrug.

The apartment is small but there is a large closet. I take Jim's Heathkit into the closet with me and rest my hand on it. I just sit there and listen to myself breathe.

CHAPTER 53

MY FAMILY—MOTHER, Sister, Rita, David, Laura, Hilda, and the
people from the Blue Angel—take up one whole row at the funeral
home. Jim's body is in a casket in the front and people walk in and go
straight up to see him. I want to go but I'm sitting in the middle of the
row and everyone is arguing in whispers about whether or not it's right
to let a child view the body. Sister is on my left and Mother is on my
right. Sister rests her hand on my leg. *Whatever they decide, if you move, I
will catch you. You are not going up there.*

I want to see him, I say.

*Look at me. He is not there. We are spirit and light and love. That is
what we are. What is up there is just a body.*

I push her hand off my leg and think of Jim's mustache and glasses
and his crooked bottom teeth and the little stains on his fingers from
cigarettes and the way his hair went every which way. *I never know what*

you're talking about, I tell Sister without looking at her and hide my face with my hands and cry.

Toward the end of the little service Mother walks to the front, resting her hand on the end of each pew as she goes, like she might fall down.

Sister closes her eyes like Mother is going to sing a prayer for us. Mother sings, *"Black is the color of my true love's hair. His face so kind and wondrous fair. The purest eyes and the strongest hands. I love the ground on where he stands."*

The sad in her voice pulls the sad out of me, out of all of us.

After the service, I stand with Mother in the parking lot.

I could come home with you, I say.

She puts her hand on my shoulder, which means no. *You need more than I have right now.*

No, I don't. When did I ever need anything? I raise my voice. She hugs me.

Soon, she says. *Be patient for me, okay, kitten?* I watch her walk away and she seems unsteady, like her heels are too tall or her dress too tight. David catches up to her but she waves him away.

Back at the apartment that afternoon, Sister and Rita decide I should go to school. When I get there the next day, Elizabeth has a thousand questions. *Please don't make me talk about it,* I say to her.

I'm sorry, she says, resting her hand on my arm, thinking about what to say next. *My mother has raised the ban on our friendship. Temporarily. So that's one good thing.*

Elizabeth stays right by my side, like she's guarding me. She doesn't leave my side for days.

One day while I'm at school, Rita shoves all the coats and wraps in the closet to the back, pushes the hatboxes to the side, puts a cushion on the floor and a small lamp, and makes a little desk out of a stack of photography books. *Stay in there as long as you like,* she says. I go in and look around. I like my secret room but it also seems to mean that I'm going to be here for a while, which nobody has actually said out loud. I look at my Heathkit and I want to put it together so bad. I just know if I can build that radio, I will be okay. I just know it and cannot wait another day.

Rita is smoking on the couch. I grab the instruction booklet for the Heathkit and put it in front of her face.

Yes? she says.

Can you help me figure this out?

She squints at it like it's something dead.

No, darling, I cannot. You know I don't do these sorts of things.

Can't you try? I ask.

Why are you asking me? Why not Idalia?

You're the only man in this house, I say, resting my finger on the head of the dad on the cover of the Heathkit manual.

I feel Rita staring at me. I wonder if she's breathing at all. Neither of us moves for a while.

I know what you're doing, she says.

I'm not doing anything, I tell her.

You're mad.

I am not, I say.

CHAPTER 54

On WEDNESDAYS, AFTER school, I go to Elizabeth's house on the South Side, where all the Negro folks live. Sometimes Mrs. LaFontaine fixes my hair. It's the first time my hair has looked good in my whole life.

Mr. LaFontaine says, *How's that Heathkit coming along?* and Mrs. LaFontaine gives him a sharp face, like no one is supposed to say anything that will make me think of Jim.

Not so good, I say. *The diagrams are hard.*

Oh, not really, he says, tossing a yellow notebook on the table and sitting down in front of it.

He draws a diagram that makes more sense to me than the one in the manual. Then he explains what all the parts do—resistors, capacitors, diodes, transistors—and how to read the chart so I know where they go.

Is this what sociologists do? I ask him.

He thinks. *In a word, yes.*

I work on the radio as soon as I get home. Sister peeks in to see if I'm doing my homework and just smiles when she sees that I'm working. She and Rita have an argument about how I'm falling behind and how they're responsible for me now.

Sister says, *Let her do what she needs to do.*

You coddle her. Did that go so well with Naomi? No, it did not, Rita says as she marches around the apartment in heels, watering the plants with a bright pink watering can.

The buzzer sounds.

Oh, what now, says Rita.

She pushes the intercom button and says, *Yes?*

It's me, darling, says Mother's muffled voice.

She's come for me, I think, running to the door.

Rita pushes the small black button on the brass plate.

When Mother walks in I feel my body lean toward her like she's a giant magnet and I'm a shard of steel. She rushes me with her arms open wide. *God, I miss you.* She takes my head in her hands, kisses my face, and smells my hair. I know by her voice that she's not here to take me home.

Are you taking me home?

Soon, sweetie, says Mother. *Real soon.*

I brought you something, she says, her voice a little hesitant. She reaches into a yellow envelope and pulls out a magazine and hands it to me. I take it. It is *Look* magazine. Jim's *Look* magazine, and there, on the cover, is the picture of Mother in the blue night-sky dress, her hair big and stiff, all her makeup on, crouched down holding me by the hips, looking up at me like she loves me. "Chicago's Beating Heart," it says above our heads.

It came in the mail today with a note from the editor. He said the story was just going to be a little article in the back, nothing much, but when he heard what happened to Jim . . . She stops and can't continue, holds a small, embroidered handkerchief close to her face.

Sister and Rita stand behind us and look over our shoulders. We all stare at the cover in silence.

There's more inside, says Mother.

No, I say, standing up. *I don't want to see it yet.* I can't start to look now, look again, at us, at what used to be our life.

You don't have to, says Mother. *This is yours.* She sets the magazine on the table. *Someday.*

Sister brings her coffee.

Rita says, *We're talking about coming to see you this Saturday. It is your last show, this Saturday?*

It is.

Well, we'll be there, then.

We wouldn't miss it, says Sister.

You, too? Mother asks me.

I don't know.

I would love it if you came. I need you in my wings. I really don't do so hot without you.

Okay, I say, wanting to be there for her.

Rita says, *Darling, why don't you show Mama your office?*

I walk to the closet, Mother following.

I open the door and Mother steps in and squats on her haunches. *Oh, look. Is this the kit Jim gave you?* She reaches for the Heathkit plate, which is lying on a sheet of newspaper.

Don't touch that.

Sorry, she says. *It makes me so happy you're working on it, it really does. We've got to keep him alive however we can. He made me a better person . . .* Her voice trails off.

I can't stop crying, I say.

Me neither. She looks up and the fixture lights her face. It seems wherever she is, a spotlight appears.

I wish you would take me home.

She thinks. *I've got to get through this weekend. Then I have to find a new gig, really pound the pavement, you know? I just want to be a little more settled.*

You won't even know I'm there, I—

Sophia, no. I said no. Not now. I just can't.

I wait a little while for her to change her mind, then I sit down on the floor and look at the diagram.

Oh, I almost forgot. She pulls a brown paper sack out of her bag and hands it to me. *Some batteries. For your little radio? And some candy. Atomic Fireballs and Mary Janes.*

Thanks.

Don't be sore at me, kitten, she says. *We'll be together again soon. Real soon.*

CHAPTER 55

AFTER SHE LEAVES I get the *Look* magazine and the soldering iron and take them into the closet, closing the door behind me.

Rita says, *You're being careful with that, right?*

No, I say. *I'm melting all of the shoes.*

I lean the magazine against the wall, the cover facing it. There is an ad for a Plymouth Barracuda on the back, a happy couple standing by it.

While I wait for the iron to heat up, I pick up the magazine and flip through until I find the article. At the beginning is a little blurry black-and-white photo of Jim. I look at it a long time and it makes me smile. I pretend to fight with him, whispering, *Be quiet. No, YOU be quiet; no, YOU be quiet.*

I fold the magazine on itself and lean it against the wall so Jim is watching me.

I can do it myself, I tell him.

The iron heats slowly. I hold my hand above it until I think it's hot enough. Then I press some of the wires between my forefinger and thumb to flatten them and push them through the holes; they come out the other side of the plate. I touch the iron to a piece of solder until it softens into a small glistening bead, which I drop between the wire and the plate, holding still until they harden. With Jim watching over me, I work a long time.

Finally, Rita taps on the door. *I'm unplugging you*, she says.

I set the soldering iron on a small ceramic stand Rita gave me. She said it was for resting chopsticks but *when do I ever get to use chopsticks?*

I wait for it to cool. I never leave the closet until the iron is cool. I imagine these rules for myself and imagine Jim telling me the rules with a cigarette in his lips.

I pick up the magazine again and turn the page and there we are, all of us, Elizabeth and I, Rita standing with my birthday cake, and Sister and Mr. LaFontaine looking seriously at each other, Mother in the middle of everything, her mouth open in laughter or singing, shining like a sun at the center of us all. Everyone but Jim is in the picture and it takes up two whole pages.

I put it down, make myself into a ball, and hold my face in a coat that's on the floor and scream into it as loud as I can, stopping only to breathe. I scream as loud and long as I can, kicking the wall of the closet as I do. I scream and cry. Sister rushes in and tries to get close to me, saying, *Baby, baby*, but I keep kicking, so she can't get anywhere near me. Then Rita is there telling her to leave me alone. *Let her do this*, Rita says, and I do it until I feel like I can't move anymore. They wait for me outside the closet, and when it's over, they put me to bed and Rita holds me tight until I'm asleep.

The next day after school, I go back to the closet to look at the rest of the article. There are pictures of the Armory, the church on Belden, all the old places now gone. There are more pictures of Mother—onstage, in the dressing room, at our home—smiling, singing, worrying. There's one of me sitting on a cooler at the grocery store, handwritten signs hanging above my head: GRAPES 14¢/LB. GREEN PEPPERS 5¢ EACH. And a broken egg on the dirty floor. There is a photograph of Mother backstage, her hands on her hips and her head down. Underneath it the sentence reads, *The struggling artist takes a breather backstage.* In the bottom corner of the photo, I can see one of my feet.

On the last page of the article is a small picture of the Chicago Stock Exchange before it fell. A sentence on the page reads, in bold letters, "As One Star Rises, Another One Falls." The last few paragraphs are all about Jim and include an interview. He talks about the failure of urban renewal, whatever that is. Someone asks him, "It appears as though your chief areas of interest are Chicago architecture and this unknown singer. Why this odd combination?" And Jim says, "Not so odd, really. I'm interested in vulnerability, especially in the people and things that appear to be tough, who appear to be here for good." The interviewer responds, "How poetic." The writer goes on to say that in the end, the truly vulnerable one was James Piccolo himself. I can't read any more after that and close the magazine.

CHAPTER 56

THE DAY *LOOK* magazine hits the stands, the whole city discovers Mother. *Like she wasn't right under their noses for ten whole years*, says Rita. Mother's last night at the Blue Angel threatens to be the biggest show she's ever had.

On the phone she tells me, *I'm holding seats for Sister and Rita but I need you backstage with me. Can you do that for me? Will you help me out tonight?*

I guess I can, I say.

In the audience are the LaFontaines, their friends, and Elizabeth. I wave at her from the wing and she waves back. Even though her mother keeps tugging at her dress, she can't sit down. She just pops back up and watching her makes me laugh for the first time in weeks. I've never seen so many people at the Blue Angel, the crowd is so loud.

I realize I'm waiting for Jim to show up and make me do something or scold me. This happens over and over. I'm sure he's just going to walk around a corner or duck out from behind a curtain with his camera. Then I remember. I walk quickly to the backstage corner, where it's darkest, and lean my head against the ropes.

Mother appears backstage in the new dress. It is the color of her skin and covered with rhinestones. The front drops low and the back drops low enough to show her whole spine. It's straight and long and in it she moves like she's floating. The guys backstage go quiet when they see her.

She stands in the wings, absolutely still, and waits. I stand behind her. She whispers to herself, *How do I do this without you? Help me.* I touch her naked back and she jumps a little.

You're going to be great, I say.

She straightens and takes a deep breath. *Of course I am, darling.*

Mother's voice is clearer and stronger than I've ever heard it, it seems like she's controlling every note. She used to sing like she had no idea what her voice was going to do, but that has changed. She seems to know now.

I watch her and listen and the wonder settles over me. I feel lost in her voice, more than I ever have. On the heels of that, a small, slow-moving panic rises in me. I think, If I'm feeling this, everyone is feeling this, and it makes me happy and it makes me afraid because once they see her like I do, love her like I do, they will take her away. I just know it. I sit down on my *X* for the very last time.

During the intermission, Mother hums and rolls her shoulders in her room.

Pretty good so far, I tell her.

It better be, she says, staring at herself in the vanity.

There's a knock on the door. Mother doesn't even blink. *Tell them no.*

I open the door and when Mother sees who it is she changes her mind. It's a man from some record company. He sweats when he talks to her.

319

Eventually, Steve pages Mother to stage right. She smiles and says good-bye to the man, waving his business card as she does.

Let's go, she says.

On the way down the hall, Mother stops and leans against the wall for a moment. I stop, too.

She lowers her head so her chin is touching her chest. The top knobs of her spine poke up on the back of her neck.

Mom?

I miss him terribly, she says. *I just miss him so terribly much I sometimes think I can't breathe.*

Miss Hill, stage left, Steve says over the page.

And here I am with an offer from Canary Records. I'm taking off, kitten. And all I want is to tell Jim. We did it, Jimmy. Finally, huh?

The second half of the show is even better than the first. It's like she's shoving every feeling she ever had into the notes, making them so full they burst. *Oh, man*, I say to the air, *I wish you could see this.*

After two encores, the backstage floods with people. I watch a man walk up to her and introduce himself. He is handsome. Mother smiles and touches her hair while she talks to him. I get closer. Not because I want to, but I feel I should be prepared. He is talking about radio, television, magazines, *The Ed Sullivan Show.* More people come backstage and surround them until I can't hear anymore, and as she is whisked away, I wave at her and she blows me a kiss.

CHAPTER 57

SISTER, RITA, AND I go straight home afterward. I call Elizabeth, who talks so fast it makes me smile; I can hear her parents laughing with their friends in the background. I hope that tonight will buy me more time with her.

When I hang up the phone, Rita and Sister are drinking wine on the couch. I plug in my iron. *May I?* I ask.

Of course, darling, says Rita. *It's a Saturday. You can fiddle all night.*

It's not fiddling.

You know what I mean, kitten.

I know, I say, and kiss them both on the cheeks before heading into the closet. I solder until the apartment is absolutely still and my eyes sting.

A few days later Mother stops by to fill us in on all the good news. Recording, radio spots, job offers, etc. The craziness of it all, the last show, *Look* magazine.

So you're getting settled, I say.

Well, I sure don't feel settled! She laughs. *I feel like I'm in a whirlwind! It's all too much to believe.*

Rita clasps her hands in front of her and shakes her head. *Oh, my darling, I could cry.*

They talk about all the details, about music, about clothes, about venues. I slip away to the closet. The radio is so close. A few more solders and I can slide it into its neat little box.

I hear Mother say, *Are you sure it's no trouble? You know, I just can't be worrying about her right now with everything going on.*

Before she leaves, she comes to find me in the closet. *We have to talk*, she says.

I heard you. I know.

It's just for a little while, love. And when we come together again, we'll have a whole new life. A brand-new start.

I liked our old life, I say as she turns to leave.

CHAPTER 58

SISTER TAKES ME to Mitchell's for supper. She puts her fork down and folds her hands in front of her. I don't look at her.

We need to discuss something, she says, smiling. *I've been talking with your teacher. You're not doing well in any of your subjects.*

I know, I say.

There's still time. You can pull your grades up if you perform well on the end-of-year exams.

I shrug, turning a french fry round and round in a pool of ketchup.

Sister is seriously considering holding you back. I really don't want that to happen.

I watch her talk. The only thing I think is that if I get held back, I won't be with Elizabeth.

I have a plan, of course. I've spoken with Mrs. LaFontaine and was thinking Elizabeth could help you catch up. I think it would be easier that way. You don't seem to want my help right now, she says, mostly to herself.

The waitress comes, Sister pays, and we leave.

Will you help me finish the radio? I ask on the way home.

Sister smiles. *I'll do anything for you, Sophia. You know that.*

Elizabeth is so worried I'm not going to pass she quizzes me on something or other the whole time we're together. Mostly we work in a study room at her father's university after school. She makes little tests for me and paces up and down the stacks while I take them. If I do well, she lets me look at microfiche on fallout shelters.

Mother calls every day and then every other day and then sometimes.

Sister peeks into my closet. *What can I do?* I make her solder diodes. We leave the door open so it feels like there's more room. Rita says, *You're both crazy people*, which makes Sister jump up and say, *You know what I'm thinking*. She pulls a record from the stack and plays "Crazy People" by the Boswell Sisters.

Oh, your mother loved these girls when she was young, says Sister.

I listen to the song on the couch, watch Rita dance to it, and then I cry for a little while right in front of them.

A few days later, I come home from school to a note that says Rita has to work late and Sister has a meeting and there's a sandwich in the fridge. The number to Rita's club is scrawled on the bottom next to *In case of emergency*. When it gets dark, I call Elizabeth and talk to her for a few minutes but she has to get off in order to go to a dinner at her church.

I go into the closet and study the radio plate, the instructions, and Mr. LaFontaine's notes. There are a few parts left but they are extras. I slide the plate into the brown leather case and snap it shut, reach for the knob, but then pull my hand away. What will I do if it doesn't work? The last thing he gave me? I hold it for a long time, until I can hear Jim's voice in my head saying, *Oh, for Christ's sake, turn it on already.* I turn the knob. Nothing happens. I shake it a little. Nothing. I feel a sinking in my stomach and look at the magazine against the wall. *I did everything I was supposed to do,* I tell Jim. And then I remember the batteries. I pull them out of the brown sac and unsnap the case and place them. I take a deep breath and turn the dial. There's static. I can't believe it. I turn the knob slowly and hear voices. *It works. It works, it works, it works,* I shout out loud. I keep turning until I hear a man's voice, it is low and nice. He's talking about songs he likes like they're girls he wants to go with. His voice makes me smile. I hold the radio on my lap and listen to him talk. It's warm. I made this, I think. Jim, I did it. Listen!

The low-voiced man says, *And now for something really sweet. Hot off the press.* I hear a needle touch and the band begin to play. I feel like it's a song I know by heart but it can't be, coming from this strange home-made thing on my lap. Then I hear her, her voice. Mother. On the radio. Singing to me in my closet. *"I'll be around,"* she sings. *"No matter how you treat me now."* I hold the radio in front of me, like it could break any second, like a bit of solder might simply lift off the plate and leave me in silence.

I place it very slowly on a hatbox and curl up right next to it and close my eyes.

Here she is.

AUTHOR NOTE

IN MY RESEARCH for this book, I spent many days wandering the streets of Chicago and countless hours in the city's libraries. I was trying to build in my mind's eye a vision of Chicago in the sixties, and as I poured over photographs, I kept returning to the images of Richard Nickel. Nickel's chief work as a photographer was to capture, with the hope of protecting, the city's architecture. He made countless appeals to city leaders to save buildings slated for destruction, and he staged protests. His aesthetic scope was broad enough to capture the slightest detail—a banister, a touch of ornamentation—to the entirety of buildings and the blocks on which they stood. He infected my imagination and increasingly insinuated himself into the character of Jim. Nickel, like Jim, did perish in the Chicago Stock Exchange Building but that building didn't come down until 1972, not 1965 as it happens in the novel.

I am indebted to Nickel for his work. He ignited in me the awareness of, and the desire to illuminate, the life of a guardian, and this story would be lost without the history he preserved so beautifully and the passion he embodied.

ACKNOWLEDGMENTS

To WHOM AM I not indebted?

I don't know many agents and editors but I know I have the best. Thank you, Henry Dunow and Jessica Williams, respectively, for being smart as hell and fierce and honest.

My humble gratitude to the teachers, Bob Grunst and Jonis Agee, who expected so much, to the Nebraska Summer Writers Conference which led me to Timothy Shaffert, Maud Casey, and David Ebershoff, excellent artists and guides. To the kick-ass nuns (Servants of Mary, Sisters of Mercy, and the Sisters of St. Joseph of Carondelet) for being tireless advocates of education, justice, and unblinking acceptance. To Kathy Havlik for holding my indecipherable poems, and my heart, for twenty-five years now. To Sara Koch, for asking, since we were little, to read more. To Mimi, for sharing her Chicago. To the other writers in the family—Ron Hansen, Bo Caldwell—you show me, so beautifully, how to do it well. From this tribe of Omaha artists—the dear musicians with whom I spent so many hours stitching together songs (Air, Brad, Quinn, Al), the writers with whom I share so much, least of all work (the luminous Lindsey Baker and the penetrating Todd Robinson)—I have learned both discipline and a commitment to what we must do, despite the outcomes, and whether or not anyone is watching. To Bruno and Melanie, for taking us to sea during the saddest year and filling me with enough sunlight to finish the book. My dear friend Amy Loyd with her huge talent and huge heart has inspired me forever. To the early readers—Emily Danforth for paving the way and pushing me, Jack Phillips for teaching me narrative via the life of trees (and for firing me four hundred times), Karen Chaka for her nagging and support, and Jim Shepard, the greatest most underappreciated writer on the planet, whose generosity and patience moves me as much as his talent.

To the people around the tables, especially my Northside family, the Grat Girls, and Tuesday Process, for giving me a safe place to unfold myself week after week. To Leslie Jeffries for fielding four million phone calls, Marilyn Cady and Shirley Huerter for telling it like it is, Father Michael for teaching me over and over that we are loved as is, Kirstin Kluver for shining her big redheaded light all over the place, and to Bernie Devlin who said thirteen years ago, come in, sit down, here's some coffee, and has been my compass ever since.

I am nothing if not the product of my mother's artful life and my father's cowboy courage. What grace they showed in supporting me whether or not they understood. My brother Wil has made me laugh at myself all my life, and I love him for it. My sister Nik's big brain and constant inappropriateness are a beacon in the dark. My big extended clan—the Roterts, Hansens, and Shaws—are all stories of compassion and eccentricity and getting back up, and they provide more support (and material) than I can stand. And little B, who will not read this book until she's at least thirty-eight, you gave me Sophia and you give me wonder.

Finally, I thank Bud, my love, my toughest crowd and steadiest hand, for crying when I read you scenes and dancing with me in the kitchen.